"What kinda scapegrace you 'low in here, Rusty? Look at him. Seems the town dump was his tailor."

The two cowboys at the bar laughed.

"Hey, saddle bum—move to the far end of the bar."

Dane ignored the bullyragger.

"I said, mister, this is a place for gennelmen. . . ." Metzger approached Dane, hand on the gun in his belt.

Dane looked at him and said nothing. He waited.

Metzger shoved the "saddle bum."

Dane slid instantly into a strange state of mind. It was as if his body took over from his brain.

He snatched his own pistol from under his coat, flipped it so he held it by the barrel, and, in almost the same motion, cracked Metzger in the forehead with the butt of the gun.

Dane whirled, flipping the gun around again, catching it neatly so it was pointed toward the two cowboys. They turned tail and ran out the front door, shouting for the sheriff. Feeling strange, Dane holstered his old Colt. It really felt as if someone else had done all that business with the gun. . . .

RALPH COMPTON

BROKEN RIDER

A Ralph Compton Western by
JOHN SHIRLEY

BERKLEY
New York

BERKLEY
An imprint of Penguin Random House LLC
penguinrandomhouse.com

Copyright © 2020 by The Estate of Ralph Compton

ISBN: 9780593102305

First Edition: August 2020

Printed in the United States of America
1   3   5   7   9   10   8   6   4   2

Cover art by Dennis Lyall
Cover design by Steve Meditz
Book design by George Towne

THE IMMORTAL COWBOY

This is respectfully dedicated to the "American Cowboy." His was the saga sparked by the turmoil that followed the Civil War, and the passing of more than a century has by no means diminished the flame.

———◆———

True, the old days and the old ways are but treasured memories, and the old trails have grown dim with the ravages of time, but the spirit of the cowboy lives on.

———◆———

In my travels—to Texas, Oklahoma, Kansas, Nebraska, Colorado, Wyoming, New Mexico, and Arizona—I always find something that reminds me of the Old West. While I am walking these plains and mountains for the first time, there is this feeling that a part of me is eternal, that I have known these old trails before. I believe it is the undying spirit of the frontier calling me, through the mind's eye, to step back into time. What is the appeal of the Old West of the American frontier?

———◆———

It has been epitomized by some as the dark and bloody period in American history. Its heroes—Crockett, Bowie, Hickok, Earp—have been reviled and criticized. Yet the Old West lives on, larger than life.

———◆———

It has become a symbol of freedom, when there was always another mountain to climb and another river to cross; when a dispute between two men was settled not with expensive lawyers, but with fists, knives, or guns. Barbaric? Maybe. But some things never change. When the cowboy rode into the pages of American history, he left behind a legacy that lives within the hearts of us all.

—*Ralph Compton*

CHAPTER ONE

1876. The Smoky Hills. Kansas.

W HEN HE FIRST rode up, Dane did not know the town's name. He'd seen no city-limits sign. But after all the dusty trailing he'd done from Abilene, the greenness of the place appealed to him. In the October dusk the place looked pleasantly sleepy and well shaded. Its few streets were laid out to either side of a tree-lined river. This time of year, the river was awash with silt from the thunderstorms in the hills, so it seemed the color of saddle leather. The rolling hills to the west of the town were yet green for rich grazing. Most of the birches and cottonwoods hugging the river still had a passel of green leaves, though the oaks were going golden red. A soft breeze ruffled the treetops, a sight Dane found soothing. There was little enough comfort in the world, and this place might offer him a spoonful or two before it urged him on.

The town didn't seem large; nor was it too small. Large towns made him nervous. Small towns made him feel overly conspicuous. He couldn't remember why he felt that way any more than he could remember what his full name was, or how old he was—or even where he had been born.

He was almost a stranger to himself. *Dane* was the only name he could recall, though it seemed to him he'd had more than one, sometime in the curtained-off past. He thought he might be from Missouri, because folks sometimes remarked that he had an Eastern Missouri accent.

All that really mattered, most times, was where he'd just been and where he was going. For a while he'd cowboyed for a big spread in Kansas. Lately he'd been working on a small ranch a half day's ride from Abilene, Kansas, just a hired hand fixing fences, digging irrigation, taking care of the small herd, even hoeing the vegetable garden. They'd paid him scantly, but they'd given him two meals a day along with a bunk in a lean-to, and they'd put up his mule, Gravy, even giving her grain. Still, eight months on that dusty, unfriendly High Plains spread had been enough. He was not a talkative man, but working for German folk who knew just enough English to boss him—who made their own beer and never offered him any—had been even lonelier than he was used to. Dane had saved a small poke of silver, and six days ago, he'd climbed on Gravy and ridden out with his few possessions: the clothes on his back, the old Colt Army revolver—Dane couldn't recall how he'd come to have it—exactly three bullets, one lariat, a harmonica, a saddle and saddlebags, a comb made of elk horn, a tin pan for cooking, a tin coffee cup, an iron saucepan he used for boiling coffee, a tinder box, an Army canteen with a bullet hole halfway up it, and a skinning knife. He'd stopped in Abilene for coffee and bacon, hardtack and dried apples, and a handful of matches. He had finally bought a new canteen, too, because the bullet hole—he had no idea how it had come to be there—meant his old canteen could be filled only halfway.

Dane had fifty-five dollars left. He needed new boots, but he was reluctant to part with the price of them. He suspected he might need to buy another mount. Poor old Gravy might give out on him. For a good long time, before he'd bought her for three dollars and seventy-five cents, she'd been used to pull plows and buckboards. Mules were tough, but she had been seventeen years old when he bought her; now she was nearly twenty, and her working life had fair worn her down. She was beginning to be swaybacked and complained more than she used to when he mounted her. Dane was afraid she wasn't long for the world. He would miss her. She was a kindly animal, for a mule, and his only friend, now that Old Keggum had died.

Dane had hoped to stay in Abilene longer—but found himself unsettled when Marshal Freeman had accosted him with questions.

"Seems like I saw you out to Bull Run," Freeman said. "You don't remember me? I was provost marshal."

"No, sir, I don't remember if I was in the war or not," Dane had said. He was careful to be polite to the notorious gunman. "I don't remember much, till startin' three years ago."

"Is that so? What's your name?"

"It's Dane, Marshal."

"Dane what?"

Dane shrugged. "The one name's the only name I know."

Freeman had scowled, seeming to think Dane was covering up some shadowy past—perhaps as a deserter from the Army—and gave him twelve hours to leave town.

It was often that way. Some lawmen distrusted him, though he avoided trouble. Dane knew he looked rough, knew he seemed a saddle tramp. Hilda Weber, the wife of his boss, had made him shave and cut his hair once every two months so he didn't scare the children. Perhaps he was indeed a mere saddle bum.

Thinking that maybe, somewhere on, he could be something better, he trotted his old mule on into this new town.

T HE FIRST TIME Suzanne Marrin saw Dane, she took him at first glance to be a skulky vagabond of the lowest type.

It was getting on toward sunset as she walked from the dress shop, where she'd bought a pattern, to the mercantile, for a bolt of dark blue cloth and a little lace. She'd saved her egg money for the makings of a new dress so that she would no longer be embarrassed when she went to church. Just now she was wearing a much-worn tan walking skirt, one of her mother's hand-me-down white blouses, and a rose-pink sweater her mother had knitted for her. Her old button-up shoes, which had also belonged to her mother, clipped rapidly across Main Street. The town council, in a fit of pride and concern for the tendency of the street to flood, had sprung for brick pavement with drainage. She paused partway to let a costly brass-and-fringe-trimmed surrey clop past, drawn by a fine, neatly groomed quarter horse. It was driven by Jess Willoughby, the dapper owner of the Horseshoe W Ranch. He was a narrow-faced, sandy-haired man with a vinegary expression on his face most times, but now he managed a smile and tipped his homburg at her. She nodded in return, not meeting his eyes. He'd twice asked for Suzanne's hand. But to the frustration of her mother, Suzanne had politely but firmly said no.

"You're thirty-three, Suzanne," her mother had said. "Folks think you a spinster!"

Now Willoughby clucked at the Kentucky mare to quicken the surrey out of Suzanne's way, and she made her way hurriedly to the wooden walkway in front of the mercantile. She heard a distant rumble of thunder; she'd seen clouds gathering on the northern horizon. It wouldn't do to be caught in a downpour.

She had one hand on the glass knob of the mercantile's door when another clop of hooves made her glance over her shoulder—and she stopped, staring.

A stranger was riding in on a gray mule that snorted with weariness. He was a big man, almost too big for his mule. No doubt he was a trail-traipsing drunkard, for he had holes in his old Stetson—the sort that come from taking off a hat by the crease for a couple years—and his boots were down at heel, the sole on one of them peeling off. His blue trousers were scuffed open at the knees, and he wore an open duster over what might have been a ragtag red flannel shirt, the shirt so dusty itself, it was hard to have an opinion as to its original color. He had the kind of beard that comes from ignoring his razor, and brown hair past his grimy collar. And his face . . . his eyes . . .

Suddenly, she found herself unsure of her first estimate of the man.

His gray eyes were intelligent as he glanced her way. They were sensitive eyes, even kindly—but haunted, too. His weathered face creased in a sad smile, and to her surprise, the saddle tramp doffed his hat to her and nodded, his manner marked by a gentlemanliness that belied his appearance.

Realizing she was staring, Suzanne turned away, blushing, and hurried into the mercantile.

THE SUNSET WAS just starting to make a scarlet outline of the rolling hills, when Dane dismounted at the livery. A sign on the whitewashed building read *R. K. Gunderson, Hostler.*

Dane patted Gravy, feeling the sweat on her trembling withers, and looked down the street, reading some signs: *Smoky River Dry Goods . . . Smoky River Inn . . . First Bank of Smoky River . . .*

"Gravy," he said, "could be we're in a place called Smoky River. This is a corner of Kansas I don't know. But clues lead me to the conjecture."

"Mister, you want to put up that mule here?"

Dane turned to see a roosterish red-faced little man in overalls and a leather apron; he had an imposing brown beard stained yellow from tobacco. "You'd be Mr. Gunderson?" Dane asked.

"I would be, and I am," said the hostler. "Roy K. Gunderson."

"My name's Dane."

"You didn't answer my question. You puttin' up the mule or not? I don't want him blocking the door for real trade."

"I would indeed like to put him up, Mr. Gunderson. Let's say for one—no, two nights. And maybe longer."

The hostler quoted his price for a stall, and the cost of hay and grain and a rubdown. "Water's for free if you take the stall."

"I'll take it, sir, but I'll rub Gravy down myself. We're old friends, and she expects it of me."

"Same price!" Gunderson stuck his hand out for the money. He wasn't going to wait on payment from a saddle tramp.

Dane nodded and paid it over. "I take it this is the town of Smoky River?"

"It is that. Named after the Smoky Hill River, which you can see yonder. Town council thought Smoky Hill River too much of a mouthful for namin' a town."

"Is there a saloon that also serves a man fair grub?"

Gunderson hooked a thumb to his right. "'Cross the street and two doors down. Rusty's Saloon. He offers grub that won't lay you out with a bellyache. Most times."

"I thank you, sir. I'll take Gravy inside."

Gunderson stepped aside, and Dane found a stall next to a sleepy-looking mare where he put Gravy in a harness. He fed and watered her and rubbed her down himself, Gunderson watching with a frown.

"That old mule," he said, tamping tobacco into a corncob pipe, "is on its last legs."

"Well, I don't know. Likely she's just tired out."

"Don't tell me I don't know mules! If she falls over dead in here, you'll be responsible for hauling her away. But you know"—a certain craftiness entered into the hostler's voice—"I have a stock horse for sale. Good cow horse. I'll give him to you for thirty dollars. Then you can shoot that mule—somewheres else!—or put it out to pasture. In fact, I've got a pasture you can use. Fifty cents a month."

"You seem pretty eager to sell this horse to the first feller you meet, Mr. Gunderson—I say it respectfully. I'm sure you have your reasons." He smiled. "What are those reasons, may I ask?"

"You speak with peculiar nicety for a drifter," Gunderson said, scowling. He lit his pipe, flicking a match alight with a thumbnail. His thumb was discolored with tobacco, too. "Well. This mustang's powerful choosy about who sits on him." He puffed the pipe alight, blew smoke at the cobwebbed ceiling, and said, "He'll take a fella on, and if he doesn't much like him, he'll carry him a short way, then wait for a chance to shake him off. Usually into the mud. What're you chucklin' for? It ain't funny; that's a good horse going to waste!"

"I would not mind having a look at this cow pony, Mr. Gunderson."

"Right over here."

Gunderson went to a stall on the other side of the stable, took hold of a bridle, and led the horse out. It snorted in a way that, to a man with horse sense, sounded its irritation at being separated from its grain. He was a brown mustang with a black mane and tail, a white blaze. Fairly young and muscular. An unremarkable creature, except that he had a sort of dangerous stillness. Dane felt the horse was assessing him the same moment he was taking stock of it.

"What's his name?"

"Got none that I know of. Just a remuda horse."

"Must be a troublesome one." Dane stepped closer and looked the horse in the eye. "Hey, pard," he whispered. "You want out of here? I can get you a better stake than this ol' stable. My name's Dane. Don't know much else to tell you except I always know when I'm makin' the acquaintance of a good horse." The horse had its ears perked toward him; its dark, lustrous eyes were watching him closely.

Dane remembered a couple of old horehound drops in his duster pocket. He took them out, held them on his palm for the horse. The mustang sniffed at them and then lipped them up and set to busily crunching the candy drops.

"You like that? I get a sweet tooth myself now and then. . . ."

He held the back of his hand in front of the horse's muzzle, let it snuffle at him. The mustang tilted its head, and the taut muscles under its hide seemed to soften. It let him stroke its muzzle.

"Why, by God, I think the damn hammerhead has taken to you!" Gunderson said. "Now you *got* to buy him!"

"Got to? For thirty dollars? Well, that's more than half what's in my poke, Mr. Gunderson. How's about eighteen? And I'll hire that pasture for my mule."

"Eighteen! Why, you're soaked!"

"I have not taken a drink today. How about nineteen?"

They finally settled on twenty-three. Gunderson seemed relieved to be shed of the mustang.

Dane felt foolish, buying the horse without trying to sit it first, but he had a hunch. "I'm gonna call you Pard," he said, scratching behind the horse's ears. "I think we'll do fine."

HALF AN HOUR later, Dane was finishing a couple of pickled eggs and a cut of ham in Rusty's Saloon. He was standing at the bar to eat and washing down the food with a schooner of beer, when one of the other men at the bar began to bullyrag him.

"What kinda scapegrace you 'low in here, Rusty?" the man blared. He was a round-faced man, leaning back on his stool, looking at Dane over his long nose, mouth agape, chin poking toward Dane. He had one hand on the bar, the other on the check vest over his broad belly. There was a small silver gun in his belt, not far from that hand. "Look at him. Seems the town dump was his tailor."

The two cowboys at the bar laughed. The cowboys were at Dane's left; the man in the broad check vest was lolling a couple stools away on Dane's right.

"Oh, I dunno about that, Metzger," said Rusty as he poured Old Overholt in a whiskey glass for an already drunk cowboy. The barkeep was a tall man in a white shirt and apron, his thick black hair greased back, a perpetually quizzical expression on his lean, mustachioed face. His accent sounded Texas Panhandle to Dane. "I myself was a time or two down on my luck and had my toes sticking out of my shoes. I sold my horse and got into a poker game, and had it not been for my three aces and the other man's busted flush, I'd not have had the money to buy this establishment. I might still be tying my shoes closed with rags. My policy, therefore, is that any man that pays can find his refreshment here."

"You were never so ragged as this saddle bum, Rusty! Hey, saddle bum—move to the far end of the bar. I can smell goats—and there's no goats in here!"

Dane ignored the bullyragger. He drank the rest of his beer, wiped his mouth, and thought about sleeping at the livery, alongside Gravy. He needed to save his money.

"I said, mister, this is a place for gennelmen. . . ." Metzger approached Dane, hand on the gun in his belt. "Not goats."

No one was laughing now.

Dane looked at him and said nothing. He waited.

Metzger shoved the "saddle bum."

Dane slid instantly into a strange state of mind, then—something that happened to him from time to time. It was as if his body took over from his brain.

He snatched his own pistol from under his coat, flipped it so he held it by the barrel, and, in almost the same motion, cracked Metzger in the forehead with the butt of the gun, just hard enough.

Metzger's eyes crossed. He fell back, stumbled over a spittoon, and went heavily to the floor, out cold.

"Look at that!" one of the cowboys shouted. "He's killed Tom Metzger! Busted his head open!"

More cries rang out, and the other two men at the bar backed away from Dane, their hands hovering over their pistols.

Dane whirled, flipping the gun around again, catching it neatly so it was pointed toward the two cowboys. They turned tail and ran out the front door, shouting for the sheriff as they went. Feeling strange, Dane holstered his old Colt. It really felt to him as if someone else had done all that business with the gun.

"What's all this ruckus on what should be such a peaceful night?" cried a silhouette at the doorway backlit by the lanterns hanging outside. The lanterns inside the saloon shone off the silver star on his chest.

The lawman stepped into the room, one hand on the butt of a holstered Colt. The other hand was operating a gold-headed walking stick. He was a good-looking blue-eyed man with a slim mustache, dressed in a three-piece chestnut brown suit, polished Spanish boots, and a maroon bowler. Across his middle was a gold watch chain. *Fancy for town law,* Dane thought. *And young for the job, too.*

The man with the badge looked analytically down at Metzger. "Rusty, someone's cold-cocked Metzger, I take it?"

Rusty cleared his throat. "Well, Bat, Metzger was four whiskeys down, and he was callin' this gent here names. The gent ignored it, and Metzger gave him a shove and duly received a sockdolager on the forehead with a gun butt."

Metzger was groaning, his eyes fluttering open. "Whuh? Where . . . ?"

Bat chuckled. "I don't see as his head's busted open as some reported," the deputy said. "And he's breathing just fine. Real peaceful." He looked Dane up and down. He frowned and shook his head.

The cowboys were looking through the door behind him. Bat half turned to them, keeping his gaze on Dane, and said, "Boys, help Mr. Metzger here over to our good Dr. Greeley. I think Tom'll do all right, with some willow bark and a rest."

Bat stepped aside, still watching Dane, as they helped Metzger up and half dragged him out the door. Then he pointed his walking stick at Dane. "Mister, I'm a deputy of the town police. W. B. Masterson. Who'd you be?"

"My name's Dane, sir. That's all the name I've got."

Bat put his hand on his own gun butt. "Put your gun on the bar there, real slow. Keep your fingers clear of the trigger."

Thunder rumbled as the rainstorm drew nearer.

Dane took out his gun, moving syrup slow, and placed it on the bar.

"Any more weapons?" the deputy asked.

"I got a skinning knife, but it's in my saddlebag."

"Did Rusty tell the story as it happened?"

"Yes, sir, he did."

"Metzger is not my delight, but he is the town gunsmith—imagines he knows something about the use of firearms, too—and some regard him as an upstanding man. But for his fits of drunkenness, he would be on the town council. We cannot have you buffaloing our citizens with your gun butt."

"If you want me out of town, I'd like to leave in the morning, if I may. There's a rainstorm coming."

"What's your profession?"

"Hired hand. Cowboy or farmhand. Did some buffalo hunting. Didn't like it much."

"Did you? So did I. Me and my brother, Jim. And Wyatt. I did not care for that job either." Bat glanced at the Colt Army on the bar. "That old Civil War iron, there?"

"So they tell me."

"Does it still do its work?"

"I haven't fired it in two years. Fired a shot to scare a road agent away. But I believe it still works."

Bat gave a short nod. "Tell you what. If by noon tomorrow you have cleaned yourself up—a shave and bath and clothing that doesn't elicit insults—I'll risk you a while longer. If you solemnly swear not to bust any more citizens in the noggin."

Dane hesitated. He wasn't quite sure how he'd come to bust Metzger in the noggin. But he nodded and said, "Do my level best, Deputy."

"That doesn't ring of committal," Bat observed.

"He showed more forbearance than many a man would, Bat," Rusty put in. "Some would've shot the damned fool. Metzger had his hand on his gun."

Bat took off his bowler, swept his hair back with the other hand, then replaced the hat with an air of decision. "I'll keep a close eye on you. But you clean yourself up, first chance. Before noon tomorrow! The sheriff likes me to run tramps out of town."

Dane nodded. "I understand, Deputy." Dane was considerably older than W. B. "Bat" Masterson, but he was unfailingly respectful of honest lawmen, and this young fellow seemed like a straight shooter. He had a lawman's air of authority, but there was no bullying about it.

The rain was bucketing down now. Bat turned and swore softly. "Going to soak my new hat." He strode hastily out, boots loud on the walkway.

Dane turned to Rusty, who was ruminatively polishing a glass. "Rusty, I thank you for speaking for me."

Rusty shrugged. "See you live up to it. You want a whiskey? I'm going to have one."

"No. I thank you. I do not drink the hard spirits. But I'll have one more beer if that'll suit you. . . ."

Rusty drank his whiskey, Dane quietly sipped his beer and listened to the rain *rat-a-tat* on the roof.

Dane, sir. That's all the name I've got, he'd said. Was it true?

It had been bothering him lately, more than it ever had before. Not knowing for sure . . .

Who *was* he?

CHAPTER TWO

THE PASTURAGE OUT behind the livery was a few acres, with the river beyond it. The Smoky Hill River was rushing now, Dane saw; it was brimming with last night's storm, looking golden brown in the morning light. "Anyhow, you won't hurt for water," he told Gravy, who was contentedly cropping the thick grass. He patted her and looked around. There were two swaybacked old horses sharing the pasture and a milk cow. "Looks like you'll have company. That Gunderson—I have a feeling he's got a softer heart than he lets on." Dane smirked at himself. "Talking to a mule again. But you're about all I've had to talk to, since Old Keggum passed. You've been a good friend, Gravy girl, and I'll come and see you again."

He turned away and went through the gate into the livery.

"Where you headed?" Gunderson called, getting up

from his coffee. "I'm looking for someone to throw a
horseshoe with."

"I'm a good hand at horseshoes," Dane said, "and
I'll bet you a penny a throw, first chance I get. Right
now I'm on a big job for Deputy Masterson. He wants
me bathed and suited up—if I fail at the job, I'm to
leave town."

Gunderson made the creaking sound that passed
for laughter with him.

D ANE HAD RUN through most of his savings now,
but there was still enough for bacon, bread, and
coffee and a few nights at a boardinghouse.

He put his coffee cup down and wiped his mouth
with a cloth napkin. He felt good—bathed and in his
new clothes—because no one was staring at him; no
one was wondering what a tramp was doing in here.

When Dane bathed, it was usually with the aid of a
rag, a cake of soap, and a bucket of water. Not pleasant
on a cold winter's day. Before today, he'd only had one
hot bath over the last three years, when he'd bathed for
Elias Keggum's funeral, and Dane had forgotten how
pleasurable it felt. The shave and haircut felt good, too;
and he felt renewed to be wearing new Levi's work
trousers, new socks, and a pair of new boots, a new hat,
a new shirt. Not the best hat, and not the best boots in
the shop, but sturdy. He had a belt, too, and a charcoal
black shirt, because it wouldn't show up dirt much.
He'd even cleaned up his duster.

He looked at the other folks sitting at the tables in
the little café. Nearby was a prosperous farmer—or so
Dane guessed, from his sun-weathered face and his

gnarled fingers—hair oiled, wearing a suit jacket over his denim, with his very pregnant wife, who wore a long white cotton dress. In a corner, two tittering ladies in gingham bonnets were drinking tea and whispering secrets. A bespectacled man in a rumpled suit sat at the window, reading a newspaper.

Dane felt more right with the world than he had in a good while, but he also felt the lightness of his money poke. He needed a job and quick. Maybe Masterson would know who was hiring.

He got up and stretched, nodded to the friendly Chinese fellow who ran the place, gave him the price of the meal and ten cents more, and went outside to have a look at the day.

A soft, cool wind was blowing. Good to feel it on his face. It was a fresh day, with racing clouds and enough sun to make it feel bright and cheerful.

"You new in town, mister?"

He turned and saw Bat Masterson surveying him with a cocked eye.

"You truly don't recognize me, Deputy?"

Bat grinned. "I know who you are. But in a way I don't recognize you. Shined up like a bright new penny. A grand improvement!"

"Thanks—am I shined up enough that I can call you Bat?"

"Certainly. I prefer it to Bartholomew, which my mother calls me, and there's too many Williams about." Bat was wearing a tailored black suit today and a red silk string tie.

How did he afford them on a deputy's salary? Dane wondered. He could well picture the man at a card table. Could be he was lucky at cards.

"Here." Bat reached under his coat and drew out Dane's old Army pistol. "Saw you out here, decided you can have this back, but don't fire it in town except in desperation. And think twice before you crack anybody in the head with it."

My hand didn't have time to think twice, Dane thought. "Thanks again." Dane tucked the gun away. "Know where I can get a job, Bat?"

"You can always shovel horse apples for Gunderson."

"I'll do it, too, lacking better work."

Was that music he heard in the distance? An organ and a choir?

"There's ranches in the area. They hire sometimes. Horseshoe W might be looking for a hand. Willoughby is a sourpuss, owing perhaps to his having lost a leg in the war, but he's fair enough. Hell, his ramrod is a Confederate captain, and it's the Rebs that took his leg. So he does not hold a grudge. What's that look on your face, like a dog listening for a squirrel?"

"Thought I heard some music."

"Oh, it's Sunday. That's the Doxology Works. First and only Church of Smoky River. Come on with me. I was going over there to gaze upon the dolled-up ladies."

Y OU SEE THAT? It's that killer from Steeple Rock. The one who shot Johnny O'Hara."

"Can't be, Squint," said Hans with his mild Scandinavian accent. "That man is dead. Yah. More than three years now."

Squint Brewster clenched his little Mexican cigar in his yellow teeth and growled, "I swear it's him."

The two men stood across the street from Dane and

Masterson, in the shade of a porch roof beside the door of Clemson's Silver Goddess Dance Exhibition and Game Emporium.

Brewster kept his eyes on Dane. That was him, wasn't it?

Hamish "Squint" Brewster had one eye always squinted. He'd made a feeble attempt at a clipped beard about his face; it was the soft, nose-reddened face of a man who liked his drink overmuch. His lips were so thin, they were almost not there. He wore his best duds—a clean shirt, a vest, a string tie—because of the mission Shine had sent them on.

Hans Husman, sometimes called the Swede, contemplated the man strolling cheerfully down the wooden walkway with Masterson. "It's not him," Hans declared. "I put a ball in him myself."

"You shot him from a distance with a rifle. Me and the others, we know him up close. Anyhow, I know him. You never met him—you were new to the bunch then."

Hans was almost a foot taller than Brewster, a clean-shaven, big-jawed blond giant. He wore a suit that was about two inches too small for him, all around his limbs, and glossy black boots. Both men were armed, but Brewster's was a hideaway under his vest; Hans had his pistol holstered under his coat.

"Sure as hell looks like him," declared Brewster. "And no one found his body."

"He fell right off that Squaw's Cliff. I could see that much. Seemed like wolves must've dragged his body away. We heard 'em howling out there. Wolves, they like to eat a man when he's still alive if they can." He licked his lips, and his eyes shone at the thought. "They like to tear him apart."

"No proof he's dead."

"We shot him three times, Squint."

"I swear that's him. I never forget a face."

"Shine will be very surprised if that man's alive," Hans said.

"He won't be happy."

"No."

"He'll want something done about it."

"He will. But we got to know for sure. And we got to tell Shine before . . ."

"Well, we're almost done here. Clemson seems like he wants to shake hands on that deal with Shine. Once that's done . . ."

B AT AND DANE strolled through sunshine and shade, depending on where the hurrying clouds were, and down the wooden sidewalk toward the edge of town. The way Bat used the walking stick, it seemed to Dane that it wasn't mere decoration. He favored his left leg.

Bat noticed him looking at the walking stick. "I like to pretend it's just high fashion, but I do need it some. Fella shot me in the hip, about the same time I shot him, last January. That was down in Sweetwater. I came out alive, and he didn't, but I was crippled up for a time."

"I've been through Sweetwater with a herd. That's a tough town."

"It surely is. Mostly con men, cardsharps, thieves, snake-head whiskey, and drunken buffalo hunters. Well, I'd had enough of it. I went to my folks' farm in

Sedgwick to heal up. And my papa heard they were looking for a deputy here. And so here I am. But I may not stay a whole lot longer."

"This town doesn't suit you either?"

"The *pay* don't suit me. Nor does— However, I won't go into that." He shook his head. "I've got a friend on the police force in Dodge City. Better pay, more card games. He'd like me to join him there. I might do it."

Dane felt the rough makings of a friendship with Masterson, and he'd be sorry to see him go. Dane didn't make friends easily.

As they strolled along, he looked down a lane that started across the main road. It led to a wooden bridge stretching over the Smoky Hill River to the other half of town. He could make out small, ramshackle houses, their chimneys trailing smoke, on the farther bank. "Haven't been across the bridge yet."

"Most of the best side of Smoky River is here, on this street. Over there it's cabins, small houses, even some still in tents. One or two fancier houses. There's a cattle pen, a couple of warehouses, and a saloon that the town should probably close down."

"What's wrong with the saloon?"

"Hasn't been approved. They need to sign a paper with the town. It isn't much more than a lean-to. The lady who owns it has a little house back of it occupied by sporting women. I don't hold against a bawdy house, but that one's too flagrant for this town. Couple of them tried to hook men from Main Street here and tow 'em over there. That is not protocol, my friend. Had to put a stop to it. Ah—for a pleasing contrast, here's the church."

They'd come to a stone path leading through sere grass to a shingled one-story building with a cross over the open front door. A large brass bell hung in an oaken stand beside the stone porch.

Bat put a finger to his lips, and they went quietly to the open door, hats in hands, and looked through to see a preacher—a cadaverous man in a black frock coat—intoning solemnly in front of a tolerably full congregation, everyone in Sunday best. To the preacher's right, a hefty lady in a feathered hat and a flowery dress sat at a pump organ, with her back to the congregation. Behind the minister was another cross, and to the right on a small wooden stage, a row of eight people stood with hymnals in hand. The choir. One of them looked familiar—a woman in a dark blue dress trimmed in white lace. That was the woman he'd seen yesterday, wasn't it? She had stood at the mercantile door and met his eyes. For a moment she had seemed to him like a picture from a magazine, a living tableau. She had long copper-colored hair, creamy skin, green eyes, a heart-shaped face. He'd impulsively lifted his hat to her.

She was listening gravely to the preacher.

"As it is written in Isaiah: 'Behold, the Lord is about to come out from His place to punish the inhabitants of the earth for their iniquity. And the earth will reveal her bloodshed, and will no longer cover her slain.'"

"He's a fire-breather, this one," Bat whispered.

Something flashed in Dane's mind as he contemplated the verse from Isaiah. He seemed to remember a battered field, wreathed in smoke. A shattered cannon. A weeping man bleeding out from the stump of his missing leg. The rattle of rifle fire. Muzzle flashes through the smoke. His horse screaming as a bullet caught it and—

He shuddered and banned the vision from his mind—one of those orphan images that sometimes came to him. Maybe a memory. Maybe a kind of dream.

Dane closed his eyes, sickened, and was about to turn away from the church when he heard an angel singing. He looked for the source of the singing. . . .

It was the young woman from the mercantile, singing solo.

In a sweet, slightly husky voice, she sang,

Abide with me; fast falls the eventide;
The darkness deepens; Lord, with me abide.
When other helpers fail and comforts flee,
Help of the helpless, O abide with me. . . .

The choir came in then to join her. What a glorious sound it was. How long since he'd heard something of the kind.

But when *had* he heard a choir before? He couldn't remember.

Still, the sick feeling he'd had a moment before was swept away by their voices, and as he gazed on the woman leading the choir, he felt a sweet warmth rise inside him.

"Say," Bat whispered, "you'd better close your mouth before bees make a hive in it. Good God, man. You never heard a choir before?"

"She . . . she's . . . like a . . ."

"Oh, is that it! Come on, Romeo." Chuckling, Masterson tugged him away from the church. "Get a job, work a time, buy yourself some church clothes, and go to the Doxology Works to meet her, if you want. She'll probably say nay to courting, however. That's Suzanne Marrin. And she's been asked by many a gent. She always says no. Even to me, if you can believe it! Course, I'm a mite younger than she is. Why, she's all the way to thirty-three!"

And how old am I? Dane wondered. *Late thirties, maybe?*

They fell silent, walking back to the center of town.

A man crossed to their side of the street and stopped, staring at Dane. It was Metzger. He was cleaned up and wearing a butter yellow suit, but there was a red knot on his forehead.

"Uh-oh," said Masterson under his breath.

Metzger strode up to them—and beamed at Dane. "A stranger in town! Just come in today?" Before Dane could answer, Metzger gave him a card. It read, *Tom Metzger, Gunsmith, Smoky River, Kansas.* "If you're looking for a gunsmith, I'm your man"—he winked—"because I'm the only one in town!"

He laughed—and then winced. The laugh had hurt his head.

Dane looked at Metzger to see if he was in earnest. Did he really not know that Dane was the man who'd put that knot on his head?

Metzger continued to smile and touched his hat to Masterson. "Deputy!"

"Tom."

"Mr. Metzger," said Dane, "I'll surely stop in sometime."

"Say, Tom," said Masterson. "That's a fine goose egg on your bean there."

Metzger scowled. "You should know. Rusty says

you run that saddle bum out of town last night! Hell, you should have arrested him!"

"Well, now, the story I had was that you were a bit soaked and came at him with your hand on your gun. But I sent the, uh, saddle bum . . . on his way."

Metzger grunted. "If he ever comes back here, he'd better not let me see him." He turned smilingly to Dane. "See you soon, sir! Ah—what was your name?"

"Just call me Dane, Tom."

"Dane—I shall see you in the shop."

Metzger crossed the wooden sidewalk and went into the apothecary shop.

Bat shook his head in amazement, laughing softly. "Well, by God, he really did not recognize you, Dane! Course, he had swilled considerable oh-be-joyful in Rusty's."

"And just as well he didn't know me, too. I reckon he's gone in to get himself a headache remedy. . . ."

"And he's got you to thank for the necessity."

They walked on, their boots making a slow drumming on the wooden walk. Dane noticed that Bat maintained his usual air of genial unconcern, but the striking blue eyes were taking in everything on the street. Bat paused at a closed grocery and tried the door to make sure it was locked. *He's a natural lawman,* Dane thought.

They were almost at Rusty's Saloon when Dane noticed two men coming toward them on the sidewalk. One was a tall, barrel-chested blond man with a lantern jaw; the other, squat and seamy, came to a sudden stop on the walkway, glaring at Dane. All four men stood there, taking the measure of one another.

The shorter, squint-eyed man looked familiar. And yet Dane couldn't remember having seen him before.

The squint-eyed man seemed to nod to himself. Then he walked into the saloon, followed by the blond man in the ill-fitting clothes, so tall he had to duck his head at the door.

"You know those two, Bat?" Dane asked.

"I was just going to query you the same."

"One of them looked familiar. But I don't know from where. He seemed to recognize me."

"Well, I'll get their names later. They're new here, and I like to keep track. And I don't like the looks of them." He clapped Dane on the shoulder. "You ought to head out to the Horseshoe W. Ask Gunderson to tell you the way. Right now I've got to talk to the sheriff, see if I can get some time off tonight. There's a fine fat card game awaiting me. What do you figure on doing?"

"Do some riding, look around some. Tomorrow I'll head out to the Horseshoe W. . . ."

S O FAR, THE mustang hadn't bucked him off.

Dane rode north, between stands of dusty, autumn-dyed oaks, along a rutted dirt road, staying in the grassy margin so that the horse didn't twist an ankle in those muddy ruts. He was thinking, mostly, about the girl in the dark blue dress singing in the choir. *Suzanne,* Bat had said. A grown woman, not a girl. Would she talk to him? Absurd.

This road would take him to the Horseshoe W, if Gunderson was to be believed. Dane wasn't sure of Pard yet, remembering the hostler's story of the horse allowing a rider for a time before choosing an opportune spot to buck him off.

"You going to pull that one on me, Pard?" he asked, his voice soft, patting the horse's neck. "It's up to you. It's not going to discourage me. I'm in for every toss you give me."

Pard drew to a stop as if about to take the dare. But instead the mustang perked up his ears and looked toward the west, whinnying softly.

"You hearing something?" Dane peered out west and saw only grassy rolling hills spotted with oaks and rippling with the shadows of passing clouds. But he kept watching.

There they were. Two men, one on an especially big horse, riding parallel to the road about three hundred yards away. They were looking his way. One of the men, tall in the saddle, had blond hair.

It was the two men who'd almost braced him on the sidewalk. He had a feeling they might have jumped him if the deputy hadn't been there. And here they were again. . . .

Could be they were just riding the same way. But why weren't they taking the road?

After a few minutes of clopping along on Pard, Dane was sure the riders were watching him. Likely trailing him. He could feel it. He racked his brain, trying to remember who the squint-eyed one was. But long ago he'd learned that trying to force a memory to come just didn't work. Not if it was from more than three years past.

Sometimes he had dreams that might stem from his life—before. The scenes from war. And in smoke-blackened saloons. Blazing guns, screaming horses, drunks firing at him in honky-tonks. But all murky. Nothing clear. No faces ever emerged from the dreams into daylight.

The two riders rode into a copse of trees and underbrush, and he lost sight of them. Were they setting up an ambush?

Crazy thought. He had no reason to fear anyone from his past.

But how would he know that? He couldn't remember his past but for three years. No way to know what he'd done before that. Sometimes it troubled him that what he'd done, back in the time before he could remember, might have been bad.

No use chewing it over now. He had a job to get.

Dane patted Pard's neck. "I knew you were a good horse. Thanks for keeping watch."

He gave the mustang a slight nudge with his bootheels, very gently, and Pard responded, setting off in a trot. Dane nudged him again, slightly harder, and the mustang took it to a good canter.

Be interesting to see if those riders troubled to keep up. Dane was about a mile and a half on before he saw them again, riding parallel, in the hills.

He thought about riding up there, asking their business. But maybe that was what they wanted. The fact they were showing themselves made him think maybe they'd like him to come away from the road and into rifle range.

Dane shook his head. They were probably just out hunting for strays. Still—an inner uneasiness warned him to wariness.

Dane made up his mind when he saw sycamores off the road between him and the riders. He drew his pistol with a flourish, wanting them to see it, and turned off the road, galloping toward the stand of trees. He was among them in moments and dismounted. He peered between the tree trunks and could no longer see the riders. They might still be up there, hiding in the brush atop the ridge. Gun in hand, he slipped between the boles to an outcropping of rock and hunkered there, scanning the ridgeline. He had a good view of the terrain here, all around; he'd see them if they tried to flank him.

He waited fifteen minutes and saw no further sign of them. The riders were gone.

Dane holstered his gun, returned to the mustang, and rode off toward the Horseshoe W, wondering if he'd been foolish to think he was being tracked.

But he seemed to see Elias Keggum, then, shaking his head, warning him, *"There are men out there, looking for you, Dane. The ones who left you out there, busted up and bleeding . . ."*

CHAPTER THREE

PARD TOOK A long curve in the road, and Dane was suddenly in front of the gate to a ranch. A wooden plank over the gate proclaimed *Horseshoe W Ranch.* The brand of the ranch, a W over a horseshoe, was burned into the plank beside the words.

Pard quite sensibly slowed and stopped at the wooden gate, all on his own, and Dane looked up at the hills. He didn't see the riders. But he had a suspicion they were out there, watching, maybe in that grove of oaks. He wondered what history they had with him, and if it was the kind that led to gunplay. Or simple back shooting.

Half expecting to catch a bullet from a Winchester, Dane swung out of the saddle, unhooked the rawhide latch of the gate, and led Pard through. He closed and latched the gate, mounted, and rode west another quarter mile to the ranch house.

The main ranch house was two stories, rude boards

cut from logs but neatly placed and properly chinked. To the north were a blacksmith's shed, a windmill for pumping water, a bunkhouse, a long low building where the hands took their meals, some outbuildings, and a big corral for breaking horses. Beyond that was a large pasture—the far side of it was over a hill—where a herd of horses grazed.

A group of hands ringed the breaking corral, as a young cowboy was bucked from the hurricane deck, tossed summarily to the ground. The onlookers laughed and hooted at the fallen bronc buster.

A stocky, grim-looking Indian wearing a blue flannel shirt over fringed buckskin trousers was stationed between the corral and the road to the ranch. He had long, braided black hair, and he carried a rifle in the crook of his arm, which he took into his hands as he watched Dane approach.

Dane reined up not far from the Indian, raised his hand in a peace salute, and said, "Howdy. I'm looking for Mr. Willoughby."

"I'm afraid he's not here," said the Indian in perfect English. "He's in Abilene, selling a string of quarter horses. What is your business here?"

Dane was a little surprised at the Indian's precise English. It wasn't usual. Probably grew up in a mission school.

Dane touched his hat. "My name's Dane. That's all the name I've got. Deputy Masterson said Mr. Willoughby might be hiring."

The Indian, expressionless as he assessed Dane, gave the faintest of nods. "He might. We lost a hand."

"You know my name now. Can I know yours?"

"My name's Blue-Snake Thompson. You can call me Blue."

"Blue, seems this is a horse ranch."

"Expecting to find cows?"

"I was. But I'd be pleased to work with horses. Better company than cows."

The Indian gave the faintest smile. "Rand Binch is bossin' till Mr. Willoughby gets back. And he's the ramrod anytime. You got a pistol on you under that coat?"

"I do."

"If you want to ride in, take the belt off, hang the gun over the saddle horn. Then ride up to the corral. I'll get Mr. Binch over. I'll be watching you."

"Sure."

A nervous outfit, thought Dane as he slung his belt and gun over the saddle horn.

At the corral the same lanky youth on the hurricane deck of the bronco was once more headed to terra firma. The cowboy landed on his rump as the others laughed. Someone shouted, "Not bad for a green kid!"

Keeping an eye on Dane, Blue turned his head enough to call out, "Mr. Binch!"

A tall man with a bushy gray mustache turned frowning from the corral and looked Dane up and down. "What's this, Blue?"

"A hand looking for work, Rand."

Rand Binch scowled and shook his head as if such a thing was impossible, but he sauntered over to look at Dane more closely. Binch was a middle-aged man with a mustache and beard that seemed descended from Robert E. Lee's. He had a weather-reddened face that seemed to have conformed to go with his scowl; he wore overalls, a low-crowned ranch hat, and a red flannel shirt, "Well, step down, mister," Binch said. A southeastern Texas accent, so it seemed to Dane.

Dane dismounted, keeping hold of the reins, and put out his hand. "Name's Dane. Just looking for a job."

"Rand Binch. Foreman." They shook hands, Binch testing Dane's grip. Binch was wearing well-worn leather gloves.

Binch stepped back and literally looked Dane up and down, from his head to his toes. "Don't look like you've done any work in those clothes."

"No, sir, I haven't. Just bought 'em with the money I earned at the last job. Weber ranch, up by Abilene."

"What they have you doing?"

"Just about all of it. Cow punching, hunting, hoeing gardens, feeding pigs, and tending horses. Fence and building repair."

"You handy with wood, are you?"

"Handy with hammer, nails, and saw, right enough. Did my share of cow punching on a drive from the Brazos to Abilene. I can rope. And I managed the remuda on that drive, too."

"Did you? Good, this spread's mostly all about horses, though we have a small herd." He was eyeing Dane's mustang. "Looks like a good cow horse." He walked over to Pard and tugged at the saddle to see if Dane had it on properly. Then he took off a glove and ran his hand over the horse's withers. Pard snorted and shifted his hooves, but stood it. "Seems in fair shape. You ever catch one of these knotheads wild?"

"Caught a couple of bangtails a couple years back, yes, sir. We broke 'em and sold 'em into a remuda."

"Who sent you out here?"

"Deputy Masterson gave me the hint."

"Masterson's a good egg, though little more than kid." Binch pushed his hat back as if that helped him take a closer look at Dane. "As Masterson sent you, and you don't seem a complete fool, I won't pretend we don't need another hand—last 'un got his head busted in chasing bangtails. Roped one, got dragged off his horse, and a big ol' wild stallion 'bout the size of a daddy elk stepped on him."

Dane nodded. "Man's got to be careful, keep his rope cinched, and take a good horse to the job."

"Yep. Well—sounds like you'd do, only I can't hire on my own. Mr. Willoughby won't allow it. Has to approve each man. Won't let you so much as grain a horse till he meets you. I expect him back day after tomorrow."

"I'm at Galvado's Boardinghouse in Smoky River, Mr. Binch. I can come back in a couple days."

"Good. Well, we got to get back to . . ."

"Somebody's coming down the road," Blue said, shading his eyes to peer past Dane. "Buckboard. Two ladies."

Dane turned, surprised, and saw two figures blurred by dust and distance on a wagon pulled by a draft horse. "You've got good eyes, Blue. Can't tell from here." But after a moment he made out two bonnets, yellow and checked red.

"He's got an eagle's eyes, right enough," Binch said, squinting at the buckboard. He shook his head. "We don't usually get to entertain ladies. Not a female on this ranch that's not a horse. Could be they're lost."

"How big's this spread, Mr. Binch?" Dane asked.

"Twenty-eight square miles or close. Not the smallest but not big."

Dane nodded. He'd seen ranches in Texas that went on for many hundreds of miles.

"Twenty-seven acres of pasture, separated into two fields, to the west here," Binch went on, gesturing in that direction. "Wild ones to be broken and sold in the farther field. Nearer field, Mr. Willoughby raises some sport horses and gait horses. Got a couple of Arabians. But they're harder to sell hereabouts. He's sold a few in Kansas City."

They spoke for a few minutes of horses, and Dane's preference for a riding horse sixteen or seventeen hands high, with a deep chest. The cowboys began to gather around them, realizing that more company was coming. "This tall drinka water going to be working here?" drawled a slim young cowboy in leather chaps as he gave Dane an appraisal. It took the slim cowboy twice as long as most folks would to speak the question. He was about a foot shorter than Dane, and clean-shaven but for handlebar mustaches as blond as his hair.

"We'll see what Mr. Willoughby says, Buck," Binch declared.

Dane noticed the dirt on Buck's pants. "Looks like you're the bronco buster that took the spills."

Stretching the assertion out slowly, Buck said, "Why . . . that's just how I dismount."

Dane laughed, and even Binch almost smiled.

Two almost identical cowboys, in chaps, dusty Stetsons and tattered flannel shirts, crowded close, giving Dane frank once-overs.

They had the same spray of brown freckles over their long noses and gaunt cheeks, the same badly cut sandy hair, the same bright shade of blue eyes. And mostly the same skeptical expression. Dane took them for brothers, one maybe a year older and slightly taller than the other.

"Could be an owlhoot, Rand," said the older one. "Got a scar on his head there." Dane didn't take offense. The young fellow seemed the kind who was rarely serious.

"I've got scars on parts of me, some you can't see, and on my head, too, Ben Quinlan," Binch said. "Don't make me an outlaw."

"Hell, I'll take a chance on 'im," Ben said, sticking his hand out to Dane. They shook. "Ben Quinlan, this here's my brother, Ducks Quinlan," he said, hooking a thumb at his shorter brother.

"*Dirk* Quinlan!" the other boy declared, elbowing his brother hard in the ribs. "I told you not to talk that way about me!"

"Do you *duck* when called for night watch or not?" Ben demanded, giving his brother a shove.

"The devil I do!" snapped Dirk, taking a swing at his brother.

Ben slipped the blow and raised his fists.

"That's enough, you damned fools!" Binch growled, stepping between them. "There's ladies coming!"

They forgot their quarrel, which Dane reckoned to be not much above horseplay, and turned to gape with the others at the buckboard trundling up to them, drawn by a snorting, loudly clopping sorrel draft horse.

"Why it's Mrs. Marrin and her Suzanne!" exclaimed Binch.

Suzanne wore a yellow bonnet and a yellow blouse. Dane noticed that Suzanne was driving the rig, and he wasn't surprised. She struck him as a woman who drove buckboards, sang solos in church, and generally did things her way.

Now how do I know that? Dane wondered. Yet he'd known it the first time he'd seen her.

She tugged at the reins, called, "whoa," and pulled the wooden brake handle.

"Why Miz Marrin, what brings you all the way out here?" Binch asked, reaching up to help her down from the buckboard.

Suzanne climbed down on her own—jumped down, really. Suzanne's mother, a plump woman with a pronounced air of determination, was wearing a long rose-pink calico dress; Suzanne wore work jeans and walking shoes. Her hair was piled loosely up on her head under the bonnet, and there was a delicate little tuft of coppery hair growing from the back of her neck.

Dane shook his head. Why was he noticing such details about the woman? What foolishness.

"It's a simple thing, Mr. Binch," said the older woman. "The Lord has this season gifted me with a surfeit of strawberries, and I discovered we had put up too many strawberry preserves. I have taken some to the church, and some to Mrs. Aquino, who's been short on supplies, and seeing as there are but men out here who likely don't put up strawberries . . ."

"Way-ll," Buck drawled, "ma'am, you shore got that right."

Suzanne laughed. Dane thought it a lovely sound.

He found she was looking at him, then, frowning slightly, as if trying to place him. He took off his hat. "Ma'am," he said. "My name is Dane."

"Suzanne Marrin," she said. "And—and this is my mother, Elana Marrin."

He gave a faint bow to Mrs. Marrin, who returned a sour smile.

Suzanne nodded to Dane and went to the rear of the buckboard. She quickly returned with a wooden crate of jars filled with red preserves.

"Here's the goods, gentlemen," she said.

"Saints!" Binch said. "Are those for true *ours*? Why, I'd pay most any price for strawberry preserves!"

"They are yours without cost, Rand Binch," said Suzanne's mother grandly. "I'm sinfully prideful about my preserves, and you can reward me with compliments if you like them."

"Ma'am, I had some of your strawberry preserves at the harvest picnic, and they took me back to my mother down in San Antone. Almost had me blubbering." He glanced at the other men and noticed Buck staring wide-eyed at Suzanne with his mouth hanging open. Binch pointed a finger at Buck. "You! Stop ogling the ladies in that shameful way and take this box to Cookie Ike. Tell him we'll have them with hot bread, first chance."

Buck, grinning, took the box from Suzanne, muttering thank-yous.

Binch turned back to the ladies, remembering at last to take off his hat. "Miz and Miss Marrin? If you wanted to come to the grub hall, why, I could make some— Oh, I have no tea! But we've got some elderberry wine." He hastened to add, "Scarcely fermented at all!"

Mrs. Marrin did not deign to answer immediately. "Is Mr. Willoughby about?"

"I am sorry. He is not," said Binch. "He is away on business."

Clearly disappointed, Mrs. Marrin cast a sidelong look at Suzanne, who seemed relieved.

Dane figured the situation as Mrs. Marrin wanting Suzanne to have a visit with Willoughby, the prosperous rancher who might be a suitable husband for her daughter, and Suzanne preferring not to. The gift of preserves took on a new meaning.

"I think we'll be on our way," Mrs. Marrin said with a weak smile. "Please tell Mr. Willoughby that Suzanne and I are sorry we missed him."

Ben Quinlan, humming to himself, hands in his pockets, sidled up to Suzanne. "Ma'am, you sure look fine in that bonnet. Why, I could take you on a stroll round the—"

"Quinlan!" Binch barked.

Quinlan jumped a little and looked at him. "Boss?"

"Your turn on the hurricane deck! Get on over there!"

"Rand, these ladies here, it's a rare thing when—"

"Quinlan!"

Ben snorted and stalked off to the corral. Suzanne hid a smile behind her hand.

"I'm sorry, ma'am. He's young. He's got no manners," Binch said.

"That's all right," Suzanne said. "May I have a gander at your new horses? I heard about them in town."

"That you can, ma'am!"

"We've got no time, I'm afraid," Mrs. Marrin said sharply, gazing at the cloudy sky. "I expect it'll rain on us before we get home." She turned to her daughter. "Come along, girl. It's a good ways t'home."

Suzanne glanced longingly toward the horses, then shrugged and went back to the buckboard.

"Pleasured and honored to have you here, ma'am," said Binch. "You've brightened up our day a parcel and a peck."

Suzanne smiled at that as she climbed into the buckboard. "You are a courtly man, Rand Binch."

"Oh, ha-ha," he laughed, his cheeks reddening.

Dane scanned the hills. There was no sign of the two riders who'd trailed him, but they could still be up there. And these women were proposing to take the buckboard alone back to their ranch. "Mrs. Marrin," he said as she climbed up beside her daughter.

She frowned at him. He was obviously a mere ranch hand. "Yes?"

"I am riding back toward town. I'd be honored to escort you ladies to the gate of your home."

Everyone looked at him then. He had suddenly sounded like an educated gentleman.

He had surprised himself, speaking up like that. It was bold, and he was embarrassed. But to Dane, it seemed a necessity. Those riders in the hills could have been outlaws.

"I don't see why not," Suzanne said brightly as her mother hesitated. "If you're Mr. Binch's friend, I'm sure you're a good 'un."

"Why, I only just met him, ma'am," said Binch. "But if I'm any judge, he'll do. Wise for you ladies to have an escort. Bat Masterson judges him a good 'un."

"Mr. Dane," Suzanne said, her gaze frank as she looked Dane in the eyes, "if you're ready."

"Yes, ma'am." He climbed on Pard, turned the mustang around.

"Suzanne!" her mother hissed. But Suzanne clucked at the horse and twitched the reins, and the buckboard swung toward the town. Then the two women and Dane headed back down the road toward the town of Smoky River.

WALKING BEHIND THE saloon on the wrong side of the river, Sheriff Daryl "Jipps" Jipsell had made up his mind that he was not going to take any more guff from the madam of a bawdy house. He had his quirt in his right hand and a sawed-off ten gauge in his left. He meant to make an impression. And he'd made sure that Bat Masterson was out of the way that afternoon, playing cards. The young deputy was all too prone to be in the way, frowning with disapproval, hinting he might have to go to the higher authorities if anyone played what Masterson called "a crooked game." Oh, Masterson never accused the sheriff of extortion, not outright. But the message was clear enough. Jipsell would have fired him for putting on such airs, except Masterson did all the lawing that the sheriff couldn't take the time for.

The construction behind the saloon was two stories, with a peaked roof, and even a couple of curtained glass windows on the front—all the windows it had— but it was still a shack. A large, gray, roughly nailed shed disguised as a house. Behind it was an outhouse, which Jipsell could smell from here, and to one side was a pile of wood for the stove. It had one room upstairs, divided into two with a blanket on a rope, and one back room downstairs, these quarters occupied by sulky soiled doves, two of whom Jipsell had sampled.

Inside the bawdy house, someone was playing an accordion. It was hard to make out the tune.

"Sadie Danniger!" he called, stepping onto the porch and hammering the door with the muzzle of his shotgun. "It is Sheriff Jepsill! Make yourself decent and make yourself known!"

Muted cusswords were heard from within, then footsteps on a squeaking floor. The door creaked open and a tall, heavy-hipped woman appeared in a nightgown; her round arms like loaves of bread, her chestnut hair in some disarray, her makeup from the day before a bit smeared. In one hand, she held a coffee cup.

"I am just risen and have not completed a single cup of the Arbuckle," she said, in a raucous, fierce voice, her brown eyes narrowed. "What is it you'd have of me? I am not prepared for gentlemen!"

"You have never been prepared for a gentleman, I'd wager, Sadie," declared the sheriff, "and I am here on official business. This establishment, as I told you the last time, has been named a house of ill repute."

"And I paid you the . . . the 'fine'!"

"You said it was all you had! But it was not! Information has come to me that you are sending a power of money to a bank in St. Louis!"

"I send money to my sick auntie! And I do without so I can send it!"

"You will not dazzle me with lies this time," the sheriff insisted. "I will have seventy-five dollars from you . . . in fines . . . or I will call my deputy and rush you to jail!"

"Why you bloodsucking horsefly! I will give you not a penny more than forty-five dollars! That is ten dollars more and—"

"Sheriff Jipsell?"

The sheriff whirled to see two men stepping down from their horses. He knew the sight of them. Hamish "Squint" Brewster and Hans "the Swede" Husman. They had the look, and so did their horses, of just coming from a hard ride. He'd seen them at a meeting with Clemson. They worked for Shine O'Hara. "What do you two want? I'm engaged in law business!"

"Is that what you call it?" Hans asked innocently, looking at the thinly clad madam.

"We're here, Sheriff," Brewster said, wiping sweat from his brow with the back of his hand, "because we're heading back to Steeple Rock with our report, and we need a word with you before we go. Having to do with your business with Mr. Clemson, and ours."

Jipsell sniffed and turned to Sadie. "Sixty dollars and not a penny less."

"Fifty!"

"Fifty-five!"

She sipped her coffee, twitched her nose, and then said, "It's a deal. Or you could take part of it out in trade." She jerked a thumb up toward the second floor.

"I'm still paying the price for the last one! Fifty-five it is! Close the door and gather up the money, and I will have a chin-wag with these, ah, business associates."

Jipsell walked over to Brewster, who said, "I'm starting to wish I was a sheriff. Putting that money in your pocket and your—"

"You shut your sauce box! It's all accordin' to law!"

"Now listen to me, Sheriff—we have a deal between Mr. Clemson and Mr. Shine O'Hara. Shine is going to buy one of Clemson's saloons and one of his gambling halls for twice what they're worth—and Clemson agrees to let Mr. O'Hara call the shots in town. But you've got an enemy of Mr. O'Hara's here in town. And he's a fly in the ointment, sir; he's a bug in the bed."

"Now who would that be?"

"Well, we don't know what name he's going by here—but when we knew him, he called himself Dane. He might be working at a horse ranch. Got a horse-shoe in its brand."

"That'd be the Willoughby place. Horseshoe W."

"This fellow's a newcomer—so a cowboy told us after we saw him. And if he's the man we think he is, he's a killer, and he's a danger to us all. What we ask, Sheriff, is: What are you going to do about it? You're part of Mr. Clemson's association—and we're for Mr. O'Hara. Shine O'Hara will not countenance this man, and I don't think Clemson will either!"

"You don't even know for sure it's the man," Jipsell said, shaking his head in disgust.

"We'll find out who he is. And suppose it's *him*? Suppose he's here to ruin the smart-laid plans of Mr. O'Hara and Mr. Clemson?"

"We cannot just gun a man down on your whim, Brewster! But—if he shows himself a problem, then he'll either be run out of town or go missing out in the woods. I'll kill him myself if I have to. Are you satisfied? Or will you continue to trouble me when I'm doing business?"

"I have your word he'll be taken care of?"

"*If* he's the man—*and* he proves a problem."

"I told you, he's Mr. O'Hara's enemy. Don't matter if he's not a problem for you yet. He will be in time."

The sheriff spat in the dirt. "Shine's enemy is Shine's responsibility. But if this 'Dane' gets in the way of our plans here, then whatever name he goes by, he won't live long enough to put a wrinkle in the blueprint, boys. Not a wrinkle or a blot."

IT WAS A slow ride, following the buckboard back along the rutted road. Dane rode just a little behind, not wanting to impose himself on the ladies. Occasionally Mrs. Marrin turned her head to glance worriedly back at him. He was, after all, a stranger. She doubtless wondered if they could trust him. He remembered to smile at her or touch his hat when she did it.

The sky rumbled, the clouds tumbled together, and Elana Marrin's prophecy came true. It began to rain fairly hard up ahead. They could see it like a gray broom sweeping toward them. "Did I not say so!" Mrs. Marrin said.

"You did, Mama," Suzanne replied calmly. "There's a clean blanket in the back. We could use it as an umbrella."

"You do have some sense, after all." Mrs. Marrin reached back, tugged the blanket to them, and draped it over them just as the heavy rainfall arrived.

The rain pounded down, making Pard snort and lower his head and inducing Dane to button up his duster. They made another half mile, the rain drenching the road with remarkable alacrity, and then a wagon wheel struck a deep rut filled with mud and half blocked with a stone. The buckboard shuddered and lurched to a stop at an awkward angle.

"Dang it all, Sherman!" Suzanne yelled, snapping a buggy whip over the draft horse.

Dane smiled at how she sounded like an annoyed bullwhacker. Truly a woman of the Western frontier.

The horse tried to pull free and failed. "You'll just have to give him a good whipping, Suzanne!" Mrs. Marrin said.

Suzanne shouted at Sherman again, and the draft horse tried once more to tug the wagon free. Then Dane heard a troublesome sound from the axles.

He rode hurriedly up beside Suzanne. "Ma'am, if you keep on, he'll break the axle this way!"

"What other way do you know in a fix like this, Mr. Dane?"

"If you'll give me a moment, I believe I can make it easier."

She nodded, blinking against the rain as she peered up at him.

Dane looked around, saw an outcropping of gray rock, and rode up to it. He climbed off the mustang and quickly tied him to a leatherwood bush. Rain or not, Pard took to cropping at the roadside grass as Dane rushed to the rock pile and picked up the smoothest pieces he could find. He found some stout bark, too, on a nearby fallen log, broke it off, and carried the whole of it over in his arms to the stuck wheel. His boots sinking deeply in the mud, he dropped the rocks and bark beside the wheel and hunkered down to shove the pieces in place, topped by a long piece of walnut bark. He fitted everything in place in the muddy trench the best he could at the front of the wheel; then slogged back over to Pard. He got his lariat, went to the hitch tackle at the front of the wagon, knotted one end firmly on the side away from the stuck wheel; he was so focused on his work, he scarcely noticed that the rainstorm had moved on. Carrying the other end of the rope, he went back to the mustang, untied him, and climbed into the saddle. He tied the rope around the saddle horn and rode up beside Sherman. The big draft horse looked at them, shook its head, and nickered.

"I'm gonna start pulling, ma'am!" Dane called. "Then you start up soon's I got the tension in 'er!"

He started Pard forward, fearful the horse would balk at the job. But the mustang had pulled loads before, and Pard dug into the mud and started forward.

Suzanne snapped the whip and shouted, "Let's go, Sherman!"

The draft horse pulled, the wagon creaked—and now it moved forward a little and then a little more. Suddenly its wheel lurched free, and the buckboard rattled ahead.

"That's got it!" Suzanne said exuberantly.

A strange vision cut across Dane's mind's eye then—a mule pulling a wheeled cannon across a stream. Getting stuck in the sand. He was there, pushing a wheel with his bare hands and shoulder. . . .

The memory, if that was what it was, faded as quick as it had come. Dane shivered from disorientation. And suddenly he felt all the wetness from the rain down his back, the water in his boots, the chill of it.

Pard was still tugging—they pulled the wagon a few yards more and then came slack in the rope. Dane turned, raised a hand for a halt. Suzanne called to Sherman to stop, and Dane unhitched his lariat—much stretched out now, near to breaking.

"Ready to move on, Mr. Dane?"

"Yes, ma'am," he said, climbing on his horse. He

was relieved Pard hadn't wandered off when he'd let
the reins go. He was still getting to know that mustang.
Pard was shaping up to be a darn good horse.

"Will you not ride beside us, Mr. Dane?" Suzanne
asked. "That way you can see from your higher vantage any holes we should drive around. I can scarce see
around Sherman."

"Yes, ma'am."

"You don't have to call me ma'am," said Suzanne.
"You have done us a service—least we can do is be on
a first-name basis."

"I'd be honored, Miss Suzanne."

She smiled at that and snapped the buggy whip.
They started out again, Dane riding beside Suzanne
and suddenly conscious that a little sun was breaking
through the clouds, and there was a fine smell of land
and greenness rising as happens after a rain. He noticed a few late-season yellow flowers. *That's what
being out in the world beside a lady does for you,* he
thought.

The ladies put the blanket aside, and now Dane
could glimpse Suzanne's copper-colored hair over her
forehead, even a flash of hazel green eyes as she glanced
up at him. He had scarcely been near a woman other
than to raise his hat when passing on a sidewalk these
last few years. Twice he'd accepted extra biscuits from
the cook's daughter on a drive, and she'd smiled at him.
And he'd been jostled by a bar girl when he'd gone in a
saloon. But he didn't take to saloon girls. He levied no
judgment against them, for life was hard on the frontier
for a woman alone, but he knew he was just a run-down
cowboy to them and of no use past the money he might
unbelt.

Searching for conversation, now that he was riding alongside Suzanne, he managed, "How comes it, ma'am—Miss Suzanne—that Sherman there got his name?"

"Why, my late papa was in the Civil War. He served under General Sherman, and when this big old draft horse was a yearling, he named him Sherman because he said, like the general, that horse will go straight on till he gets where he's going. He'd have pulled us free from that hole, have no doubt, but like as not broken the axle, had you not helped."

"Your father has passed, then?"

"My papa fought three years in the war and was scarcely hurt. One small wound. Then he came home and was killed by Cheyenne renegades within a year of his return."

"That does not seem fair."

"Not much is, I find. May I ask what your given name is?"

"You may, Miss Suzanne. But . . ." He sighed. This would surely be the end of his time with Suzanne. She would set him aside on hearing this. "But I don't know my Christian name. Could be that Dane is my first name—but I'm not sure." It all came tumbling out then—the facts he tried to hide from everyone else. "Miss Suzanne—a bit more than three years ago, I woke up in a Colorado canyon, in a blizzard, and found I had no memory of anything but the name Dane, which I was pretty sure was me, and little else. I had no papers on me. I did not know how I came to be there. I had a deep, bleeding crease on my scalp, and it may be that whatever gave me that mark drove the memories of my life away. I don't know who my parents were or where I was raised or where I was schooled." He had encountered only one person who seemed to recognize him—and the man had run from him on sight. That was not a memory he cared to share with Suzanne.

"You remember nothing more?" She gave a gasp loud enough to be heard over the creaking of the wheels.

"I do know I can read and write. Sometimes certain passages of William Shakespeare will come to me, so I reckon I was fairly well educated. I do remember some American history, the kind of thing you learn when you're a boy, and how government works. Abiding by laws and manners seems a part of me. I know how to work with stock—always had a good feel for horses—and I can ride and rope and fire a gun properly. I know I have a sweet tooth, and I don't like asparagus much. I know I prefer the countryside to a town. I don't care to wear bright colors, and I recognize certain songs. Hymns, a few other things. That's about all there is to me."

"I suspect there's more to you than that. But it must be hard—to not remember family!"

"Sometimes pictures come to me. A kindly older woman's face. Is it my mother? I'm not sure. And—I suspect I was in the war, on the Union side." He sighed. "My memory since that blizzard in the canyon is full enough—but only of what has happened in these last three years. Little else do I know."

"And you really don't know if Dane is your first or last name?"

"I do not."

"I—I shall assume it is your first name. And I will call you that. I'm sorry that you have been stricken in this way, Dane. That, too, does not seem fair."

"I can't recall if it's fair or not, Miss Suzanne."

They were silent for a time. Mrs. Marrin whispered something to Suzanne, but he could not hear what it was.

"Mother!" Suzanne said. "The poor man! Have some Christian charity!"

"Oh, Lord!" Mrs. Marrin said. "Listen to the child!"

They rode on in silence. "Ma'am . . . Miss Suzanne . . . I heard you singing at the church. Sure made me feel good to listen."

She looked up at him. "You were there?"

"I was walking with Deputy Masterson, and we looked in. I thought I might come next Sunday."

"You flatter my singing, but thank you, Dane." She paused, cleared her throat, and said, "I teach Sunday school before the church service."

He was puzzled as to why she told him this—then realized she thought he might ask to take her to church. Such an idea was far beyond his hopes. He felt lucky just to be talking to her.

"Oh, well, I . . . I'm just . . . I'll be sitting with the congregation."

The sky was darkening a little, and there was a rusty glow at the western horizon by the time they reached the Marrin farm, about a mile south of the town of Smoky River.

"Dane," Suzanne said, "you're soaked from the rain, and it's been a long ride. Perhaps—"

"*Mr. Dane!*" interrupted Mrs. Marrin loudly, stepping off the buckboard. She fixed Dane with a look he'd once seen in the eyes of a cat threatening to wallop a dog on the snout. "Thank you for escorting us to our gate—and for your help with our wagon." Her voice was as harsh as an unoiled hinge. "I shall tell Mr. Willoughby you are a worthy ranch hand!"

"Ma'am, he hasn't yet hired me—"

"We bid you good day, Mr. Dane!"

She turned to the gate, unlatched it, and said, "Suzanne, drive through, and I shall latch after you."

Suzanne looked at Dane, and he thought she might speak—but he knew he must go. He had admitted he was a broken man who did not know his own full name or where he came from. Mrs. Marrin had heard the story, too.

Suzanne's mother was right. He wasn't someone to invite in. He could have any history at all. For all she knew—for all he knew himself—he could have been the worst of men before he lost his memory.

Dane touched his hat to Mrs. Marrin and rode quickly away toward Smoky River.

CHAPTER FOUR

"ONE DAY'S WORK or two?" said Gunderson, tapping the dottle from his pipe. "And then you aim to depart my employ?" He blinked at Dane in the morning light. "You ain't too much use, are you?"

"Not much, I expect. Do the best I can for you. Only need five dollars for the two days."

"Five? Boy, you are loco. Three!"

"Four."

"I'm always a-givin' charity, and who gives it to me? But four it is. Except if you lose two games out of three when we play horseshoes, why, I pay three."

Dane grinned. "Done!"

They were leaning on the wooden fence behind the livery barn, watching Gravy cropping grass contentedly beside Pard.

"Gravy seems happy as a spoiled child in a candy store out there."

"Happy as a mule gets. Wish I had a pasture to retire to. All right, if you're a-going to work, get started. Hold on, now—you had your breakfast?"

"I did." Dane rolled up his sleeves. "Thought I'd clean out the stalls first, get that done."

"Well, you know where to find the tools and the manure pile. Have yourself a good time."

Dane was just finishing that chore, throwing the last forkful on the manure pile, when Sheriff Jipsell sauntered up to him from the back door of the barn.

Frowning, one hand on his holstered pistol, Jipsell asked, "You the man Dane?"

"That's my name, Sheriff." He had seen the sheriff on the street but hadn't met him. Dane stuck out a hand to shake.

The sheriff seemed taken aback. After a long moment of Dane's hand hanging there, he reached out and surrendered a limp handshake, then quickly dropped the other man's hand.

"Someone told me you might've killed a man back at Steeple Rock, fella," said Jipps.

Dane was surprised. "News to me, Sheriff." He took off his hat, scratched his head with the same hand, and said, "You got a circular with my face on it?"

Dane was genuinely interested to know if he was on a wanted poster. For three years he'd checked them on the rare occasions he was in a town just in case he was there. Never found his face.

"Haven't found you on a circular so far. Nor anybody with your name," Jipsell admitted. "You got any papers? Birth registry, military record, anything confirming who you are?"

"Not a thing, Sheriff. You can go through my things,

such as they are, over in Minnie Galvado's place. My saddlebag hangs yonder. Make free with it."

"You're not wearing a gun, I see. . . ."

"Don't need it for cleaning stalls. Forgive me for asking—you got a warrant for me, Sheriff?"

"Don't need one to throw you in a cell if it suits me."

"I expect that's so. Does it suit you?"

"More inclined to send you packing. You could leave town and save me the trouble."

"Sheriff—if I have to leave town, I'll go. But I have no memory of killing any man anywhere. Who was accusing me?"

"You don't need to know that."

Keeping his voice and his face affable, even humble, Dane said, "I believe the law gives a man the right to face his accusers."

Jipsell went beet red. "Who are you to tell me—"

"Something I can help with, Sheriff?" It was Bat Masterson walking up with Gunderson beside him. Dane suspected Gunderson, seeing the sheriff, had fetched Masterson.

"I don't need you poking your nose in, Masterson."

"I made a determination that this man Dane was all right for Smoky River, long as he keeps himself shined up and fragrant."

"Not too fragrant at the moment," Dane said.

"Masterson," Jipsell said, "how many times do I have to tell you, you're a *deputy* here. I'm the sheriff."

"Never doubted it, Jipps," Masterson said mildly. "Did I hear you say something about a killing?"

"A . . . a concerned citizen said he thought this man might've killed somebody up in Steeple Rock, over to Colorado."

"Who said this?"

Jipsell seemed uneager to answer. Bat looked at him expectantly. Finally, the sheriff said, "Squint Brewster."

"Anybody decent and reliable say it? That is, anybody besides Brewster? I met him. Didn't think much of him."

"You a lawyer now as well as a deputy?"

"No, sir. Just don't want the office of the sheriff to get into trouble over a false accusation. Who was it was killed in Steeple Rock?"

"He didn't say."

"When was this?"

"He didn't say."

"How'd he get killed? Gun, knife, beating?"

"Didn't say, blast you!"

"Seems mighty tenuous, Sheriff."

"Mighty what?"

"Ah—foggy, uncertain. And it happens I've taken a liking to this man Dane. If you fling him out of town, I reckon I'll ride off with him. I'm just a burr under your saddle anyhow. . . ."

Breathing hard, opening his mouth to speak and shutting it again, the sheriff stared at Masterson. Finally, he said, "This is on your shoulders, Masterson. You're responsible for this . . . this stranger. Far as I know, he's just a wanderer. Maybe running from something. You keep an eye on him."

"Yes, sir, I'll do that."

The sheriff stalked off. Gunderson chuckled.

Masterson said softly, "Well, was it not that Suzanne Marrin spoke up for you—"

Dane was startled. "She did?"

"You were seen escorting her close to town, and I asked her how you behaved," Bat said, studying the gold head of his cane. "Also, was it not for the fact that I interviewed Mr. Brewster and found him to be a lying varmint and most likely a thief, and indeed a man I suspect is a certain Brewster wanted in Iowa and Ohio . . . and was it not for the fact that I enjoyed the way you knocked that bully Metzger on the noggin . . . why, I would have helped the sheriff run you out of town. As it is, you are on notice, sir, to behave like a sterling citizen or take yourself away from here."

"That happens to be just my plan, Bat."

"Very good. The only reason the sheriff let me have my way, you know, is that he's lazy. If I leave, he'd have to do all the work I usually do—which is, in actual fact, all the work."

There came a gunshot, a hoorah, and a shout from the direction of Rusty's Saloon.

"And indeed, I am called to duty," Bat said, tipping his hat. He hurried off.

"You brought Bat over to back me, Mr. Gunderson?"

"Suppose I did! I had my reasons. First being I cannot bear Sheriff Jipsell. Second being— Well, never you mind."

They were silent for a moment, Dane leaning on his pitchfork, the hostler looking at Pard who was now trotting over to the river.

"Well?" Gunderson asked at last.

"Well, what?" Dane responded.

"You going to put fresh straw in the stable or not?"

S HADOWS WERE STRETCHING across the street as evening crept up on Smoky River. The town, so Gunderson told Dane as they played horseshoes, had no railroad as yet and was not a town for the delivery of cattle. A railroad was coming, and its workers often came into town and spent their money. Drovers brought herds close by, stopping a mile away to water and rest their cows, so the local merchants benefited from the cowboys; the road through town was useful to travelers, who spent their dollars at the inns and saloons; small barges came down the river and stopped at the town's docks; there were numerous prosperous ranches and farms in the area, and small herds of cattle, sheep, and horses were temporarily held for market close by. In consequence of all this trade, the town was thriving, and that meant that saloons and gambling halls had fastened to it like leeches. The town council had been discouraging any more gambling or saloons, especially with women of uncertain virtue attached to them—had been discouraging it until someone started passing out bags of gold eagles to the right people.

"And who did that?" Dane asked as they finished their early-evening game of horseshoes in the dirt alley alongside the livery barn.

"Rumor says it's a gambling hall hustler name of O'Hara from Steeple Rock," Gunderson said. "Buying into Clemson's string. Going to put in some new gamblin' mills."

The name O'Hara, tied with Steeple Rock, caught Dane's attention. It sounded tantalizingly familiar. But he had no idea why.

"You going to toss the durn horseshoe, or *ain't* you?" Gunderson asked.

Dane had discovered over the last few years that he was good at horseshoes—at anything that needed fine coordination of the hand—and he had been handily beating Gunderson at the game for more than an hour. The old fellow was growing sullen, so Dane decided to miss this shot. He tossed and missed.

"Ha! I knowed you couldn't keep throwing that good!" Gunderson crowed.

"You win this round and I'll buy you a drink, for I'm building a thirst," Dane said. "I win, you're buying."

"You're on!"

Dane made sure that Gunderson won this round, and they were off to Rusty's Saloon. Outside the saloon, Rusty was tacking up a flyer on a post holding up the saloon's porch roof. A group of men and two women had gathered to look on, as a man in a brown suit, standing on the wooden sidewalk, addressed them. He was a solemn man, about forty with curly brown hair swept back from a high forehead and small spectacles on his prominent nose. He had a full brown mustache to go with his hair and his suit. "That's Joe Hanrahan," said Gunderson. "Local printer, does a weekly newspaper, goes in fer politics. Ran for city council and didn't quite get there."

As they reached the group Dane read the headline on the poster. *IS SMOKY RIVER BEING SOLD TO SCALAWAGS? Come to a meeting and hear the facts tomorrow morning at Hanrahan's Print Shop, nine a.m.*

"I'm calling a meeting," Hanrahan said loudly, "to talk about how the town council's plans to allow three more gambling halls. We may certainly expect women of ill repute working these vice emporiums! We may expect baggy-legged cardsharps chiseling the hard-won earnings of inebriated citizens! And I suspect that certain members of the town council are being paid off to let it happen! Paid off by a criminal element from Colorado!"

"I believe the man's right," Rusty announced, turning to the small crowd.

"Oh, you're just agin' any more competition, Rusty!" called a man in the crowd to general laughter.

"I don't mind competition," said Rusty firmly, pointing at the heckler with his hammer. "I mind gangs of scalawags taking over this town!"

He turned and strode into the saloon. Hanrahan said, "That's all I've got to say now, folks. But you'll hear it all at the meeting! Good day to you!"

He walked into the saloon. Dane and Gunderson followed him.

"Buy you a drink, Joe?" Gunderson said, bellying up to the bar beside Hanrahan.

"Thank you. Just a beer."

"Beer for me," said Dane. "And I'm paying for all three drinks, Rusty."

"I'll have a whiskey, Rusty," Gunderson said.

Dane turned to Hanrahan. "Those are some tall accusations against the town council, Mr. Hanrahan! Can you back them up?"

Hanrahan gave Dane a narrow-eyed look. "Who'd you be, now?"

"Dane." They shook hands.

But still Hanrahan frowned at him. "Roy? Is he...?"

"You can trust him," Roy said. "Anyhow, I do. Masterson seems to think highly of him."

"All right, Dane— Yes, I can back it up!" Hanrahan said, slapping a hand on the bar. "I have a witness who heard the bribery being discussed and saw it being paid! Andy McCutcheon! Co-owns the dry-goods store, with Bill Sharton. McCutcheon's on the town council himself and . . ." He glanced around, to see who else was in the saloon. No one was there. "I've told you enough for now. What I said—best keep under your hat. Be safer that way."

Dane saw a shadow at the saloon's window. Someone was right outside. Could they have heard Hanrahan's talk of a witness?

Dane kept his voice low when he said, "Mr. Hanrahan. I'm thinking of making Smoky River my home— if there are no objections from the folks I respect. So I'll be there tomorrow."

"Me, too, by God," Gunderson said. "I got the same notions about these kinda outsiders. New folks is fine with me, long as they're decent. But from what I hear . . ."

"What did you hear, Roy?" Hanrahan asked in a low voice as he leaned close to Gunderson.

Dane took two quick steps to the door and looked out—whoever'd been there was gone now. He returned to the bar in time to hear Gunderson say, "Brewster and the Swede were talking when they put up their horses with me. Said they had to hurry. 'Got a bill to pay at the town council,' he says."

"Did he say that indeed? Who's this Brewster?"

"Squint-eyed gunman—at least, he wears his gun that way, tied down low on his hip. Deputy Masterson said he thought the man was wanted somewhere out of state. Out of Masterson's jurisdiction. No circulars on him here. But he thought this Brewster was a bad 'un."

"Masterson's young," Rusty put in. "But he's a natural judge of character."

"Good enough for me. Would you speak tomorrow, too, Roy?"

"I'll say what I heard. It don't amount to proof, but a meetin' ain't a courtroom neither."

JOE HANRAHAN WAS just going to the door of his print shop to lock up when a man pushed it open and came in.

"I was just closing up," Joe protested, taken aback by the big man.

"I've got some printing needs doing. Yust announcement." He had a slight foreign accent. At least a head taller than Hanrahan, who was not a small man, the stranger was fair-haired with a torso as daunting as his height.

Joe shrugged. "Leave your text on the counter there, sir, and I'll do it in the morning— if you give me half the fee as a deposit."

"It is real urgent, friend," the blond giant said. He turned quickly to the door, closing and locking it.

"Now, wait a minute there!" Joe said as the man tugged down the shades.

Instinctively, Joe reached for the gun on the shelf under his money box—and then froze as the muzzle of a .45 revolver was shoved against his cheekbone.

"You pull your hand back empty, mister," the big man said.

"Less than five dollars in the box there," Joe said, his voice trembling. "Not worth shooting a man for. All the rest of my money, which isn't much either, is in the bank."

"Not interested in your pennies, Hanrahan," the stranger said. "Go over to your printer there. Get that . . . what you call it? The letters for printing."

"The type?"

"Yah. Set it up for my message. Just two lines—big-sized words, yah? We will be done right quick."

"Very well."

Joe was a bit relieved. Seemed he was not to be shot or robbed. He went to the type box beside the printer and said, "What's your text?"

"It'll read, 'I am leaving town, for I'm ashamed of lying. Signed, Joe Hanrahan.'"

"What!"

The big stranger raised the gun, pointed it at Joe's forehead, and cocked it. "You can do it or you can die. Which you prefer?"

Joe swallowed and turned to the type box. It didn't take long for his practiced fingers to set the type. "There you are."

"Now print it. One page only."

"Sure. Why not?" Anger was rising in Joe. He was sure this man was working for the combine that wanted to take over Smoky River. But what could he do? The man had the drop on him.

Joe made sure the paper was in place, reached for the lever, and printed the page. He drew it out, blew on it, and turned to hand it to the stranger.

"No, you carry it over to the front of the counter. Hang it there on the front. Hold the top down with that money box."

Anger turning to outrage, Joe started to the inside of the counter, hoping to make a grab for the gun, perhaps throw himself aside and take a shot, but he felt cold steel press against the back of his neck. "That gun's staying right there on that shelf. Take the paper round the front."

Joe did as he was bid, his heart pounding, hands trembling with a fine mix of fury and fear. His mind cast about frantically for some way out of this.

Maybe Masterson would come along, check on him.

But no one came as he draped the poster in place, weighting it with the metal money box. Now a sign misrepresenting his intentions hung on the front of the counter.

"Unlock that front door, but don't go through it. You try, and I'll shoot you in the back."

Joe unlocked the door and hesitated, thinking of running for it. But the stranger couldn't miss his shot at this distance.

"Now come back here," said the big man. "Go to the back door."

"There isn't a back door," said Joe, stalling.

"You're a liar. I saw it from outside. Go on."

Wait for a better chance, Joe told himself. He walked stiffly to the back door.

"Go slowly through that door. You run, I won't shoot you. No, I'll chase you down, and I'll cut your throat. That'll hurt more. Kinda wish you'd run."

Hand trembling, Joe opened the door—feeling the loom of the big man close behind him. Too close to run from. Outside it was dark but for a pool of light from a lantern hung by the back door. The stranger must've put it there.

"Where we going?" Joe asked.

"Why, I'm escorting you out of town. You're leaving here for good. You're going far, far away."

Licking dry lips, Joe stepped out and saw that two horses were tied up to a post outside.

"Get on that Injun pony there," the stranger said.

Joe climbed up on the small, nervous paint. The big man untied the horse, took the reins, and, one hand still training the gun steadily on Joe, climbed up on the big horse beside him.

"Yah." The man tossed Joe the reins. "Now you ride slowly on ahead. Yust a little more than a trot 'less I tell you different. Remember, I shoot a moving target—easy. If you see anyone, anyone speaks to you, you say nothing. Maybe wave, that's all. I will hide this gun, but I can pull it fast."

Vowing to himself that he would not be run out of town for long—he would be back, with a US marshal—Joe nudged the pony into an easy canter, and they started off, the blond giant just a few steps behind.

Behind the row of buildings, parallel to Main Street, was a dirt road that passed a series of outhouses, some for a man to relieve himself in, other, bigger ones for storage and tools. To the left was a stretch of weedy ground cut by a wooden fence; beyond that, the plains stretched, flat for a good ways till the land rose to the low hills. All was dark but for a little moonlight.

"How far you going to . . . to escort me?" Joe asked.

"Plenty far. Got to make sure you leave."

They reached the end of town, then turned onto a dark side road that led north through a copse of oaks. They rode a mile, then two more. Soon they'd come to farmland owned by Hank Peterson. It was surrounded by an orchard of peach trees Peterson had planted himself, some years back. There was a distant light, at least a quarter mile off, that might be the farmhouse. Joe wondered if he could spur his horse and ride through the oaks to the farm, call out to Peterson for help.

He was about to try when two horsemen rode out of the near row of the orchard, one behind the other, blocking the way. A few more yards and Joe saw who it was. Andy McCutcheon, a big man with a gray spade beard, the moonlight striking his bald pate; behind him a swarthy man with a squint and a gun in his hand. Must have been that man Brewster.

"Oh, God, not you, too, Andy," Joe said.

"Joe—they mean to kill us! Ride!" So saying, Andy spurred his horse, leaning forward, and the horse got but a few paces before Brewster fired. The horse screamed—Brewster'd missed and hit the mount. The animal buckled, whinnying, dying, trapping Andy under it.

Hoping the blond giant was distracted, Joe spurred his pony and lit out—he had just time to see Brewster shooting Andy McCutcheon.

Then two bullets struck Joe in the back, and he was knocked clean from the horse.

But he didn't live long enough to feel himself hitting the ground.

CHAPTER FIVE

IT WAS A windy, overcast morning, as Dane joined the party milling in front of the print shop. Gunderson was there, and Rusty, and so were Minnie Galvado and her husband, Rafe, and a number of men Dane didn't know. Bat Masterson came out of the shop, shaking his head, Sheriff Jipsell behind him. Rusty had a notice in his hand, just two lines on it in big letters.

He ruefully held it up, and Dane read it. The statement was all alone on a newspaper page.

I am leeving town, for I'm ashamed of lying.
Sygned, Joe Hanrahan

"Boys, don't seem like there's going to be a meeting today," said the sheriff. There was considerable muttering discussion.

"Anybody seen Joe Hanrahan this morning?" Rusty asked.

Heads were shaken. None had seen him.

Dane spoke in a low voice to Gunderson, "Is Mr. McCutcheon here?"

"Nope. Seems to have disappeared himself. I heard he left a note about some woman he was leaving his wife for."

"Kind of a big coincidence, isn't it?"

Gunderson nodded grimly. "Sure is. And I'll tell you, I knowed both men ten years and more—neither man would just up and disappear on this town."

Masterson had taken the page and was staring at it. "Now hold on! Hanrahan put out the weekly paper. Not much to it, but I read every word. He never misspelled a thing. He was an educated man. But he's misspelled 'leaving' and 'signed'! It's absurd. He would never do that."

"You think he wanted us to notice the misspellings, Bat?" Dane asked.

"I do! He was forced into printing this foolery—and taken from here under duress! And I've got no doubt McCutcheon was, too!"

Men swore and called to the sheriff, "Do something, Jipps!"

"Let's go find him!"

Jipsell shook his head. "I forbid any such rash action. Why, if he was kidnapped—which I doubt—he might be in the hands of an outlaw gang who would surely be waiting to ambush the posse! I can't be responsible for my good friends here dying that way! No, sir! Now, was I convinced he was forced along, why I'd go after him myself, careful-like. But—I believe I heard him say he might do just what he said here!"

Bat stared at Jipsell. "You don't mean it."

"I do! I heard him say—somethin' of the kind."

"When?" Bat asked coldly. "I saw him half an hour before his shop closed, saw him through the window, whistling to himself, tidying up. He did not seem like a man ready to light out."

"Masterson," the sheriff growled, glaring at the deputy, "are you calling me a liar?"

"I cannot be certain enough to make such an assertion, Jipps. But I'll tell you what . . ." He took a folded telegram from his pocket and showed it to Jipsell. "I got a telegram from a friend yesterday. Wyatt Earp is now assistant marshal in Dodge City, and he's offering me a job there as a deputy. Got a faro job lined up in my off hours, too. You've made up my mind, Jipps. Like Wyatt said about another burg, this town isn't my size. I'll be taking the stage to Dodge come Monday."

Bat Masterson turned and walked away, carefully folding the telegram and tucking it in a pocket. Everyone stared after him in shock. Dane and Rusty hurried after him.

"Bat!" Dane called.

"Catch up, then," said Bat, his voice taut with a fury barely held in check. "I'm not stopping."

Dane loped up to match Bat's stride. "Where you headed?"

"Got a telegram to send. And then I'll find something to do. Going to do anything I can to stay away from Jipsell till I get on that stage. If he pushes me to lose my temper, it'll end badly."

"Bat," Rusty said, catching up to them, "I'd back your play if you want to go after McCutcheon and Hanrahan."

Bat stopped in the middle of the street, blinking in the morning sunlight as the clouds broke. He looked back toward the men still speaking heatedly around Jipsell. "I wonder if we'd find Joe and Andy alive."

Dane nodded sadly. He, too, suspected the men were already dead. "Still, I'd ride along if you'd have me, Bat," he said.

Bat shook his head. "I can't go against Jipsell—he's the sheriff. If I resign and go off half-cocked trailing those scalawags, he'll find some ordinance to throw at me. He was *elected* sheriff, Dane. Most of the town still backs him. I'm merely the young outsider he hired as a deputy. I overlooked him squeezing gold from Sadie and her girls. Now this—he's trying to pull the damn wool over our eyes! Legally, I have no authority to defy the man. But I don't have to work for him. I'll remain a few days to take care of some personal matters—I am still hoping Melody will say yes—"

"You've been courting the schoolmarm?" asked Rusty, smirking. "Why, you devil."

"All has been genteel, but the lady has not been unresponsive. I don't think she'll come along with me when I go, how-some-ever. It's just as well—she does not hold with gambling."

M RS. GALVADO WAS giving Dane that look again when he came in for lunch. Eating here was a little more expensive than at the Chinese café, but Dane liked the feel of being in something akin to a home. The boarders ate their meals in a dining room if they paid an extra fee, and it made Dane feel less the saddle bum.

"Well, Mr. Dane, you're going to work for that rascal at the livery again?" she asked as she laid the sand-

wich plate down before him. She did that odd thing with
her lips—pretty lips, to be sure—a kind of half-kissing
motion, and that indefinably sensual look with her eyes.
She put her hands on the table and leaned over a bit to
exhibit her substantial cleavage. She wore a senorita's
white blouse, but she was, in fact, a woman with honey
brown hair and creamy skin and not a whit of Mexican
ancestry. Her husband, Rafe Galvado, was half Mexican, hailing from one of the Texas border towns.

"No, ma'am, I did some work this morning graining
and brushing down the horses for Roy, but I'm going
out to the Willoughby ranch, try to firm up a chance
for a job this afternoon."

"I'll be sorry to see you move out. Are you sure . . .
you don't want to spend a little more time here?" And
she put her hand over his.

"Minnie!" shouted Rafe from the kitchen. "Come
in here!"

She frowned but went to the kitchen, and Dane was
relieved. He was as red-blooded as the next man, and
having been a long time without the intimate company
of a woman, he would likely have given in to the temptation, if not for the very clear fact that Minnie was
married. That was a line he would not cross. It occurred to him, with some satisfaction, then that now he
knew something about himself he hadn't known for
certain before. . . .

He wiped his lips with the napkin, got his hat and
coat, and went to the street. A gusty wind was driving
a thin rain. A wagon rumbled by, piled high with pump-
kins, and the year's last field corn. Down the street a
stagecoach was pulling up in front of the Smoky River
Hotel, and a lady in a long pink bustle dress and match-

ing pink hat was getting off, helped by the bearded driver. A couple of boys, ignoring the slight rain, were playing kick the can over by the livery. Dane decided to look in at Rusty's Saloon before heading out so he could ask Rusty if there was any news about Joe Hanrahan. The boardinghouse door opened behind him, and Rafe stepped through. He was a squat man with an apron draping his big belly; he had oiled-back brown hair; his dark brown eyes were snapping with anger. "You! Are you making plans with my wife?"

Dane shook his head. "Mr. Galvado," he said mildly, "my only plan is to ask for a job at a horse ranch. Maybe say goodbye to a couple fellas before I ride out."

Rafe seemed taken aback by Dane's friendly calmness. "But—she was making eyes at you, warn't she?"

"Why, no. She was nothing but ladylike." The lie didn't feel right in his mouth, but he thought it for the best. "I know how you feel. Being lucky enough to have a pretty wife like that, I'd be careful of her, too. Nothing to worry about this time, and that's my word on it. I paid my bill to your missus this morning, Mr. Galvado. Already moved my gear to my horse. I won't be coming back." He touched the brim of his hat. *"Hasta la vista."*

Dane walked without haste toward Rusty's Saloon—listening for, and hearing, Rafe Galvado going back into the boardinghouse. He was glad to hear that sound. He didn't want any more dustups in Smoky River. Metzger had been enough. He had to grip his hat against the wind just before he turned in at Rusty's.

In the saloon a couple of farmhands looking to hoot and holler on their day off were getting an early start at it, working on a bottle as they played a hand of draw poker at a rickety table set up in a corner. A big jowly man, his jowls accompanied by muttonchops, his enormous hands clasped around an unusually large German beer stein, was wiping beer from his lips. The stein had an image of an elk on it. He had a platter with scraps of cheese and meat at his elbow. His nose was red, his eyes glazed. Like as not he was already drunk. Dane remembered seeing him in the church congregation. He'd seemed very pious indeed there, nodding at every word preached with his bowler hat clutched in his hands.

"Who'd you be?" the man asked dourly.

"Howard," said Rusty, "this is . . . Dane. Only name I have for him. He's on the prowl for ranch hand work. Dane, you won't find it at Howard's shop. Mr. Armbruster here owns the confectionary."

"Also own the bakery," said Armbruster, clanking down the beer stein and wiping his mouth. "Don't use ranch hands there either."

"Happens I was thinking of kids in candy stores this very morning, Mr. Armbruster," Dane said. "I saw that stein there on the shelf under your mirror, Rusty, but I thought it was a decoration!"

"Nope, Howard keeps that here. I could use it to water my horse if he decides he wants to sell it."

Armbruster turned to glower at Rusty. "What do you imply?"

"Just that it's a mighty big beer stein. And that's your third swillin' from that pretty beer bucket. That from the old country?"

Armbruster grunted. "Yes, my father's. He brought it from Munich."

"Can I get you a drink, Dane?" Rusty asked.

"No, I thank you. Can't stay. Just wanted to know if anything more was heard of Hanrahan and Mc-Cutcheon."

"Not a word. It's a marvel how no one in charge around this town wants to look for those men."

"Why, he explained himself in a note," said Armbruster. "They both did. Could be they're skipping town with someone else's money. Some scheme. Never trusted either one. I saw that harlot Sadie—I have forgotten her last name, but it's probably not real anyway. I saw her talking to McCutcheon in front of that gambling hall on First Street. The place with the disgraceful painting and the unclad women serving drinks!"

"*Half* clad," corrected one of the farmhands, coming up to pay his bill. He slapped down a coin, weaved his way to the door and out into the blustery day.

"Half clad?" Dane said musingly. "Disgraceful paintings? I seem to have missed seeing the important sights hereabouts."

Rusty laughed. Armbruster scowled.

An imposingly dressed man came in, sidling expertly past the drunk farmhand; the newcomer wore a cream-colored suit with scarlet lapels, silvery vest, yellow string tie, and shining black boots. He had his top hat in his hand to save it from the wind, and with the other, he smoothed back closely barbered curly blond hair. He had small blue eyes with crinkles at the corners and a wide mouth that split in a big smile for Rusty. His mouthful of large teeth displayed several gold overlays.

"Rusty! We've got business to talk," he said, clapping his silk stovepipe on his head.

The barkeep shrugged. He didn't seem to be looking forward to the talk. "Clemson—this here is . . . Mr. Dane. He's new to town, hopes to stay a while. You know Howard Armbruster."

Clemson nodded at Armbruster and thrust a hand at Dane. "Clement Clemson, Mr. Dane." He gave Dane a business card printed with silvery ink. It read:

Clement Clemson
Clemson Entertainments and Refreshments

And it gave an address on First Street. "Come by the Silver Goddess sometime, sir, right there on First. It's my establishment, and I'll stand you a drink."

"I'll do that when I'm—"

Clemson didn't wait for him to finish. He turned to Rusty. "My friend, I'll have your best brandy and a word with you."

"My only brandy, but I guess that makes it my best, too," Rusty said, pouring.

"Timing is everything in the world of commerce, Rusty!" Clemson drank off half his liquor and continued. "Strike while the iron is hot! Now, me, I struck silver, as you know, ha-ha! And don't I know it! Got to the Comstock Lode in time for one of the last veins of silver. Just enough to get me in business. Took a stagecoach bound east, stopped in Smoky River to have lunch while the horses were changed, and by God, I decided to stay! This was an up-and-coming town with almost no entertainment! People was just waiting for some music to dance to!"

"Sometimes I whistle a song for folks here in the saloon," said Rusty dryly.

"Well, whistle this one—money's a-comin' to him who goes drummin'!"

"Don't know that one."

"Rusty—money is coming to town! There's an investor—wants to take a place like this, turn it into a big concern. A band, girls, the works, Rusty. Get in with him and he'll get you rich!"

"I heard something about it. I'm plumb not interested."

"You won't lose a thing! He'll keep you on as a partner. That's *my* deal with him. He's going to turn this town upside down and set it up right. What do you say?"

"Tell you what—I've got a deal for *you*," Rusty said.

"Yeah? You want to know what your percentage is?"

Rusty shook his head. "Here's the deal, Clement— you give me a dollar, I'll give you another brandy."

The chummy glow drained out of Clemson's face. He looked like he'd shoot Rusty if the two of them were alone. Then he forced a smile. "There's still time—just a little time for you to get right with us. You think about it, Rusty. Think hard."

He tossed two silver dollars on the bar, nodded brusquely to Dane and Armbruster, and walked out.

"Seemed like he was trying to drive you into a box canyon, Rusty," Dane said. "That slick was sure proddin'."

"He was. Has been."

"Did it sound to you like there was a threat to it?"

Rusty nodded. "A desperate man's threat. You know, bartenders and barkeeps—one drinking establishment to another—they talk. We hear things, and sometimes we share 'em. Clemson didn't weigh in as much silver over to Virginia City as he likes folk to think. He over-

extended his capital when he came here. Got himself
in debt to builders and the merchants in Kansas City
who sent him the fancy furnishings. Had to sell out to
this man O'Hara in Steeple Rock. . . ."

O'Hara, Dane thought. *Steeple Rock.* He felt that
curious chill again.

Rusty went on. "Makes him not much more than
manager of his own dance hall. Partner? In a pig's eye!
And he's got Clemson pushing to get the other saloons
to sell out to him." Rusty shook his head. "I didn't work
my fingers to rags to get this place just to become some
tinhorn's lackey."

Dane nodded. "That's what I figured." He took off
his hat and abstractedly ran the tips of his finger over
the scar on his head. 'Timing,' he said. After what we
heard this morning. There was some timing!"

"I was thinking the same thing, Dane. Joe Hanrahan gets routed out of town—maybe worse—on the eve
of his hosting that town meeting. Maybe routed out by
the same people holding the reins on Clemson."

"Yep." Dane put on his hat. "Well—I'll look in when I
can. Got to go out to the Horseshoe W. See if Willoughby
is back."

"Good luck, Dane. See you round the mountain."

Dane grinned. "You would if there were any mountains in Kansas." He waved and headed for the door—
having to stop because Armbruster was already there,
rocking on his heels and staring out into the street.

"Look at that!" the merchant bellowed at no one in
particular. "The very harlot I spoke of and there she
is!" Armbruster took one big stride out onto the walk.
"Sadie Danniger, showing herself where only decent
women are allowed, by heaven!"

Dane stepped out behind Armbruster. Coming along the wooden sidewalk—carrying an empty basket, her head ducked against the wind—was a tall, wide-hipped, blowsy woman in red and black satin. She wore a red-and-black silk hat tied in place to cover her chestnut-colored hair. A little gray showed at the roots. She came to a standstill, seeming both disgusted and sad, taking in the spectacle of Armbruster with his big hands raised, fingers splayed, between them.

"Satan's harlot! Get off these boards and into the muck where you belong!"

He stepped in and grabbed her right wrist, making her totter beside a deep mud puddle as he tried to push her in. "On your knees in the slime that bore you!"

Thinking about it later, Dane was a little surprised at how fast and instinctive his own reaction was. How he took Armbruster by the back of the collar and by the back of his trousers, pulled him away from Sadie and then shoved him belly down into the mud.

"Whuh—!" Armbruster sputtered, floundering. "Who—!"

"Reminds me of when we was moving fattened bullocks" came a voice at Dane's elbow. He turned to see Bluc-Snake Thompson carrying a brown paper package of goods under his arm. "They had a way of getting into the quicksand. Hell of a time getting them out." He chuckled, low and deep.

Armbruster struggled to his feet, splattered with mud, and turned to face Dane. "You!"

"Sorry about the necessity there, Mr. Armbruster," Dane said, genuinely trying to sound reasonable. "But I cannot stand by and allow a drunk to manhandle a lady. It's just not in me. Kinda can't help myself. If you send me a bill, I'll pay for that suit—it'll take some time to earn the money, I expect."

"You—I—!"

"But I'm sore afraid that if you accost the lady again, why, I'll have to *hit* you next time."

It'd happened once before in the course of the last three years. On a dark night in Hays City, he'd been passing an alley where a young woman was pressed struggling against a shadowy wall by a drunk, cackling cowboy who had one hand over her mouth and the other yanking at her dress. Dane had spun the cowboy around and hit him hard on the point of his chin so he fell into the alley, out cold. The young woman ran away, weeping, and Dane had gone about his business.

Today, Armbruster just stood there, clawing mud off himself, cursing under his breath.

Sadie was rubbing her sore wrist and looking at Dane in openmouthed astonishment. "I . . . thank you."

"That's all right, Miz Danniger."

"I guess I'm not what you'd call a lady, but he had no right to . . ."

"No, ma'am, he didn't."

"I have business at the general store like everyone else!"

"Sounds natural enough to me, ma'am."

Dane stepped aside, taking off his hat. She took a deep breath and walked on by, her head held high.

Watching her, he noticed someone else across the street in front of the livery. It was Suzanne Marrin, looking at him with her head cocked as if she'd never seen him before. She wore a long black walking dress, a white blouse, buttoned-up shoes, and a simple black tied-down hat, beneath which her coppery hair swirled in gusts of wind.

Dane had a sinking feeling. She'd seen him rough up a man. Suzanne couldn't approve of that.

A bitterness rose in him. What difference did it make? A man like him who didn't even know who his own family was—he had no right to the good regard of a woman like Suzanne. Let alone . . .

Let alone what? Had he been actually thought she might let him court her?

He looked away from her. *Don't be a fool,* he told himself.

"Mister!" Armbruster declared. "I should take you apart!"

"I wouldn't try that, Armbruster," Rusty said from the doorway. His apron snapped in the wind. "I saw him crack a man over the head and knock him flat quicker'n a rattler's tongue. I don't think you'd come out of it with your noggin intact."

Armbruster ground his teeth, his fists clenched and shaking. Then he stalked diagonally across the street toward his shop and, Dane supposed, clean clothes.

But Armbruster stopped partway, turned back, and jabbed a finger at Dane. "I am about to be a much bigger man around here!"

"If he eats much more," Blue murmured.

"And I'll tell you something," Armbruster continued. "I'll see you get your comeuppance. First off, I'm going to the sheriff!"

"I saw the whole thing, Armbruster," Rusty said. "Dane was in the right! You can't go tossing the local women into the mud, whatever their profession might be."

"I saw it, too, mister!" declared Blue. "I think he saved your bacon! I've seen that lady pull a hideaway gun on unruly gents!"

"And you—*Indian*!" snarled Armbruster. "You'll get yours, too!"

Then Armbruster turned and hurried toward his shop, shaking his fist at two laughing Texas cowboys sitting their horses.

"Ha, he sure gave that fella a good look at the rich Yankee soil!" one of them chuckled.

"Dane, I don't think he'll go to the sheriff, given the tenor of things," Rusty said, "but best you ride out for a while. Till he cools off."

Dane nodded. "Could be I . . . might've handled it different."

"It was her in the mud or him," Blue said. "You coming to the Horseshoe W?"

"I am."

"You can ride out with me if you have five minutes. I have to put this on the wagon and pick up my horse at the livery. Then I'll side you."

"Meet you at the livery, got to saddle up my horse anyhow."

Dane glanced across the street, saw that Suzanne wasn't about, and started off, stepping over puddles, one hand holding his hat on his head as the wind abruptly got pushier. He'd never been one for tie-on hats, but he was starting to reconsider.

Inside the livery barn, he headed right for Pard, who was dozing in a stall. He whistled softly to the horse. "Hey, Pard, how about we ride out and meet some of the fancy horses? You might meet a filly."

The mustang raised its head, ears perking up at his voice, and gave a soft whinny.

This was followed by the sound of someone clearing their throat. In a rather feminine way.

He turned—and saw Suzanne backing a horse out of a stall. "Hello, Dane."

He took off his hat. "Ma'am."

She patted her horse and gave Dane a small smile. It made her eyes crinkle in a way that stirred up his pulse. "I told you, you have the privilege to call me Suzanne. I do not extend that privilege lightly, so please do not let it fall to waste."

"Suzanne . . . I am a mite embarrassed that you saw that tussle. That's the second local businessman I've run afoul of. I . . ." He didn't know how to say it.

"Embarrassed?" She raised her eyebrows. "I thought it was magnificent! These local men make use of Sadie's girls—and Sadie herself—and then belittle her in public! The hypocrisy is fouler than the mud in that street, Dane." Suzanne sighed. "She's a lost woman, I suppose. But it's hard for a woman out here. Who knows what she's been through? And the Gospel says, 'Judge not . . .'"

Dane nodded. "'Lest you be judged.'"

Now her smile lit up the livery. "So you remember your Bible at least!"

"Old Keggum gave me a copy. I read it over a long drive, by the campfire mostly, and quite a few verses sounded familiar."

She took her horse by the reins and led the mare over to him. "I am riding a ways toward the Horseshoe W. Turning off after a couple miles. Rumors have it outlaws are carrying people off, right out of town. Gunfire from out in the orchards. No bodies found, but . . ." She shrugged. "These are uncertain times."

"I'd be honored to escort you to your ranch," Dane said, moved by her compassion—her kindness for him and for Sadie. He felt as if a great weight had been lifted from him. "Blue is riding along with me if that's . . ."

"That'll be just fine. Two guards are safer than one."

T HE SKY HAD mostly cleared, but the wind still gusted, rippling the late-season grasses on the plain to either side, dappled with yellow dandelions. Clouds chased other clouds, as if after stragglers from a herd, and Dane thought: *Sun always comes out, eventually, if she's there. . . .*

Then he chastened himself, inwardly, for foolish sentimentality. But the feeling remained.

"Now, who was this Old Keggum you spoke of?" Suzanne asked as she trotted her mare beside him. Blue had been riding closer, but for some reason, he had dropped back a couple of rods.

"Why, ma—Suzanne—he was a man who saved my life. Elias Keggum. We mostly called him Old Keggum. He was a runaway slave, in fact. Run away when he was a boy, out in Northern Arkansas, long before the war. They had trained him to be a house slave, and the lady wanted them all fine in livery and able to talk nicely, so she had them learn reading and writing, even sums. It wasn't even lawful to allow that in some states, but she did it, and the books gave him a notion of—this is how he told it to me—just how wonderful big the world is. So, when the rest of his family was sold off, and they wouldn't tell him where they were sent, he had no desire to stay on. He found his chance and lit out to the Missouri River, took a job with a bargeman who didn't hold with slavery. He worked for him some, and then, when slave takers were looking for him, he headed west. Worked for anybody who'd take him on, as far west as he could go. He took skins in the mountains, too, and sold them, used the money to buy himself a horse and learned ranching work."

"You know his story well!"

"He was my only real friend, these past few years. Though perhaps I might've met a friend or two—if I'd come here."

"Tell me the rest of his story. For I deplore slavery, and it cheers me to hear that some got themselves free, even before the war."

"After the war he made his way to Colorado—and that's where he found me, you see. Keggum's the one found me half busted up and shot in that canyon. He was caught out in a snowstorm, and he saw me there in the trees. Said it looked like I'd fallen off a cliff over that stand of trees, and they broke my fall. I couldn't remember how I'd come there. . . ."

"You were—shot? How badly?"

"Three rounds. One in the back, under my right shoulder. One in the front—upper left leg. One creased my head pretty good. The scar is there on my head, mostly hidden by my hair."

Her eyes wide, she said, "Sounds like they were firing on you from front and back both!"

"Could be. Sometimes a bullet will spin a man around though, and then—" Dane broke off, wondering how he knew that. He hadn't seen it happen. Not that he could remember.

She shook her head, looking up at the racing clouds as she said, "You seem to know a lot about such things—but of course, you said you'd been in the war. You are lucky to be alive, Dane, after two such wounds."

"Old Keggum dug the bullets out. He had learned about how to do such things with a steady hand, fighting Indians for a spell. Spent two years in Oklahoma as a scout for the cavalry. He saved my life and took me under his wing. Treated me like I was as good as he was—though most of my life was wiped away. Because someone had been trying to kill me, he counseled me to keep away from towns, much as I could. Said I should plain avoid Colorado, try to keep to sparsely populated places where there were fewer who might recognize me. They might, after all, be the ones who'd shot me."

"Wise counsel. He was a good friend."

"The other fellas mocked me some because I didn't know where I was from, so I kept to myself. But Keggum didn't care about who I had been—only who I was right then. He taught me much, Suzanne. I lost him about nine months ago. Trampled to death in a stampede."

"A terrible way to die," she said gravely. "I'm sorry you lost him."

Dane nodded and observed, "Here we are, once more at your gate. Does the ranch have a name?"

"Surely! It's has the unassuming name of the Marrin Farm. Not much more than a farm and thirty acres of grazing for a small herd of sheep. We have some pigs. We spin our own wool, raise most of our own food. We have a small apple orchard, too."

They paused at the closed gate, and Dane looked around. The fence around the property had been badly repaired quite a number of times. There were a few cottonwoods to the east; to the south was a copse of small oaks. The Marrins had begun a rose garden in front of the dilapidated one-story house, he saw. The roses had lost their petals. The roof of the house was missing shingles; its chimney had lost some of its stones. A lean, stooped man in overalls, his lank white hair streaming in the wind, slammed a hoe angrily into the garden to one side of the house, weeding the last of the season's goods. There was a square-walled well made of brick. Chickens pecked freely in the weedy yard. Dane saw a barn, beyond the house, tilting out of true a little, supported upright by propping timbers; a large pigpen stood beside it, and a corral where the draft horse stamped. A yellow dog trotted out from behind the house and barked at Dane.

"Quiet, Tulip!" Suzanne said, and the dog sat down obediently, only softly growling, keeping an eye on Dane.

Dane contemplated the old man toiling in the garden. "Who's the old gentleman?" Dane asked. "An uncle?"

"No, no, he's a hired man," said Suzanne ruefully. "That's Matthew, the one farmhand who'd take our rate of pay, which is three fairly scant meals a day—we eat the same—and a cabin out back, plus a dollar a week. He hails from Florida, Missouri. Been here ten, no, eleven years. Sometimes plays accordion. Gets drunk on his own corn whiskey once a week whereupon he declaims about the Book of Job. He usually gets his work done. Can't be trusted on a roof, however. He had the temerity to ask my mother for her hand last year."

"Possibly thinking how he didn't have much hard work left in him."

"I expect so. That's why I pressed her to keep him on, despite his foolish proposal."

"I've met many who claimed to be Christians, Suzanne," Dane said. "But you're the real thing."

"And now you flatter me. And not the flattery I'd hoped—" Then she caught herself, her cheeks flaming red, and hastily added, "Well, I'd best go in. Mother will be waiting for me. I've got the ingredients we need for supper in the saddlebag."

There was suddenly a great deal Dane wanted to say. He had, in his short memory, chased Comanches away from a herd, turned a stampede, swum into a raging river to save a young fool of a cowboy, run off road agents, entered into a burning cabin to save a cook, and once, on a dare, ridden the biggest, meanest bull in the herd, only to be tossed contemptuously into a patch of nettles. But he didn't have the courage now to say what he wanted to say to Suzanne Marrin.

Instead, he lifted his hat to her and rode off with Blue toward the Horseshoe W Ranch.

S QUINT AND HANS were in Shine O'Hara's office on the main street of the Rocky Mountains town of Steeple Rock that late afternoon. The sun had busted through clouds and was bulling its way through the window, right into Brewster's face. He slanted his hat brim down to block it

"You saw him, Squint—and you didn't *shoot* him?" demanded Shine O'Hara.

"Well—well, boss," Brewster stammered. He was always a little shaken when O'Hara glowered at him with those steel gray eyes. "We were in town when we first seen him, in broad daylight."

He and Hans were standing before Shine's desk, hats in their hands. Leaning against the wall, nosily chewing tobacco, was a sloppy man with a matted beard, Ferry Johnson.

"I don't think it t'were him, boss," Hans said, making a massive shrug with his big shoulders.

"Hans, you never saw him up close!" Brewster said. "I worked right beside this fella, damn it! I saw him clear—he was walking alongside Bat Masterson. Most likely it's that fella Dane."

"Masterson?" Shine grunted at that. "Were they friendly?"

"Seemed like it. Shine—I do think it's the man who killed your cousin. I do."

"Couldn't be," said Ferry Johnson. "We shot that man right off a cliff."

"No one found his body!" Brewster reminded them.

Johnson shifted his chaw from one cheek to the other. "Next day we looked—we found wolf tracks and blood! But I reckon there's no knowing for certain, us not seeing the man's body."

"You can't know much from what's left after a wolf's eaten a man," Hans observed, seeming to enjoy the idea. "I think he's dead, Shine."

Shine was a nickname from O'Hara's real first name, Shawn, lent strength by his tendency to wear large gold rings and diamond stickpins. He was leaning back in his desk chair, glowering at the two men standing uncomfortably before him. "Well, what name's he going by? What did folks tell you?"

Brewster shifted his feet uncomfortably. "We asked a couple fellas. They just said he might be the saddle bum who buffaloed the gunsmith. Cracked him over the skull with an old Army revolver. No one seemed to know his name."

"You didn't ask enough people, you fool! I need to know for sure if it's him. But that old revolver . . . that sounds like the one who gunned Johnny down." He shook his head, ran one hand over his slicked-back russet hair as the other one tugged at his green silk tie, and said at last, "There's nothing for it. I'm going to have to go to Smoky River earlier than I'd planned and see for myself. Did you ask that thievin' Sheriff Jipps about him?"

"Jipsell hadn't noticed him. Said if he caused trouble for the new arrangement, why, he'd see he was left dead in some canyon."

"*If*? I'll tell you something—if it's him, he'll be the worst kind of trouble. If it's Dane, we will choose our time, and then we will kill him all over again."

CHAPTER SIX

"Y OU'LL DO," SAID Jess Willoughby, having asked
the same questions that Binch had. "Rand will
give you your work. We need a good hand with sawing
and nailing now. Horse work will come later. Welcome
aboard, Dane." And they shook hands.

So it was that Dane, the Quinlan brothers, and Blue
were now out on an almost treeless stretch of prairie, a
mile from the ranch house on a hot Indian summer
afternoon, building a series of horse sheds for the coming winter. Dane having carpentry experience, and
older than the Quinlans, Willoughby had put him in
charge of the job.

The three of them made an out-of-rhythm drumming with their hammers as they drove the penny nails
into the wooden shingles, pausing only to wipe sweat
from their eyes, and talking from time to time of noth-

ing useful. Mostly, the Quinlan boys complained.
Cowboys had it hard enough, they insisted, corralling
horses or cattle, breaking broncos, roping what needed
roping, and repairing the occasional fence, without having to crick up their backs hammering sheds together.

A little tired of the complaining, Dane said with a
straight face, "Lazy riders like you are lucky to have
any work. Why, Dirk, you think you can bust a bronc?
You can't even ride a half-broken horse."

Dirk Quinlan threw his hammer onto the roof and
stared at Dane. "Is that right?"

"That's right," Dane said mildly. "My horse is no
more than half broken. Hellfire, I barely stay on him. No,
you couldn't ride him. He's getting bored over there,
drinking from that pail, cropping grass. You show me
you can ride *him*, I might think you'll make a bronc
buster."

"Is that *right*?" Dirk immediately jumped down
from the horse shed and stomped over to the mustang.

Blue shook his head, smiling faintly.

Pard was standing in the shadow of a lone oak, the
only tree around for half a mile. Beside it was a tumble
of rocks, moved there when someone had cleared them
off the land. Dane stared at the rock pile and suddenly
found himself worried.

He jumped down from the roof and said, "Hold it,
Dirk!"

But the cowboy ignored him. Patting the mustang's
neck, he stuck a boot in a stirrup and swung into the
saddle. Pard stood it. Dirk took up the reins and nudged
the horse into motion with his bootheel. Pard trotted
obediently forward.

"Ha, this some kind of a joke?" Dirk demanded,

smirking. "Lookee here, he's like an old trained mare, half asleep!"

Apparently having decided it had been long enough, Pard suddenly bucked hard, giving it his all and throwing the surprised cowboy into the air. Dirk fell heavily on his back near the pile of stones. The wind knocked out of him, he gasped for air. . . .

A prairie rattlesnake reared up from the pile of stones, coiling and rattling close to Dirk's left shoulder, cocking its head to strike.

Dane heard a gunshot. And looked down to see his own pistol in his hand, smoking. It had happened so fast, the knowledge of his drawing and firing was just dawning on him.

"That's some shooting, all right," Blue observed matter-of-factly, walking over to the dead rattler. The snake's head was shot clean off, but its body whipped about in reflex for a moment. Blue picked up the snake's twitching body, holding it at arm's length so it bled out on the ground, and examined its skin. "That'll make a nice belt."

Dirk was getting to his feet. "That bullet went right through its head!" He looked at Dane. "I don't know if I should punch you in the nose for setting me up to be bucked off that crazy horse—or thank you for saving me from a snakebite!"

"Let 'em balance each other out," Dane said, holstering the gun. "That'll leave us with getting back to work."

Ben Quinlan walked over to Dane. "I'll thank you for saving that damned fool's neck. That p'isen would've hit right close to his heart. Mighta killed him. Never saw anybody draw and shoot that fast—not accurately."

Dane shrugged. "Just a kind of reflex. Kinda surprised me, too." *That sort of surprise seems to be happening a lot lately,* he thought. It was as if something buried in him was starting to come back to life. Would he remember what had happened that dusk—the day that Keggum found him?

A chill went through him. The name Shine O'Hara seemed to whisper on the rising breeze.

"How's about seeing how well you can shoot that thing at a farther target?" Ben said.

"Exhibition shooting?" Dane said, blinking. "No. I've only got two bullets left."

The brothers looked at each other, eyebrows raised. Blue pointed at Dane's gun belt. "You never noticed he's got no shells in those loops?"

"Bullets cost money," Dane said. "And I'm not one for promiscuous shooting."

"Tell you what," Ben said. "You use up those other two bullets, hit your targets, and I'll buy you a box of bullets, and me and Dirk'll have a contest to see which can work harder."

Dirk snorted. "Like the dickens we will!"

"We will," Ben said, "unless you're not man enough."

Dirk gave him a shove and showed him a fist. "You want to find out if I'm man enough?"

"Don't you two start in again," Dane said. "I'll shoot at something—but you got to swear to replace my bullets, Ben."

"I swear it! Now, see how there's only two leaves on that lower branch? Back up to the sheds and see if you can cut 'em off."

Dane shook his head, thinking, *I'm going to make a damned fool of myself whether I hit the targets or not.*

But he strode back to the shed with the other men, turned, and looked at the autumn-golding leaves fluttering in the slight breeze. Something took hold of him, and he drew and fired twice, all in one smooth motion.

The leaves fluttered down, cut off at the stem.

"You know," said Blue, "it would have been all right to aim at them first."

"I must've aimed somehow," Dane said. "Not sure."

The other two were gaping at the oak tree. Then at Dane.

"*Two* boxes of bullets," Dirk said. "I'll buy one of them."

"What do you mean, you're *not sure* if you aimed?" Ben asked, exasperated. "How can you not know how you do it?"

Dane sighed. Might as well tell them. They'd eventually figure out, as people did, that he was missing something upstairs. "Well . . . I don't *remember*, is what it is. I . . . See this scar?" He took off his hat and held his hair back so they could see the scar. "Woke up three years ago with a crease in my head there. Probably a bullet graze. But a bad one. Couldn't remember how I'd come to be where I was—nor much of anything before that day. Just one name. *Dane*. Don't know if it's my first or my last. Now—I *can* remember how to do some things. Like hammering a nail. Let's see if you boys remember how to do that, too."

S HERIFF "JIPPS" JIPSELL wasn't particularly pleased to see the three men in his office. Bat Masterson had taken the morning stage to points north, on his way to Dodge City, but there were others in Smoky

River who'd had suspicions of Squint Brewster and the Swede. And this man with them, Ferry Johnson, had the look of a man no one would trust. He was a hungry-looking, pop-eyed man with a lot of black fuzz on his face, shadowing his sunken cheeks and uniting his eyebrows. He hadn't washed in a good long while, and a shirt that might've been white once had gone dark yellow under his woolen coat. He had a six-gun tied down low, one hand casually on it.

"Take your hand off that blamed gun," Jipsell snapped, sitting up straight in his chair, one hand going to the shotgun leaning against his desk.

Ferry dropped his hand, started to put it back on the gun once more—then dropped it again. He showed blackened teeth in a particularly unpleasant grin. "Nervous, Jipsell?

"Ain't you gonna ask us to sit?" said Squint Brewster, looking around for a chair. The three gunmen were lined up in front of Jipsell's desk.

"Nope," said Jipsell. "What's your business? I've got work to do." Now that Masterson was gone, he actually had to do most of the work. He needed a new deputy but was having trouble finding one. Local muttering about Hanrahan and McCutcheon disappearing had made the sheriff's department unpopular. More election trouble. He was beginning to think that the extra pay from O'Hara wasn't worth all this.

"Need to know the name of that new man just started out at the Horseshoe W," said Squint.

"Dane something. Acts like he doesn't know any name but that. No papers on him. I remember you mentioned a man by that name. I was going to run him out of town for roughing up Armbruster, but he's out working for Willoughby. And Willoughby supported me in the election. Anyhow he's miles off. Not my problem now."

"Dane," Squint said, pointing at Hans. "What did I tell you?"

"Yah, well, if it's him, then we need to find the right time and place to send him to perdition," said Hans.

"If you do it, see that it's far away from this town," said Jipsell. "You went too far with McCutcheon and Hanrahan, and you did it too close to town. Shots were heard. Take your time with it—be smart about it. After what happened to—well, those other fellas, everyone's on edge, keeping watch like mice for the cat. Now, get out of here—don't come in this room till you've discovered the bathtub out back of the barbershop. You're making my office unfit for habitation."

DANE SPENT TWO weeks on a Horseshoe W gather, rounding up wild horses, and it was work he liked. Rand Binch was foreman on the roundup, with Dane, Blue, the Quinlan boys, and Buck driving the horses into a box canyon out in the Smoky Hills, and closing them in with the tree-branch fence they had assembled and ready. They did the job rain or shine, but Dane liked the work. Once they'd gotten the bang-tails a little calmer, they cut out the wise old mare who led the herd, roping her with two lariats between Dane and Blue. They tugged the roped mare toward the ranch and most of the herd followed her. A few bunch quitters tried to head for the hills, and they were harder to catch than cattle were. Binch let a few of them go, but they got most of the small herd to the Horseshoe W. Some they then picked out, cut out from the others, and drove into an adjoining corral. Once the horses had gotten a bit gentled down there, more used to having people around them—Dane and Blue were especially good at gentling them down—they'd be taken to the corral near the ranch house for breaking.

The weather continued to be fairly mild, and come nightfall the men sometimes gathered around a pit fire for their meals. Before heading to the bunkhouse, they listened to Buck play some old ballads on a small Mexican guitar, the young cowboy singing in a fine tenor; the Quinlan Boys threw dice and Cookie swapped tall tales with Rand. Dane just listened, enjoying the respite.

Dane was pleasantly surprised by the cleanliness of the bunkhouse. Most of the bunkhouses he'd sampled were reeking chaos that developed lice and bedbugs, forcing the men to sleep outside. But Jess Willoughby would not abide lice on his ranch, nor bedbugs, and he assigned a man every day to clean out the bunkhouse using an herbal cleanser Blue had showed him that killed bugs, along with liberal applications of lye soap. The bunks were inspected once a week; linen was boiled twice a week. The Quinlan boys grumbled over the trouble of keeping a clean bunkhouse, but Dane was glad of it.

Food was good, too. Usually chicken or mutton with vegetables, toothsomely prepared by Cookie Ike. It was the healthiest ranch Dane had ever worked on.

One morning in mid-October, as he ate ham and eggs with the hands in the small dining room of the cookshack, Dane realized he was feeling more and more like settling down in Smoky River. There were

Sheriff Jipsell and Clemson to think of, but no town was perfect.

"Dane!" said Willoughby, coming in. "Blue just came back from town—says you have a telegram there. The fool in the telegraph office wouldn't give it to Blue to bring out. I reckon you'd better go get it, and you can get us another two kegs of nails, a new crosscut saw, and ten bags of grain. Here's the money. You can dally an hour after you've loaded up but no more."

Dane harnessed a couple of stout horses to the freight wagon. Blue came into the stable with Dirk. "Blue, who was that telegram from?"

"They didn't say. Didn't want to trust anything to the Injun. Here—made you something."

He handed over a belt made of a rattlesnake skin sewn to a strip of leather. Colorful beads, red, yellow and blue, decorated the edges.

Dane gawped at it. "Is this the . . . ?"

"Same fella you shot, yes. Dirk bought the buckle and fixed it on there."

"That belt's for you!" Dirk said, grinning. "And so is this!"

He handed over two boxes of bullets fit for an old Colt Army revolver.

"Ah—now, those bullets were part of the deal!" Dane said, hefting the boxes in his hand. "But the belt—it's too fine for me, Blue!"

"I reckoned it was good medicine to make it and give it to you, and that's all there is to it," said Blue, with only the faintest smile on his face. "Try it on. That old belt you have is fair falling apart."

Dane took off his ancient belt and put the snakeskin belt through his trouser loops, tightened it up, and couldn't help grinning. "I'll be the envy of every man in town!"

"And the schoolboys, too," Dirk said, laughing.

Dane put the boxes of bullets into his saddlebags, which were hanging on the wall, taking out only a dozen shells. He put six in his gun—mostly just to please the other two cowboys—and six in his pocket.

"Well, I thank you, gents!" He shook their hands. "You'd best turn out to branding those broncs. I'll be back from town before . . . What's the saying . . . ?"

"Faster'n a hog after vittles?" Dirk suggested.

"Good enough."

Hearing Rand Binch call, Blue and Dirk went about their workday. And Dane marveled at the snakeskin belt, and the easy friendliness of the two men. Mostly he'd run into cussedness on the trail. But these men seemed to want to be his friends. A rarity.

He set out, driving the freight wagon through the misty morning toward Smoky River. He had mixed feelings about the trip. Armbruster had probably reported him to the sheriff. And who would have sent him a telegram? He'd never even seen a telegram. Not that he could recall.

It was chilly out, and today he wore a brown leather coat lined with sheep fur. Cookie had given it to him, saying it was too small for him.

The mist cleared up, driven by a cold north wind coming across the plain, and the sky was a blue of startling purity. The chill wind stung Dane's ears, but the sun was cheerful, and he found himself thinking of Suzanne. Willoughby had given him a little slack time, and he wondered if he might see her in town. If he stopped by the farm, her mother just might run him off with a shotgun.

He smiled at the thought, even though it could indeed happen that way, and snapped the reins to make the draft horses pull faster.

Picturing Suzanne made him think of someone else—someone she reminded him of. But who?

A shiver went through him. He seemed to see the girl Suzanne reminded him of then. A vivid picture—almost a vision—glimmered for him. He saw a pretty girl with coppery hair, speaking to him. He was sitting on a horse, and she was looking up at him. She was young, perhaps only sixteen. She had a shawl wrapped round her shoulders. Snow lay patchy on the ground around her. And she was crying. Her lips moved, but Dane couldn't hear what she was saying. Then it came, like a distant echo, drifting in and out of audibility "Dane . . . don't . . . let us go west. . . . Forget . . . the war. . . ."

She had been so young. Her name was . . . was . . .

The image faded. And he blinked, seeing his hands had loosened on the reins, and the horses were trying to leave the road to go to the little spring nearby. He tugged the team to a stop and took a long, shuddery breath.

What *was* her name? He was sure he had known once.

It didn't matter. He knew somehow that it had truly happened long ago. By now, if she lived, she was married, tending her house and children.

But—what had just happened? Had he remembered something—from before that day he felt Keggum pull him out of the brush and help him onto a pack mule. That had been his first meeting with Gravy, too.

He felt strange, a little dizzy but almost elated.

"Horses," he said, feeling an unfamiliar rush of hope, "let us stop for some water. Then we will hie for Smoky River."

A BRAWNY CREW OF three shaggy men was unloading large wooden crates and lumber from a barge docked beside the bridge as Dane rode across. One of the crates was marked:

UPTON'S BUILDING SUPPLIES
&
FANCY FURNISHINGS

Some venture of the new combine coming to town, he suspected, one of the new establishments that Clemson had evoked. They were losing no time.

Dane drove the team to Smoky River General Store and Hardware, purchased the goods, and loaded them as quickly as he could. He had hopes that Suzanne might be in town.

His next stop was the telegraph office, which happened to be in the print shop. There was no railway station here, and rarely was enough telegraphy going on in a small town to support a telegraphy business. The telegraph office had been a side business of Joe Hanrahan's—evidently someone had taken it over.

A bell jingled at the door when Dane entered the print shop, and a slim man in ink-stained shirtsleeves and smudged gray trousers turned to peer at Dane over the tops of his spectacles.

"Morning," Dane said. "I'm looking for a telegram supposed to be here for me."

"Oh, you're the gent!" He was a pale man in early middle age, with gray-streaked black hair and a neatly trimmed beard. He gave a rueful smile. "I'd shake your hand, sir, but they're all ink. I've been trying to make this printing press work in Joe's absence. I invested in this little venture here. But it's not my usual profession, and I know not how to make the device go. My name is Arthur Conrad, sir. I'm a lawyer when my hands are clean. And I can operate a telegraph at both ends. It was a job that supported me while studying the law."

After Dane had digested this somewhat comprehensive speech, he said, "My name's Dane."

"Ah! Come behind the counter—you'll find your telegram on the shelf there, next to the gun. Most curious, Joe quitting town without taking his gun."

"I came to the meeting Joe called—but unfortunately he didn't. You knew him well?"

"We were friends. I wrote a column on the law for his weekly sheet. I was in Kansas City when he called for the meeting—the one that preceded his departure— or I'd have attended. Do you believe that he left town of his own accord?"

"Highly doubtful. Bat Masterson pointed out that Joe was a flawless speller. He would never have written the message that way."

"You seem a literate man yourself, sir."

"No, sir, just a cowboy. Horse wrangler, lately." *Far as I know,* he added to himself. "But I can read."

"Know anything about running printing presses?"

"Only that the lever is pulled when the type and paper is in place. That much I've seen for myself. It's a lot of lever pulling. Make a man lopsided in the arms."

"Oh, yes—and setting type! A man could go blind. There really ought to be a machine for typesetting. Most tedious work."

Dane went behind the counter and found the telegram. He noticed the gun on the shelf. "Right strange, like you said, him leaving his gun behind, riding out alone." He opened the telegram.

Dane. Be assured have not forgotten deplorable state of things in Smoky River. If matters come to head wire me City Police Dodge City. Have no jurisdiction outside Dodge but wisely befriended good circuit judge.
                                            W. B. Masterson

"It's from Bat Masterson, offering help from a judge if we need one. There's none hereabouts?"

"I myself am running for the town justice of the peace, come January," said Conrad, attempting to wipe ink from his hands with a cloth. "We have one, one of our two bankers—Earl Rudge, his name is. However—he's a crook. Don't quote me on that, please. But it's so." Conrad gave Dane a close look. "Curious that Bat, who always seemed to know what he was doing, would entrust such matters as summoning a judge to a man who insists he's but a cowboy. Doesn't seem in cowboy territory."

"Oh, well, I . . ." Dane frowned. "I guess he thought I might get myself tangled in it some way."

"Interesting!" Conrad took a business card out of his pocket, being very careful so he only smudged it a little. "I read the telegram when I transcribed it, and I assumed the state of things he refers to has something to do with Jipsell and Clemson. And maybe this new outfit from Steeple Rock."

"I expect that's so."

"I trust Bat's judgment. Here is my card. If you ever want my help, call upon me. I am of Joe Hanrahan's mind: I'm very much afraid a great danger has found its way to Smoky River."

Dane pocketed the card and the telegram. "I'll do that. Tell me—there some reason you didn't trust Blue Thompson with that telegram?"

"Is he trustworthy? Armbruster was here, asking me to print a circular regarding baked goods—I am thus far failing in that undertaking—and he whispered to me that the man was not to be trusted."

"I'd trust Blue Thompson with my life. Armbruster, now—if I'm any judge, he's the kind of man who'd sell his own grandmother if he could get a good price."

Conrad chuckled. "I'll put my trust in Mr. Thompson next time, then."

Dane waved goodbye and went to the wooden sidewalk, where he found that the wind was blowing dry leaves by in a great rush, rattling them along the brick paving, and a child was chasing a paper kite. A dirty white terrier trailed after the boy, barking. Dane smiled—and his smile widened when he saw Suzanne coming out of the dry-goods store, a covered basket decorated with ribbons under one arm, her other hand holding her hat against the wind. She hadn't seen him, and she hurried along toward the south end of the street, her head down. She was dressed almost exactly as he'd last seen her, being a lady who could not afford more than a few garments.

He struck off across the street, his hat tucked under one arm to keep it from flying off in the wind. He waited impatiently for two farmhands on mules to clop slowly by, and then strode up to intercept Suzanne. "Ma'am, may I help you with that basket?"

She looked up at him, startled, her hair fluttering around her face, her green eyes bright. "Oh! Dane! Well—I suppose you can. I filled it with canned goods, and they're heavier than I supposed."

He stepped around her and took the basket, and she applied both hands to her hat—and just then a feather in it became uprooted in the wind and started on its way. But his right hand shot out—of its own accord—and he caught the red feather's quill between the tips of his fingers. "Your feather, ma'am."

Her eyes were wide. "You are quick on the draw when it comes to catching feathers, sir!" She watched him tuck it into her basket. "It was surely gone in the blink of an eye and then— My!"

Quick on the draw, he thought as they walked on. The rattler on his belt was testimony to it. But that wasn't the same as shooting a man dead. He wasn't sure he could be nearly as quick to shoot a man. He knew himself to have a conscience.

"Did I say something troublesome?" she asked, looking into his face.

"No, Suzanne. Headed to the livery?"

"Why, no, I'm making a stop at Miss Gleason's house, on Second Street. I have some preserves for her."

"We've surely benefited from those strawberry preserves at the Horseshoe W," he said. "Had some of the last of 'em on my bread this morning. Sweet and . . ."

He found himself looking into her eyes. And they had both stopped on the sidewalk, not knowing why. For a moment the world seemed to stand still—but for the wind, and the leaves swishing by, and Suzanne's coppery hair whipping about her face. There was nothing else at all in the world.

"Sweet and good," he said at last, gazing raptly at her.

She was blushing then. And neither of them was sure why.

Then Suzanne started off so rapidly, he had to hurry to catch up.

They stopped in at the livery—Gunderson was there, scooping grain into a trough, but he only winked at Dane, seeing Suzanne, and went about his task with exaggerated concentration. Suzanne put the canned goods in her saddlebags, patted the horse, whispering to it, and went out to the sidewalk. Still carrying the basket, which contained three jars of jam, Dane hurried after Suzanne, but not before Gunderson chortled, "Don't you look sweet, carrying that purty little picnicky basket, Dane! Ribbons and all!"

Dane growled to himself but said nothing, and soon he was pacing along with Suzanne again. The turn onto Second Street gave them some relief from the wind.

Suzanne stopped in front of a small cracker-box house. "Dane, unless you'd like to meet Miss Gleason and discuss the choir with us, perhaps you have another errand. . . ."

"I do plan to get a bite to eat. Tell you the truth, I was hoping you'd join me. Over at the Chinese fella's place."

"Mr. Sing's Café? I rarely eat lunch, but I will have

some tea while you eat, if you will be there in half an hour."

"I will."

He lifted his hat to her and watched her go into the little house.

Deciding a single glass of beer would do him no harm while he waited out the half hour, he went to Rusty's. Best show him the telegram. Rusty might have some notions. . . .

The place was empty, only just opened, and Dane was surprised to see Minnie Galvado the only customer. She was alone in a corner, drinking sangria, and she had a pitcher of it beside her glass. The pitcher was mostly empty.

"Rusty, I didn't know ladies populated saloons," said Dane in a low voice.

Rusty nodded. "Oh, some who don't give a damn will come in with their husbands—well, not here, but in the snootier places. Minnie has taken to slipping in here for a drink when she's angry with her ol' Galvado. I'm thinking I should tell him—but maybe he knows anyway. And if he doesn't, he might beat her for it. I do not hold with wife beating."

"Nor do I," said Dane. "Well, now . . . I got this telegram from Bat. . . ."

Dane spent twenty minutes talking to Rusty, the two of them pondering Bat's offer and wondering if Joe Hanrahan would turn up alive. Both doubted it.

"Bat gives me hope for some justice, at least," said Rusty at last.

Dane nodded. "I can't do much from the Horseshoe W, but what I can—I'll do."

"Oh, Dane!" called Minnie from her table, slurring

the words. "Hello!" He glanced at her, smiled, and waved politely, then headed quickly for the door.

Once on the sidewalk, he grimaced, hearing clattering feet behind him, and turned to see Minnie coming unsteadily toward him. "Don't go, Dane! Have a drink with me! Rafe's such a bear, and I need—"

Dane put up his hands, palms spread between them. "Ma'am, I purely cannot—"

But she rushed between his arms, almost knocking him over. He grabbed hold to keep her from falling. She clung to him, nestling her head against his shoulder, sobbing about the horrid Rafe. That was when he saw Suzanne coming out of the livery—and stopping to stare at him, aghast. She whirled and rushed back into the stables.

"Oh, no, no," he muttered. It took him a minute to pry Minnie away without hurting her, and though he felt bad for her, Dane strode rapidly across the street to explain to Suzanne. But before he could enter the stables, she rode quickly out right past him, her face set in cold stone, and wheeled her horse to canter away from town.

I⊤ WAS EARLY in the day, and there were as yet no customers in Steeple Rock's fanciest dance hall.

Shine O'Hara was standing at the bar of Shine's Champagne and Whiskey Emporium, drinking a cheap sparkling white wine that almost passed for champagne and talking to Showboat Lou. He had, in fact, hired her from a riverboat when he'd been out on the Mississippi his last trip east. She was one of the ornaments of the gawdy "emporium": a willowy, busty woman with a shiny tumble of blond hair about her exposed shoulders, sleepy blue eyes, prettily pouting lips, all set off by a tight, lacy white gown with gold trim.

Shine was quite used to Lou—in truth he was becoming tired of her, especially in light of her hints that he needed a woman like her to run his household—and he was scarcely listening as she talked on and on, in her little-girl voice, about how with a little class and good taste Steeple Rock itself could become the queen of the Rockies. "Everything is so knocked together and without color out here," she said. "Yes, you have lovely red velvet curtains on the stage there. You have those musicians who're taking their blessed time tuning up, wearing their fine blue coats, but outside, this mess of a town is as gray as a cemetery, Shine!"

"No doubt," he said, watching the door. Trent Grady was taking his bloody damned time showing up.

"Now, we could start by bringing in a flower shop—greenhouses can do marvels—and some brass lampposts," Lou was saying.

"Lou—you get to rehearsing with those fiddlers and such there," Shine said, seeing Trent come in the door. "I've got to have a private talk with this man."

Lou made a sulky sound of exasperation and angrily climbed the steps to the stage.

Trent Grady joined Shine at the bar. He was a compact man, wearing a low topper hat with a silk band; adorning his round face was a carefully sculpted goatee; his suit of dark blue, with its high collar and scarlet vest, was carefully composed. He was in all things a careful man, disdaining face-to-face gunfights—which, despite tales told in dime novels, were precious rare anyhow—and always scouting for more discreet ways to eliminate men troublesome to his various employers. It was this caution that made him a desirable hireling for Shine. Squint and Hans had acted rashly in dealing with McCutcheon and Hanrahan, and Shine had grand plans for Smoky River he would not see upset.

"Trent," said Shine, "will you have a drink on the house?"

"I would not insult you by refusing, Shine." Trent Grady's round face brightened at the thought of a free whiskey. "Overholt's is good enough for me. Have you ice here?"

"Sure, I have a man who brings it down from the mountains. Goes to waste as often as not, for I can't keep it cool long. Burt! Overholt with ice for this gentleman!"

"Right away, sir!" Burt was a trim, grim-faced bartender who scarcely ever smiled—which would not be suitable in a bartender except that he could also shoot accurately, should the necessity arise.

Burt brought the drink and, another good point about him, he did not linger but went back to work polishing brass spittoons.

The two men leaned closer together and spoke in low tones. Grady knew that Shine did not waste time socializing. "That Swede of yours said you had a job for me, Shine," Trent said in a New Orleans drawl as he lifted his glass to admire the little chunks of ice in it. "Who's your problem?"

"My problem is a fellow named Dane—that's all he's going by now."

"Dane?" Trent eyebrows knitted. "The Dane from that affray in Sweetwater? And—and in Taos?"

"That's the man. You'll find him round about Smoky

River. Probably still working at the Horseshoe W Ranch out west of town. You ever see him in person?"

"Just heard some rather alarming stories about him."

"He's a big man. Getting late in his thirties. Clean-shaven. Last seen in a duster and Levi's. He was an officer in the Civil War, and he has that about him."

"Hence he's a man familiar with tactics."

"Sure, that he is. And he's a fast man. Unnaturally fast reflexes and an unerring eye. If you face him on the street, he'll kill you. I saw him do it against a tolerably fast draw in Denver. That's why I hired him. Had a war hereabouts with another outfit. But he turned against me. And he'll do it again—for he must begrudge what we did to him. I thought we'd killed him, but we never found a body, and it seems he's a hard man to kill. Your eye must be unerring, too, Trent."

The musicians had begun "Oh, My Heart Is Ever Broken," with Lou singing along, and the two men at the bar had to lean even closer to hear each other.

"Why, give me no more than fifty yards and good cover, Shine, and I shall ship him express to his Maker." Trent raised his drink to Shine and then sipped it, made a sound of appreciation, and went on. "I have lately acquired the finest telescopic accoutrements, attachable to my most admirable Springfield."

"But you just reflect on this," said Shine, pointing a finger at the hired assassin. "Smoky River is not yet a lively town. Most of its citizens are stuffed shirts. There is lately a dance hall and two saloons. And one brothel that's out of general view. I have bought a controlling interest in the dance hall and one saloon, and I have plans for my own bawdy houses; I have found a man at Union Pacific who'll take an inducement on the side to arrange a branch line to Smoky River. I have prepared, at much cost, to build a fine new saloon and a gambling palace. I've invested heavily in the local councilmen. But they are beholden to the voters, who are already not pleased with them. All of that tells us this job, in the best of worlds, needs to be done away from town and hopefully with a good cover story. Even make it look like an accident, or like Indians did it, if you can. *This man will go*, someway, somewhere, and before too long, even if I have to open the doors of hell to do it. For he killed my cousin, who was my right hand, and he cursed me to my face."

"Why," said Trent, smiling, "such a man cannot be borne. He certainly must go. I will attend to the matter." He sipped more whiskey. "But I will not conceal from you that the stories I have heard of the man make my flesh creep. I take great risks—and therefore, I must triple my fee. . . ."

CHAPTER SEVEN

"DANE," SAID RAND Binch, "you're pretty good at riding herd on those Quinlan boys. I need you to keep an eye on 'em for me."

Rand was leaning on the fence, watching Dane put some salve on the last of the horse brands, that drizzly afternoon, and gentling, as best he could, the upset wild horses out in the holding pen. Only the wild horses meant to be used as remuda ponies were branded.

In the adjoining corral, the other hands were watching Jimmy French, a professional itinerant bronc buster, snubbing a bronc to a post. It was a particularly fine stallion—strong, young, perfectly proportioned—but also particularly rebellious. Jimmy didn't hold with bareback busting; he slung a saddle onto the horse with one hand, twisting the stallion's ear with the other, the sudden pain distracting the horse long enough for Blue to buckle its saddle on. Jimmy's meth-

ods involved sharp spurs and the liberal use of a quirt.
Blue and Dane shared a gentler mean of horse training—
for them, to "gentle" a horse was no euphemism—but
their technique took much longer. Willoughby wanted
this horse "broke" and soon, so he'd brought in the
slight but wiry French to do the job. Willoughby was
sitting on the fence by the other hands, urging the men
to observe Jimmy French's rather ruthless style of bronc
busting.

The young, newly branded mare with Dane had also
been snubbed to a post so she couldn't shy away as he
treated her. Snorting and tossing her head, she let him
softly pat on the salve.

"Why, what's the problem with those boys, besides
their being young?" Dane asked. "A little nudge and
they get their job done."

"Oh, there's some suspicion on the part of Gabe
Hollander that they rustled a half dozen of his cows.
To be sure, them longhorns weren't branded as yet, for
Gabe is slow to get such things done. A loco longhorn
knocked down a length of fence, and the beeves run
off into the hills. But Gabe had reported them missing
and was looking for them. And the Quinlan boys were
caught driving them toward Burrister. Fella out there
buys cows without asking questions. . . ."

"Where might Burrister be?"

"Off in the hills east of town. Not even quite a
town—few shops, a store, a tannery, and a saloon full
of lazy cowboys avoidin' work. And also some fellas
who don't care how they fill their pockets. They'll buy
a stray cow cheap and put their own brand on it, sell it
in Abilene. Now, it's not a great big rustlin', if that's
what it is, but it'd put a hundred dollars in those boys'

pockets, so it's a temptation. Ben claimed they were driving the cows to Hollander's spread when they stampeded, and they had to chase them down near Burrister, which is hogwash."

"Jess didn't fire them?"

"He didn't know." Rand pursed his lips, looking a little embarrassed. "Well, I'm kinda fond of those idiots. So when Hollander complained to me, I dealt with it myself. And—he hasn't heard. He's not a friend to Hollander, y'see—they fought over rights to that stream a mile south there."

"They fought over Lonesome Dog Creek?"

"Didn't quite come to a fight—but Hollander waved his guns around and cussed Jess over it. Fool thing for Hollander to do. A stream running along a property line belongs to both sides, even a muttonhead knows that."

Dane nodded. "I'll keep watch on them."

"There's another thing. Once a month, Willoughby lets three hands go into town for an overnight. Ike, he just gets drunk and ogles the long-legged fillies at the dance hall. Now, believe it or not, Buck plays guitar in the saloon, drinks no more'n two beers, and next day he goes to church. His pappy was a preacher."

"I've seen him reading the Bible. He reads it slow, but he reads it."

Rand chuckled. "But the Quinlan boys, they get into trouble. Nigh every time! Fights in the saloon, fights in the dance hall, fights on the street. Mostly fistfights, but Dirk wounded a man once, and Bat took his gun and held him in the town jail till it was straightened out. Some spoke up for him, said it wasn't Dirk

started it, and the other man fired his pistol first—
missed Dirk and shot out a window—so Dirk was let
go. After that, Masterson commenced to collecting
their guns when they came to town. But . . ."

"But no more Masterson. And Jipsell doesn't care
to stay on top of things."

"I knowed Jipsell for some years now. He's afraid if
he plays with powder, he might get burned—some
drunk cowboy might shoot him. That's why he sends a
deputy to do it. Only he still ain't got a replacement for
Bat. Now, tomorrow's Saturday, and it's the Quinlans
turn to go. Blue doesn't like to ride herd on them.
Buck's too slow and uncertain. Ike's a certainty to be
too drunk. . . ."

"So that leaves me." Dane sighed. He preferred to
stay out here on the ranch. He'd been humiliated by
what Suzanne had seen and how she'd reacted. For a
time, he had toyed with the idea of going to Marrin
Farm and explaining himself. But that felt too much
like groveling, and it hurt him that she jumped to the
conclusion she clearly had jumped to.

Still—if he'd meant nothing to her, she would not
have been angry. A little disgusted maybe, but not that
cold fury. They had not made a courting agreement,
but still they had been right on the edge of it.

The question was—did she still think of him in a
courting way? She was a notoriously selective woman.
She might have given him the wind already.

Maybe she'll give in to her mama, he thought, *and
marry Jess Willoughby, after all.*

Dane figured that if he went to town of a Saturday,
he might well not see Suzanne there. She would likely

remain at the farm. And he could make up his mind in town if he wanted to see her on Sunday morning and risk being sent away with his tail between his legs.

"Okay, Rand, I'll do it," Dane said at last. "I'll collect their guns myself and ride herd on them. But I'm not much for babysitting."

"Why, just keep them from busting a bottle over some ranch hand's noodle, and don't let them pull any knives. Oh, and don't let them get between a man and his lady—that's happened twice now—and then there's the way card games turn out for them—"

Dane groaned. "It's going to be a lot of work for a day off, Rand!" He shook his head, untied the horse from the post, and led it to the holding pen.

TWO MEN WERE huddled in a recessed doorway across from Rusty's Saloon. Grady had a heavy overcoat on, but even so the night was growing bitterly cold.

"That's him," said Ferry Johnson as they watched Dane and the Quinlans walk into Rusty's Saloon. "Them's the Quinlan boys with him, so's I hear."

"You sure it's the man Dane?"

"Couldn't never forget 'im. Saw him shoot Johnny O'Hara down."

"Murder, was it?" asked Trent Grady.

"Oh, Johnny was gunning for him. This Dane feller got mad when he saw me hang that D'Enfer, old Jude D'Enfer's son. Russ D'Enfer he was. Nineteen years old. Shine framed the boy up for horse thievin', and we lynched him so's to show clear our feelings about Jude D'Enfer and his bunch. Now, me, nothing I enjoy more

than a good hangin' long as I'm on the pleasing side of
it. But this Dane, he didn't like that hanging. Called
Shine a murderer and a crook. Johnny tried to shoot
him, right enough. Come on a-shooting in the street
next day. But I'll tell you . . ." Ferry paused to spit tobacco on the walk. Trent stepped back from it. "I'll tell
you. We seen before then what kind of a shot that
Dane was. Why, he could've shot Johnny in his gun
arm and spared him! But no, that Dane put a ball nice
and neat between that boy's eyes! Now, that's the devil's work."

"I understand entirely." Every so often a wayward
gust of wind searched them out in their alcove and sent
shivers through the two men. The story about Dane's
precision with his gun—under fire, it appeared—
brought its own shiver to Grady. "Does he drink much?
A man in his cups is a poorer shot."

"Never saw him drunk—hell, I never saw him drink
't all, unless you count one glass of beer. And who
counts that? He didn't spend much time in Mr. O'Hara's
place. We boys have our own table there. Dane's a
highfalutin—!" He then unreeled a series of colorful
epithets that would've made a preacher's hair curl.

"Indeed." Grady had a sudden desire to get this job
over with. He toyed with cutting the Gordian knot and
simply walking into the saloon and shooting this man
Dane in the back. Thereupon he could run back out,
hop on his horse—Ferry Johnson could hold it for
him—and ride like the devil out of town. Would Jipsell
get up a posse? He would not. They'd had a word with
him already.

Trent owned a good fast horse. It could be done. He
could go directly to Steeple Rock, and . . .

But perhaps not. It was a good ways to Steeple Rock. "Does he have friends in town, Ferry?"

"Some—so Brewster figgers. And o' course, those cowboys he works with. You know how ranch hands are. They're pretty tight."

Grady grunted. No, it would not do. It would take days to get to Steeple Rock, in rugged conditions—and doubtless these Horseshoe W riders would be on his trail. Someone in the saloon might recognize him, too. Some itinerant gambler could put a name to him. Grady had no desire to risk hanging.

He sighed. There were always the most wretched inconveniences. And having to stand here in the cold with this ill-smelling, tobacco-squirting buffoon was just the start of them. "Let us go in, have a brandy, and reconnoiter the situation."

"Me? But he'd know me! I'm one of those that— No, tha's not a good idee. When I deal with him, it'll be my way."

"Then head to the other saloon or wherever you choose. He doesn't know me. I wish to have a look at this killer. Might overhear something about his plans."

DANE LEANED AGAINST the wall, a glass of beer in his hand. He was watching the poker game where the Quinlan boys were cursing as they steadily lost their pay.

As he did on nights when the saloon was crowded, Rusty brought in a long-bearded, half-blind fiddler who sat on a stool by the glowing potbelly stove. It was Saturday night, and every table was full of men drinking and playing poker. The bar was double crowded, men leaning on others and waving at Rusty for another drink. A drunken cowboy in denim held up by red suspenders was dancing along, a sort of buck-and-wing on the sawdusted floor, to "The Old Chisolm Trail." His friends hooted and clapped in time. Dane enjoyed the overflow of high spirits in Rusty's Saloon, but thoughts of Suzanne made his spirits as tepid as his beer. Nor had he ever been much for riotous living.

Two of the cowboys started in pushing each other, arguing over space at the bar, and Dane wished Bat Masterson was still deputy in Smoky River. Bat would most likely would have settled them down without hurting a hair on either man's head.

The room was almost too stifling for Dane, being not only heated but flush with large, sweaty men; the air was thickened by the smoke of pipes and cheap little cigars. Dane drank a little beer and loosened the bandanna round his neck.

"Hellfire and chicken droppings!" Dirk burst out, throwing his cards on the table as a cackling merchant raked in the pot. "Either someone's tinkerin' with the cards, or my luck has gone and left me for good!"

"You've failed to identify the problem," chuckled the mustachioed merchant with the slicked-back hair and garters on his shirtsleeves. Dane knew him to be Tim Rory, half owner of the Smoky River Hotel. "Man has to know when to fold 'em, and you don't know it, ha-ha! Damned fool kid!"

"I'll not be mocked by the likes of you, Rory!" Dirk declared, standing up suddenly so his chair was upset. Dirk reached for his gun—which wasn't there. Rusty held the Quinlan firearms behind the bar, as per Dane's request. "Dane, I want my blamed gun back!"

Dane clapped an arm around Dirk's shoulders and affably but firmly guided him toward the bar. "All in good time! Firstly, I'm buying you a drink, young Quinlan."

"What about me?" Ben declared, getting up. "Dirk's rotten luck has soured all my good luck away!"

"You, too, Ben." Dane wished he had a pocket watch. He was hoping he could convince the Quinlans it was time to go to the hotel and put up their feet.

He'd had a pocket watch once, hadn't he? A silver one? When was that? He could almost see it in his palm. A voice was saying, *"It's yours now, son."*

But the memory, if that's what it was, faded away, and Dane noted an open spot at the corner of the bar as the two cowboys, quitting their shoving match, stalked outside to settle their differences with their fists.

Dane and the Quinlans squeezed into the gap beside a burly man with a plug hat and a patched coat who was pouring his own drinks from a whiskey bottle he'd purchased from Rusty. To the other side was a man in a bowler hat, a blue suit, and a red vest.

The fiddler was now sawing away at "The Yellow Rose of Texas," and Dirk whistled along.

"You know what this place lacks," Ben said. "Women! I like ol' Rusty, but what's wrong with a pretty bar girl or two?"

"Clemson had the same idea," Dane said. "Not Rusty's style."

"We should go over to the Silver Goddess," Dirk suggested. "Plenty of girls and plenty of 'em to see. We gave enough of our money to Rusty and these card-sharps here. Dane'll stand us a drink over there, won't you, Dane? And we'll find you a girl to talk to! She'll come to our table 'cause I'm there and then you can charm her."

Ben laughed. "Oh, Dane's a ladies' man right enough! I heard from Blue he's courting that Suzanne Marrin."

Dane growled, "Don't talk about a lady in a saloon. And careful how you talk about that one anywhere."

There was enough warning in Dane's voice that Ben shut right up and turned to catch Rusty's eye. "We're dyin' of thirst over here, Rusty!"

Dane glanced at the sharp-dressed man to his right. He wore a glossy low topper hat and a tailored suit. His boots were shined, his chin sharpened by the point of a goatee. He had the look of a tinhorn gambler. A man quick with his fingers and smooth with his tongue.

Something about the man piqued Dane's curiosity. "Don't believe we've met," Dane said, paying Rusty for the Quinlans' whiskeys. "Name's Dane." He drank off the dregs of his beer.

"Oh, I'm just traveling through," said the man in the blue suit. He stuck out his hand and stuck a smile on his face. "Name's Edmund Earl," he added as they shook hands.

The man had a handshake like a wet sock, but his eyes were forceful and cold, despite the friendly smile. Somehow, Dane sensed the name the man had given him was a false one. "Edmund Earl? Reminds me of a name in *King Lear*." Dane suspected the man would recognize the reference.

"You're a reader of Shakespeare, sir?" said the man who called himself Edmund Earl, his eyebrows arching. "Few here this far to the west are familiar with the gentleman."

"Happens there's not much in my life I do remember," Dane said. "But much of Shakespeare comes to me from time to time. Must've read it back when."

"You're not sure?"

Dane chose not to answer.

"May I buy you a drink, Mr.—Dane, was it? I'm just finishing a passable brandy."

"A beer, if you like. That's all I go to. Tried taking a few pulls at hard liquor once. Didn't sit well with me."

"A beer. If it must be, it shall be."

Rusty served them, and Edmund Earl raised his drink. "To Shakespeare, who knew that 'When we are born, we cry that we are come to this great stage of fools.'"

Dane raised his glass and took a swallow. "Another line from that play comes to me—only other one I recall just now. 'The prince of darkness is a gentleman.'"

The stranger seemed startled by this citation. "Well, well! Ah—do you work here in town?"

"Nope, I'm working out at the Horseshoe W, wrangling horses, knocking together fences, and such. And you, sir?"

"Oh, I am a professional of the pasteboards, sir, but I look for the fat games in the bigger towns. Here I would find the pickings both too easy and too slim. You're here, I suppose, for the night and then 'ho for the trail' again, eh?"

"That's right. Back to work."

"Best a ranch is far enough from town the hands don't slip away at night, or so I've heard."

"It's some miles due west, out near Lonesome Dog Creek."

"What a colorful name for a stream! Do you spend

a lot of time out on the, ah, range, scouting up wild horses and the like?"

"Some. There's hills out west and north of the ranch— a few canyons, watering holes, good grass—good place to find bangtails."

"A most salutary air in such a place, no doubt. Preferable to the smoky miasma that is so often found in my own workplaces." He coughed. "And places like this. Do you go out to gather horses regularly?"

"Mr. Willoughby decides when." It seemed to Dane this "Edmund Earl" was fishing for information. To what end? Dane looked the gambler over more closely— and glimpsed the butt of a pistol in a hideout holster under his coat. Earl, if that was who he was, seemed to realize Dane had noticed the gun. He casually closed his coat and smoothed it in place, as if merely concerned about neatness. But there was a certain tension in the motion that sparked Dane's instincts. This man could be more than a gambler.

Dane became aware that Ben Quinlan was exchanging sharp words with the burly man in the plug hat. "I don't care what you heard!" Ben shouted. "I didn't rustle no cattle! And what would you know about it? You're a dockwalloper off the barge! You don't even live here!"

"Why, boy, I come here regular, bringing supplies from upriver, and know just about everybody who's anybody in this little pinprick of a burg!"

"You don't know me!"

"Ha! I said 'everybody who's anybody'!"

"That's the second affront we've taken tonight, Ben!" Dirk said. "I say we show 'em who they're talking to!"

"Mister," Dane said, leaning over to talk to the man in the plug hat. "You heard a rumor drummed up from a misunderstanding. These boys came across some stray cows and were trying to take them back to their owner. I've got it on good authority. Why, if you believe every rumor you hear, you could get yourself in a fight twice an hour!"

Dane looked the man in the eyes then and held them as he waited for the response.

The burly man gulped. "Just a story I heard." He turned to the Quinlans. "Boys—I render apologies, and . . ." He tipped his hat and walked unsteadily to the back door, probably headed to the outhouse.

Dirk turned frowning to Dane. "You are just *determined* to ruin all our fun tonight!"

Dane laughed. "Only the kind that might end with you in jail. Maybe it's time we go." He turned to ask the man in the blue suit if he had a pocket watch.

But the man was gone. He'd up and left the saloon.

TRENT GRADY FOUND Ferry Johnson in a dim corner of the Silver Goddess. Ferry was leaning against the wall, a tumbler of whiskey in his hand, mouth agape as he ogled the dance hall girls. Wearing what were little more than red satin blouses exposing a great deal of décolletage, and gawdy corsets with ruffles passing for skirts about their hips, the Silver Goddesses were plying the men at the bar and leaning over the gaming tables. Near the closed maroon curtains of the stage, a small band in Clemson's silver-trimmed livery was playing "I'll Take You Home Again, Kathleen."

Grady took sardonic note of one bearded farmer at the faro table openly weeping, having lost his all.

"Never trust a faro table, Ferry," Grady declared. "The odds are stacked high against you. And many a faro dealer stacks them higher yet."

"You get a good look at him in that saloon, Grady?" Ferry asked.

"Closer than I expected to. Had a drink with him. I gave out the name Edmund Earl. I'll keep to that hereabouts, so don't call me Grady."

"You figure anything on him?" Ferry asked, taking a plug of tobacco from his pocket. He held it up to his nose and sniffed at it, unwilling to break off a chaw before he was done with his whiskey.

"Oh, a couple of likely locations for an ambuscade."

"A what?"

"Never mind. Struck me as a wary and dangerous man. Seemed very sharp-eyed indeed. I withdrew before he could take too much note of me. But certain possibilities came to mind. He seems to be a guardian angel over those Quinlan boys. Gave me an idea."

Clemson emerged from a door behind the bar and surveyed over the crowded dance hall approvingly. He noticed Ferry and Grady and, seeming a bit surprised—doubtless startled by the contrast between the two men—he strolled over, hands in his pockets. "Hello, Ferry. Didn't I tell you to clean up before you came in here again?"

"Meant to. Might yet. This here man is doing that job for Shine, Clemson."

"Ah!" Clemson nodded. "I believe I heard something of the sort. Clearing out the deadwood?"

"When the time is right," Grady said. They shook hands and introduced themselves.

"What I heard, you're a careful man," said Clemson. "Discreet."

"I am that," said Grady, "and I expect the same from my associates."

"Word's just come some farmer found a couple bodies in a shallow grave." Clemson snorted with disgust. "Mighty indiscreet!"

"Don't collar me 'bout it!" Ferry protested. "Talk to Brewster and that Swede. I warn't there!"

"Keep your voice down, Ferry, if you please," said Grady. "Or even if you don't please. Mr. Clemson, I need to ask some questions about a certain rumor I heard. A man like you would hear them all. . . ."

W HEN WE GETTING our dang guns back, Dane?" Dirk asked as they walked down cold, windy Main Street beneath the yellow light from the lanterns hung in front of the shops. "I feel half naked."

"Tomorrow morning, soon as Rusty opens."

Dane and the Quinlans were headed to the hotel. They'd started work at dawn, graining the horses and repairing fences, going till midafternoon before being given the go-ahead to ride for Smoky River. All three were weary.

Dane heard a creaking come from behind, turned to see a buckboard trundling up. The driver called out, "Whoa," and stopped in front of the sheriff's office. He was a stout man with the sort of beard that ringed the face, mustache shaven away. "Sheriff Jipsell!" He called. "I got somethin' for you here!"

Dan and the Quinlans walked back to look into the buckboard. Two dead bodies were laid out, side by side, in the wagon bed. They were smeared with dirt but still recognizable.

"Why, that's Joe Hanrahan you got there, Des!" exclaimed Ben.

"Surely is," Des Conner said. "And that's McCutcheon with him! Why, I spoke to Joe about a notice on my dried apples—same day he went missing! And here he is, bless him. My old hound was digging in a windbreak out to the side of the orchard, started in tugging on Joe's arm when I caught up. Thick brush in the windbreak. I might never have found 'em otherwise. They were both in the same shallow grave."

Dane nodded. "Appears like they were both shot at least three times." A cold anger spread through him. He hadn't really known Hanrahan, but he'd admired what he'd tried to do. Joe Hanrahan had put out the town's only newspaper, and he was a bold man who stood up against corruption. And McCutcheon—an upstanding man who was working with Joe to bring the corruption to light. Two good men executed by murderers and buried in a shallow grave.

It wasn't right. It shouldn't stand, not without a reckoning.

Dane's hand went automatically to his gun, but there was no one here needing a bullet.

Seemed like that other Dane was showing up again, wanting to come out. *Who do I think I am? I'm just a ranch hand. . . .*

Jipsell strode up, scowling. He looked into the buckboard and winced, muttering something inaudible under his breath.

"We done told you they didn't just ride off to no-where, Jipps!" growled Des. "Seems to me these men were murdered in cold blood!"

"When did you get the job of coroner?" Jipsell asked. "Well, take the bodies up to Harney, and tell him to put 'em in a cold room. I'll look into it tomorrow mornin'. I'm going to bed." Shaking his head, the sheriff went back to his office door, locked it, and hurried away to-ward his house on Second Street.

"Didn't seem all that surprised to me," Dane said, as the buckboard went squeaking off.

"When's a sheriff surprised to find a man shot dead, anywhere west of the Mississippi?" Ben said.

"Who's Harney?" Dane asked.

"Undertaker," said Dirk. "Funeral director. Takes care of the cemetery. The whole shebang."

"This town got a coroner?"

"I think Doc Greeley does most of that," Ben said, rubbing his eyes wearily. "Hope I don't dream tonight, because if I do, I'm like to see those fellers lying in that wagon. I knew both of them. They were all right."

Dane doubted he'd sleep well either.

DANE WAS AWAKENED the next morning by clamor from the street. He sat up in the squeaking bed, looked around in confusion at the dank, mildew-redolent little room, then remembered he was in the hotel. It had taken him more than an hour to go to sleep, despite his fatigue, and during the night, he'd tossed and turned, sometimes wakened by the talkative bedsprings.

In the street below his window someone shouted,

"We should've set up a search party! We might've found them in time!"

"Well, hell, Rusty, why didn't you go then!" a rumbling voice replied.

"Because Jipsell gave me the feeling I'd be arrested if I did!"

There was a chorus of agreement from other voices. Dane heard Jipsell's brusque response then. "I'm investigating the matter. You can be sure of it! Now, I want you bunch to disperse! Go on, get! You're making too damn much noise for a Sunday morning!"

The grumbling died down as the men went about their business. It seemed the town had learned the fate of the men who'd shared a shallow grave. The memory of those two bodies, cast aside like trash, brought the cold anger back to Dane.

He took a deep breath. Trying to let it all be for now, Dane got out of bed and set to cleaning up. He opened the curtains for some light and went to the dresser mirror, appraised himself with disapproval. He used a cloth and soap set by the water jug, and gave himself a sponge bath. Then he pulled on his one clean shirt and a black string tie he'd borrowed from Rand. He combed his hair and thought about going to the barber for a shave. Likely closed on Sunday morning. Well, he had the soap and a borrowed razor, and he could make do with cold water if he scraped hard enough.

Dane had half a mind to go to church this Sunday morning. He'd brought the extra clothes in case. These last three years he had not gone to church, except to peep through the door. Elias Keggum, being colored, was not allowed in most churches out in the southwest, so on a drive they would read the Bible together on Sunday mornings while they drank their coffee at the chuckwagon, even reading the occasional verse to each other.

"Lookee there, it's the Reverend Keggum and his deacon," one of the cowboys had jeered to general laughter.

Dane hadn't minded. He was not a pious man, but Elias Keggum was his friend, and the ritual made the older man happy.

Today, Dane had another reason to go. Maybe though when she saw him coming, Suzanne would ask him not to soil the church with his sinful ways.

He smiled ruefully as he scraped his face. Suzanne wouldn't say any such thing. He knew that somehow. She might cut him dead though if he tried to talk to her.

Just as he was wiping the last of the soap off, Dirk commenced pounding on the door. "You going to sleep all the blessed day? There's pretty girls all dressed up a-trottin' to church out there!"

Dane put on his hat and the brown leather coat lined with wool, and joined the Quinlan boys in the small lobby. "Let's see if the café's open. . . ."

"It's closed," said Finch, the pinch-faced man running the hotel desk, when they'd got downstairs, "but the Chinaman's place is open."

They took breakfast in Mr. Sing's place, steak and eggs and a bucket of coffee. "You got a sore head, Dirk, you soak?" Ben asked.

"Not a bad one. I can eat my food. If I get a bad one, can't eat for a whole day. Pour me some more coffee."

Dane was wiping his mouth when he heard the bell ringing from the church. Curious how the clangor made his heart pound.

He got up and said, "Boys—I believe I'll do it."

"Do what?" Ben asked. "You going to get some whiskey this early?"

"I don't drink whiskey. And what's more—I'm going to church."

"Now you're funnin' me!" Dirk said, snorting.

"I am not. You boys can join me. You're not much dressed for it, but I expect they won't mind, seeing as you're lost souls and all."

"Lost souls!" Ben laughed.

Dane grinned and went to the street. The Quinlans joined him on the wooden sidewalk, and for a few minutes, they watched women in bonnets and long dresses hurrying their solemnly dressed husbands up to the church.

"We're going to be late, Samuel!"

"I'm coming, blast it all, Laurie Ann!"

Ben and Dirk laughed. Dirk opened his mouth, cupping it with his hand to heckle, and Dane jabbed him with an elbow.

"Ow!"

"Leave them be, Dirk," Dane whispered. "You two can come along, but mind your manners."

"You sure think you're riding herd on us, don't you?" Ben said, looking annoyed.

"You know, that's just how Rand put it. I'm to ride herd on you so you don't embarrass the ranch again."

They got to the church, and the Quinlans took off their hats, holding back, looking a little awed now as they watched folks go in. But when a pretty teenage girl in a bonnet glanced their way, Dirk winked at her and made a kissy sound.

"Oh!" she said, turning away and hurrying into the church.

"You boys aren't civilized enough for this," Dane muttered. "Stay outside and stay out of trouble."

He took a deep breath, removed his hat, and went in. A few of the parishioners looked at him in mingled curiosity and vague disapproval as he walked past the rough-hewn pews. Perhaps he wasn't quite shined up enough.

But he boldly made his way to the front pew, behind the organist, where he had a good view of the choir.

And of Suzanne. There she was, wearing her long blue dress and her blue lace gloves. He could see the mending on the gloves. Probably hand-me-downs from a grandmother.

He was surprised once more at the small details he noted about her. He admired the kindness in her face as she pointed at the music on the wooden stand before the choir, murmuring to a curly-headed teenage girl in a white frock, who was nervously standing beside her.

Dane had the feeling someone was staring at him, and he glanced over to the pew directly in front of the choir. There was Mrs. Marrin in a white bonnet, clutching her purse, glowering at him with narrowed eyes and pursed lips.

He nodded to her, and she quickly looked away.

Finding the church tolerably full, the cadaverous preacher in his stiff high collar and frock coat, standing a few steps behind the pulpit, inclined his head to the organist, who struck up a fulsome hymn. The tune seemed familiar to Dane—he must have been to church in his time.

The choir soon chimed in, and Dane felt his heart

melt as he picked out Suzanne's voice, singing. She was following the sheet music as she sang, but she glanced up from time to time at the congregation, and he saw her start when she spotted him. Her voice faltered a little; then she went fixedly back to singing. Sometimes feeling a bit crowded in the pew, compressed between a stout older man with the biggest beard he'd ever seen and a frail elderly lady rubbing her arthritic hands, Dane sat through the whole service. The preacher, at the climax of his sermon, raised his voice to a howl: "For as in Second Peter we are told, 'And turning the cities of Sodom and Gomorrah into ashes, He condemned them . . . making them an example unto those'"—he seemed to fix Dane with a warning eye then—" 'that after should live ungodly!'"

Dane had an urge to glare back at the preacher, but instead he looked at the floor.

A FTER THE SERVICE, Suzanne was busying herself talking to the new girl in the choir, smilingly congratulating her. The girl beamed.

Dane followed the others to the aisle between pews. He noticed Armbruster, who was standing up to leave. The big man was glowering at him. He seemed to be snorting like a bull about to charge. Dane half expected to be loudly denounced. But Armbruster contented himself with snorting.

Dane stepped into the blustery day outside, looking for the Quinlans and not finding them. The congregants lingered about the church walk, exchanging greetings, some of them cheerful, some somber, given the dismaying news of the day.

A friendly voice called out, "Mr. Dane!"

It was the lawyer, Arthur Conrad, waving to him as he stepped out of the church. "I thought I saw you in there!" In a suit that looked to have been ordered from a catalog, Conrad came over and shook hands. "I'm glad to see you here. It is a hard day—and church is the best place for us."

"Hanrahan and McCutcheon."

"Yes." Conrad lowered his voice, but the bitterness came through. "Shot dead and dumped in a hole without so much as a pine box." He shook his head gravely. "An atrocity, sir. I ache to know who is responsible."

Dane nodded. "I saw the bodies when they came in. Jipsell didn't seem to give a care about it."

"Indeed? I am not surprised. Those who wish can express their outrage at a public meeting, at eleven this morning, at the town hall." He pointed across the road to a low building that looked like a warehouse to Dane. "It's not much, but it's what we have till we can build a real city hall."

"I'll be there."

"What did you think of the service?"

"The preacher seemed to be looking right at me when he gave that warning about ungodliness."

Conrad chuckled. "He does that to any new man, especially cowboys. He feels they need extra reminding about ungodliness."

"He might be right."

"Why, Miss Suzanne!" Conrad took off his hat, and Dane turned to see that Suzanne was walking by. "Perhaps you know Mr. Dane?"

She paused. Her cheeks reddened. She nodded

pertly. "We have met. Good morning, Mr. Dane. Did you . . . enjoy the service?"

"Most instructive, ma'am. Not sure the preacher was aiming for enjoyment. But that came—with the singing."

"Yes. We have some lovely voices in the choir. . . ."

Looking back and forth between them, Conrad seemed to sense an unspoken history. He cleared his throat and said, "Ah, I must hurry back to the print shop. . . . I'm working up obituaries on the two good men we lost."

He rushed off, and Suzanne, left alone with Dane, turned away.

"Suzanne—Miss Marrin—may I walk you to . . . to the livery? That is—if you're going there . . . or . . ."

She stopped, her back still to him, and replied, "I thank you, but that won't be necessary."

He took a step closer and spoke softly. "Suzanne—it wasn't what it looked like. It never was. She threw herself—"

She turned angrily to him, and her voice, though low, was sharp. "Mr. Dane! I am not concerned to hear of a mischance in your . . . affairs. Whatever its causes. Good day, sir."

She walked quickly away. The wind sighed, and so did Dane.

She was tempestuous. Maybe it was why she was unmarried. Or maybe she was choosy. Or perhaps she'd decided she didn't require a man.

Don't lie to yourself, Dane, he thought. *You were on the road to her heart, and you let yourself be thrown.*

"She give you the wind?" Ben asked, walking up, hands in the pocket of his coat. "I coulda told ya—"

Dane whirled on him, and Ben broke off and took a step back, seeing the look on Dane's face. "I didn't mean nothing."

"Where's Dirk?" Dane growled.

"That's what I come to tell you. He's went looking for Rusty to get his gun back. We was playing dice with one of those Meagan boys from Hollander's ranch, out behind the saloon the last half hour, and Sterly Meagan accused Dirk of using loaded dice, and Dirk popped him one on the nose! Oh, but now"—he shrugged, as a man does at inevitability—"Meagan is gone to get his gun and told Dirk to get his own."

Dane shook his head in disgust. "And the day after we saw two good men shot full of holes in that buckboard, you two start stupidly grabbing your guns!"

"Me? I didn't—"

"Let's go!"

Dane stalked off toward Rusty's. They got there in time to see Dirk strapping on his gun belt as he came out of the saloon. Dane opened his mouth to shout at Dirk, but someone interrupted him.

"Quinlan!"

It was a skinny young man in chaps and a range coat, his face half covered by a forgotten black beard, long greasy black hair falling to his shoulders—and he had a pistol in his hand. He was walking across the street toward Rusty's, raising the gun level with Dirk's chest.

But it was Dane who fired his gun.

Sterly Meagan howled as his gun flew from his hand. He clutched the injured hand against himself and gave Dane an openmouthed stare. "Who the devil's hind end is you?"

"My name's Dane. I work with the Quinlan boys." He turned to Dirk, who was just now closing the buckle on his gun belt. "Dirk, keep your hand away from that gun, or I'll do the same to you."

"By God, mister," said Sterly, grimacing with pain. He was turned sideways to Dane. "I think that lucky shot of yours busted a bone in my hand!"

"Wasn't a lucky shot," Dane said. "I aimed for your gun hand. Let me show you another."

Dane fired again—and Sterly Meagan's gun belt broke apart at the buckle and dropped to his feet. Sterly stared down at it in amazement.

The Quinlans broke into hooting laughter. "He'll shoot the heels off your boots next, Sterly!" Ben called.

Someone else was chortling from the direction of the livery. Dane knew Gunderson's creaking laugh.

"I could've killed you, Meagan, and no jury'd convict me," Dane said. "You had your gun pointed at Dirk before he had his belt buckled on. Next time I see you make a cowardly pull like that, I'll kill you." Dane was in no mood to mince words. He holstered his Colt. "Now, pick up your belt, put your gun in its holster, and walk away."

"Mister—"

"If you threaten me, I'll come over and break your jaw."

Sterly Meagan's mouth opened—and then he closed it, snatched up his gun and belt, and strode toward the livery.

Dane walked over to Dirk. "You do not get in a fight over a damned dice throw! That's not what men do."

"You're saying I'm not a man?" Dirk said, eyes flashing with anger.

"Not quite yet, boy. You got the size but not the judgment. Got to learn more self-command if you want to live to be a grown man."

Self-command? Dane shook his head at his own two-facedness. He hadn't shown as much self-command today as he should have. True enough, if he hadn't drawn and fired—something he'd done without having to think about it—there was a good chance Dirk would be dead and Sterly Meagan would end up with a noose around his neck. And yet, hurt by Suzanne like a wolf with a paw caught in a trap, he had pushed it too far with the Meagan kid. Two shots was one too many.

Rusty was at the door of the saloon, looking at Dane in wonder. "You always seem to find it, don't you?"

Dane gave him a sour smile. "It's finding *me*."

People were coming out of doors down the street, looking his way, Dane saw. They'd heard the gunfire.

"Rusty, would you tell Conrad for me I can't come to that meeting. I meant to. But seems like every time I come to town, I give Jipsell another reason to run me out. I'd better ride for the ranch."

"I'll tell him."

Dane retrieved Ben's gun from the saloon, handed it over without a word, and marched the Quinlan boys to Gunderson's livery.

"Sheriff's off collecting a fine—least that's what he calls it," Gunderson remarked, lighting his pipe as they saddled their horses. "But I expect he'll be back soon. I don't think you did anything folks would object to. But best not to get tangled with Jipsell if you don't have to."

Dane nodded. "See you next time, Roy—I'll come by and whup you at horseshoes."

"Might whup me if I'm cross-eyed drunk, mebbe."

The three cowboys walked their horses over to the hotel, collected their things, then rode at a canter out of town.

The Quinlans, chastened, were unnaturally silent as they rode with Dane out toward the ranch. A couple of miles on, with the wind easing, the clouds breaking, the day warming up a little, Dirk said tentatively, "That was some unnatural-good shooting, Dane."

Dane said nothing. The silence returned. His thoughts were of Suzanne. Best he learn to put her out of his mind. The sooner she found some beau and got married, the better. When that happened, he'd learn to forget her. Foolish to dwell on her anyway. They'd never even kissed. They had come to no understanding.

So why did her rejection hurt so?

I'm like a stripling boy, agog with his first love, he thought.

He had no way to know how many women he'd sparked prior to losing his memory. It occurred to him, for the first time, that it was even possible he was a married man.

It was a shocking thought. He had never really entertained the notion. He couldn't know for sure, but he'd always simply had the feeling that he had been unmarried.

But—was he? Was some woman pining for him somewhere? Did he have children wondering when their pa was coming home?

A sobering thought. He was grateful to see riders coming down the road toward them who might distract him from it.

After a few minutes he recognized the gambler

who'd styled himself Edmund Earl, and with him was a man riding beside him, whose name Dane didn't know but whose face he recognized.

The second rider was unkempt, shaggy, and pop-eyed, and he spit tobacco at the road. They were a curious pair, Edmund Earl spanking clean and neat, and the other like some street urchin grown up to carry a gun and ride a horse.

Dane reined Pard in as the two men drew up to them. The two riders reined in, and the gambler nodded to Dane, smiling pleasantly. "Back to the laborious life of a horse wrangler, Mr. Dane?"

"That's right." Dane was looking at the other man, who was staring back at him—and had let his hand creep to the butt of his gun.

"You got a plan to pull that gun here, mister?" Dane asked, his voice calm.

The scruffy stranger blinked his pop eyes. "Me? No! But three fellers I don't know from Adam come along, why, I like to keep it under my hand."

"I know you from somewhere, don't I?" Dane asked.

"Do you? Probably mixed me up with some other . . ."

Some other grimy, pop-eyed liar, Dane thought. He knew the man's face, but he couldn't remember from where.

"What brought you two out here?" Dane asked. "There's not a gambling house within miles."

The gambler smiled. His dead eyes didn't. "I have a good deal of money saved up, and I like the area. Was thinking of building a little summer place in the country for myself. Ferry here offered to show me around."

"You know the territory—Ferry?" Ben asked. "Funny I never saw you round before today."

"I know it," Ferry said. He spit more of his quid out, making a little brown puddle on the road. "Probably from way before you got here."

Ferry. The name nagged at Dane. *Ferry . . .*

He almost had it. Where he'd known this Ferry. It was so tantalizingly close. . . .

Ferry Johnson. That was his name. But that was all Dane could remember.

"Now, if you gentlemen will excuse us, we'll be riding on," said the gambler. "I've got a hankering to embrace the comforts of civilization once more. Cold as a banker's heart out here."

Dane nodded and stepped his horse out of the way. But he didn't move on. When they'd ridden between him and the Quinlans, he brought Pard around and watched the men ride off. Maybe it was just the caution that Keggum had planted in him.

"Dane, whoever shot you is still out there. Always watch your back."

A S THEY RODE out of sight of Dane and the two cowboys, Trent Grady wondered at the curious feeling of premonition that seemed to come to him when he encountered Dane up close. Being a gambler—for so he truly was when he was not an assassin—Grady was prone to giving credence to premonition. Something was coming to a head in his life. What was it? He had saved a good deal of money—and Shine O'Hara was paying him more than he'd ever been paid before. The extra money was proportional to the danger.

Every job was a risk for Grady. He was never more than a step or two from the hangman's noose. Perhaps what he had felt looking at Dane was that this was to be his last hired killing. And why not? Why not buy that dance hall he'd had his eye on in New Orleans? Why not make his money there, selling women and liquor and opium as others in New Orleans did? Why run the risk?

Yes. Dane would be the last one.

Grady smiled.

Ferry asked, "Trent—you think he knows somethin'? Acted kinder suspiciony-like back there."

"I think he's a careful man. Like me. A man with sharp eyes, and that's like me, too. Be a shame to kill him. But the money is good, so he's going to shuffle off this mortal coil right quick."

"This mortal what?"

Grady sighed. He had indeed brought Ferry along as a guide to the countryside around the Horseshoe W Ranch. Ferry had earlier gone with Squint Brewster and Hans Husman to locate likely prospects for an ambush. But Grady was more interested in setting up a nice, neat sniping position. His father had been a Confederate sniper in the war, and he'd taught Grady the trade. Eventually, after receiving a beating from his father, Trent Grady had used his new skill on his old man.

Grady and Ferry had found several promising sites, prospects overlooking the canyons and valleys, in the hills west of the Horseshoe W. It was a region frequented by the ranch hands on their horse gathers.

Their tracks, and the presence of a crude fence blocking off the opening of the canyon, told the story.

But it might be a long time, bivouacked outside in cold weather, for Dane to come under Grady's sights. A tentative plan to bring Dane to him when he wanted him there was forming in his mind.

CHAPTER EIGHT

S O IT WAS that Andy McCutcheon went to Joe Hanrahan with evidence—that of his own ears! Evidence,
my friends, of undue influence upon the town council.
Now, both men first went missing—and have turned up
dead!" Arthur Conrad paused in his speech, seeing
"Jipps" Jipsell walk into the town hall.

Conrad knew from the look on Jipsell's face that the
sheriff was not going to be of much use—not to the
people of Smoky River. That defiant scowl told its own
story.

Fifty-five men and fourteen women were in atten-
dance. Mayor Costigan, still in his Sunday suit, sat in
the front row, listening intently. But his expression was
a picture of skepticism. He was a clean-shaven man
with a ready smile—now in abeyance—a long nose,
and a top hat resting on one knee.

Most of the merchants in town were there, some of

them women, like Carolyn Benson the dressmaker.
Melody Ortega, the schoolmarm, was in the front row.
Some of the ranchers were there, too, including Jess
Willoughby—and the neighboring farmers, Des Conner and Lucian Delroy, were leaning against the wall
to Conrad's left. Doc Greeley was there, toward the
back, scowling as usual. Some wives were there; the
Ladies Aid group had a concern for the town beyond
mere relief of the poor. Reverend Wickham was there
as well, and the undertaker Harney. Perhaps Harney
wanted to know if he was to have further business.
Clemson was not there, Conrad noted. But likely he'd
sent Jipsell in his place. Of the seven town councilmen,
three were missing—the three McCutcheon had accused. Doubtless they did not wish to hear themselves
denounced.

Conrad had the lectern; two lanterns hung from the
ceiling to either side of him; the windows were small
and it was a gloomy day outside. "And so, friends," he
went on, "a pattern emerges. This O'Hara combine
seeks to buy up key elements of the town. This Shine
O'Hara has used his influence to push aside ordinances
that would limit questionable establishments. And I've
heard rumors that he has stopped at nothing in his
crooked dealings—when he was in a property dispute
with a man named D'Enfer, there was a disgraceful
hanging, which—"

"Hold on, hold on!" Sheriff Jipsell roared, ap-
proaching the lectern. He stopped in front of it and
pointed at Conrad. "This shouldn't have gone ahead
without me here! I was off on business—enforcing the
law—and everyone knew it!" He turned and glared at
Conrad. "I walk in and hear you making wild claims!

Well, I have news, Conrad! Hanrahan and McCutcheon were killed by bandits!"

At this, there was a buzz of derision and astonishment from the gathering.

"Now, listen!" Jipsell stepped up onto the small riser that held the lectern and turned to speak to the crowd. "Both men left notes that they were leaving town—they must have left in company because they were found that way—"

"Those notes were obviously fallacious!" snapped Conrad, slamming a fist on the lectern.

"Them notes are horse pucky, and that's something I know about!" agreed Gunderson from the back of the room to general laughter. "Didn't sound like neither one of 'em!"

"Listen to me—we now *know* who killed them! A bandit was chased down and shot dead, not two miles from town!"

"What's this?" Conrad demanded. "What bandit?"

"His name was Jack Fessiman."

"I know Fessiman," said Conrad. "I defended him once. A petty thief, a shoplifter, but no murderous bandit! Why, if he had a gun, he'd have pawned it!"

"So you're still defending him!" said Jipsell, and some laughed at that. "He was found at that cabin of his, out on Piney Pond! He confessed to the murders—and then he tried for a gun! My deputies were forced to shoot him!"

"Deputies! You've no deputies, Sheriff. Bat walked out and for good reason!"

"I don't give you an account of all my doings, Conrad. You're just a small-time lawyer for small-time thieves. *There* are my deputies!"

He pointed at the door . . . where now stood Squint Brewster and Hans Husman, looking smug, for each one was wearing a deputy's badge on his coat.

Jipsell went on. "I could not get a man to deputize here in town—everyone scurried away when I asked. So I found two men who've been deputies elsewhere, and I've hired them. As for McCutcheon's accusations about the council, why would you believe the ravings of a man who suddenly left town to seek his fortune elsewhere? I aim to prove he left because he was about to be accused of embezzling—stealing money from his partner!"

Conrad had noted that Bill Sharton was there—a spindly, balding, snub-nosed man of forty, unmarried and seemingly uninterested, for he was terribly shy. But he loved the dry-goods business. Sharton hadn't spoken a word since coming to the town hall meeting though it involved the fate of his business partner.

Conrad looked over at Sharton. He sat in one of the rickety wooden chairs, holding his hat in his hand, staring at the floor.

"Bill?" Jipsell called.

Shaking—he was thirty feet away, but Conrad could see it from here—Bill Sharton stood up, cleared his throat, and said, "It's . . . it's true. He . . . I . . ." Sharton licked his lips. He looked at Jipsell, who nodded encouragingly. "He and I had . . . had *words* and . . . well . . . I suspected him of stealing from the till. And I so accused him. And . . . and then . . . he left town."

Shivering still, he sat down, looking as if he might burst into tears.

Someone's gotten to him, Conrad thought. *They threatened him. He's an easily frightened man.*

Conrad opened his mouth to say so—but saw then that the crowd was standing up, most everyone heading toward the door. Everyone was leaving, shaking their heads, convinced by Sharton's frightened testimony.

I T WAS MONDAY morning but so early, it was still dark. The rooster had not yet crowed as Suzanne was awakened by a lantern glaring from the door of her little bedchamber.

"Suzie," her mother said, "I believe that Matthew is dying."

Suzanne sat up and rubbed her eyes. "More likely he's stiff from liquor, Mama. I told him there was to be no more brewing of corn liquor, but I suppose he's got it hid somewhere."

"I've never seen him this poorly before. He came to my door and said something I couldn't hear, and there he collapsed. It could be he was stricken by apoplexy. You'll have to ride for the doctor."

By the time Suzanne had dressed, drunk half a cup of tea, and eaten a biscuit—"So that you should not grow faint on the ride, for it is brisk cold out"—it was dawn. The rooster crowed, and a gray light suffused the barnyard as she rode out.

She set off briskly, spurring the horse to a gallop when she reached the better road, and she was soon pounding on Doc Greeley's door. He answered the door wearing nothing but scarlet long johns. He was a florid-faced, thick-lipped man with heavy brows and black eyes, his long graying hair clubbed behind his head, his nightcap aslant on his hand. "Well, what is it!"

"Mother thinks old Matthew is dying!"

"Oh, for . . . !" Greeley swore for a bit, using some expressions that made Suzanne blush as he went to dress in his usual rumpled suit. He drank a cup of yesterday's cold coffee and then pushed past her to stomp down the outdoor stairs of the house where he boarded, and went to roust out his buggy.

By the time they got back to the farm, the sun was spearing roseate and yellow beams through the trees, the cow was lowing to be let out to pasture, and Suzanne's mother had brewed coffee. She offered Greeley a cup as he came stalking in. He gruffly said, "Not now, not now," and went down on one knee to examine Matthew. Mrs. Marrin had put a pillow under Matthew's head and a blanket over him, which Greeley summarily tossed aside. Though he yet breathed, the old farmhand's body was half twisted, as one would twist a wet rag, legs one way, arms the other, and his mouth was set into a horrid rictus.

"Oh, Lord," Suzanne muttered. It had gotten worse since she'd left for town. She searched her mind for an appropriate Bible verse to implore God for mercy on old Matthew, but she was much shaken herself, and nothing would come to her. She managed, "Lord, spare the poor man this!"

Greeley picked up the lantern on the floor beside Matthew and used it to peer into his eyes and mouth. He shook his head, then took the old man's pulse.

"Thready pulse . . . fluttering . . . stertorous breathing, acute catalepsy. The man has been poisoned!"

"Poisoned!" Mother exclaimed.

"He has poisoned himself! I can smell it on him aplenty." He waved a hand in front of Matthew's eyes.

"He does not see. He is blind, which oft occurs when one tries to distill liquor while already drunk—they make some idiot mistake, and you see the result."

Matthew made a sudden mewling sound and arched his back so that they could hear the cricking of his bones. Then he fell back. Limp though still twisted out of shape. His raspy breathing stopped.

The doctor checked Matthew's pulse once more, then reached out and closed his eyes. "You will need a new hired hand. I advise burying him deep, somewhere off in a corner of your property. Perhaps the old fool will do better in the world to come." He stood up and dusted his hands. "That will be two dollars, if you please. And I'll have that coffee now."

D ANE WAS RIDING side by side with Jess Willoughby's surrey, heading toward town, that same Monday. Dane wore an oiled-leather slicker against the fitful rain. They were on their way to town to pick up an Arabian stud when they came within sight of Marrin Farm. A short side road led to the gates, and Willoughby halted the surrey there. Dane reined Pard in, and both men gazed at the farm.

Both of us, Dane thought, *with thoughts probably much alike. Thinking of Suzanne.*

Then Dane spotted a woman toiling at the far edge of the property. She was at least a hundred yards off, but after a moment he was sure it was Suzanne. She was out there in the thin rain, in riding trousers and high leather boots and a rain slicker, digging with a spade. Her mother was walking out to her.

"You see her over there?" Dane asked, pointing. "Way over at the property fence, south."

"No, I . . . yes!" Willoughby exclaimed. "By God it looks like she's digging a grave!"

The two men looked at each other with the same expression of alarm. "We will not stand on ceremony," Willoughby said. "Open the gate, and I'll tie up by the barn."

Dane dismounted and opened the gate, and the surrey rattled through. He remounted and rode out across the farm toward the women. Suzanne was now up to her knees in the muddy grave, digging splashily. There was a crude wooden cross lashed together lying on the ground nearby.

Dane tied the mustang at the edge of the orchard and walked across the field to the grave. Mrs. Marrin stared in surprise. Suzanne looked up from the muddy grave. There was mud on her face and hands and caking her boots.

"Did the old gent pass away?" Dane asked.

"He did," Mrs. Marrin said bitterly. "But he was no gentleman. He drank himself into his grave."

Dane nodded somberly. "I expect they have grave-diggers at the cemetery."

"Both the grave plot and the digging over there cost money we don't have," Suzanne said, shoveling up another spadeful of wet earth.

"I see," Dane said. "Ma'am, I hope you'll forgive my presumption in asking, but I'd be obliged if you'd let me finish that for you. It's like to collapse, the way it's going, and I'd hate to see you in it when it does."

Suzanne frowned, and as the rain was increasing,

she adjusted her bonnet to cover her face better. "I . . . we . . . have no need. I have dug ditches and postholes. I can manage this."

Mrs. Marrin surprised Dane by saying, "Child, I think—we should let him do it. You're like to catch your death of cold out here."

Suzanne looked at her mother, a little startled. Dane could see Suzanne was miserable, wet, muddy, tired, and sad. It was all there to see.

"Please, ma'am," Dane said gently. He no longer felt he was permitted to call her Suzanne. He took off his hat. "It would be my privilege."

"Why, here comes Jess Willoughby!" Mrs. Marrin exclaimed.

Willoughby plodded across the wet field, holding his hat down against the rain and wind. "What is this absurdity, ladies? If someone has died, let's have them interred properly. I shall pay the bill."

"He asked me to be buried here," Suzanne said. "He said, if he died, this farm was the closest he'd had to a home for many years. Matthew served us for a long time, as best he could." She looked somberly at her mother. "He has died today, Mama. I think it's the least we can do."

"He did mumble some such thing," Mrs. Marrin conceded. "Oh, I suppose he must be buried here. It's all too much for me. His body is in the barn—Suzanne and the doctor laid him out in his coffin. He built the thing himself and kept it in a stall for an ox we had once."

Dane wasn't surprised. He'd known many a handy old-timer to build his own coffin for fear of ending up wrapped in an old sheet in a wet hole.

"Perhaps Mr. Willoughby and Mr. Dane could take turns," Mrs. Marrin went on, "and finish up for you, Suzanne. I shall prepare a pan of warm water for your feet, and we'll have some tea." She turned and trudged back toward the house.

Dane looked at Willoughby—and saw that the rancher seemed appalled by Mrs. Marrin's suggestion that he step into the muddy grave. He was looking down at his fine clothes—for he was going to a meeting with Davey Chase, a successful horse breeder, to buy the stud—and he would not have his suit soiled. "Ah—well—you see—it's an awkward time—"

"I'll take care of it, ma'am," Dane said. "I work for Mr. Willoughby—it's only fitting I should do it." He turned to his employer. "Boss, Roy Gunderson can arrange for someone to bring the Arabian back. If you were to tie it to the back of that surrey, why, not being familiar with you yet, he could bust loose or try—might do himself a mischief."

"Very true. So be it. You attend to the task here, Dane. I'll purchase the Arabian and, ah, take as much time as you need today for this."

He tipped his hat to Suzanne and hurried back toward his surrey.

Dane put on his hat and reached for the spade, and Suzanne, after a moment's hesitation, handed it over. He stuck it in the soft earth, hung his hat on its handle, then put out a hand. "If you'd just let me help you up, ma'am."

She looked at him, her face tilted up, blinking a little from the rain. Then she reached out, and he took her hand and carefully helped her out. She teetered on the edge of the unfinished grave for a moment, and he had to catch her in the small of her back, his other hand still holding hers. They were standing close together, and for a moment, something passed between them, a sort of soft spark, unarticulated but felt.

Then Dane stepped back, helped her another step, and reluctantly let go of her hand. He took up the shovel, stepped into the grave—immediately sinking three inches into the wet ground—and started to work.

Dane heard Suzanne walk away, and he was glad she would soon be back in the house, able to clean herself up and get warm.

A BOUT FOUR FEET down into the grave—a coffin would surely require six feet—Dane saw, as he'd expected, that the sides of the grave were crumbling inward. Using the spade for leverage, he climbed out clumsily, barely managing to keep from making the hole collapse on itself, and went to a broken-down fence nearby. There were a number of large rocks near it that someone had used to shore up the corner post. Privately vowing to fix the fence if Suzanne let him, he took four splintery fallen posts, carried them over to the grave, and wedged them in place in the weak spots of the grave walls, pounding them into the soft wet soil with the shovel blade. Then he brought the rocks over and piled them beside the grave. The rain had abated, but there were a couple of inches of water in the bottom of the grave.

Dane resumed work, digging two more feet down, shoveling out mud and dirt into a pile to one side. Then he reached out, took up the fist-sized rocks, and placed them along the bottom of the grave to keep the water from damaging the coffin any sooner than necessary. With even more care than before, he climbed out, having to brace himself on the posts to get leverage, and finally crawled out onto the ground. *Should have gone to see if they have a ladder of some kind,* he thought.

Dane trudged to his horse. "Sorry to leave you out in the rain, Pard." He mounted the horse and rode him into the barn. There he found the open coffin, tucked in its oxen stall, with the old man in it. They'd straightened his limbs somewhat, but he was still contorted. "Did the best I could with your grave, Matthew," Dane said. "Difficult work in this weather." He closed the top of the coffin, found a hammer and some nails in a wooden toolbox, and nailed the lid down. The old man had thoughtfully attached a rope handle to the top end of the coffin. Dane dragged it out to the center of the barn and used his lariat to tie one end of the rope to Pard's saddle horn, the other end to the coffin. He led Pard out of the barn to the grave, dragging the coffin behind. There he unmoored the coffin from the saddle horn and with a series of draggings and pushings, and tuggings with the rope, got it into the grave. " 'Scuse me, Matthew," he murmured, and lowered himself, carefully, feetfirst onto the coffin. He untied the rope, tossed it out of the grave, and climbed out. It was easier climbing from the top of the coffin.

Dane got to his feet—and was surprised to see Suzanne standing by Pard, holding his reins and patting him. He nuzzled her shoulder. He saw she had a Bible in one hand. She wore a clean dress now and button-up shoes, and she'd washed her face and hands. She hadn't troubled to put on a bonnet, the rain having abated, and her hair blew about her face like red flames.

"Didn't see you walk up, ma'am." Dane took off his hat. "Did you want to say a few words over Matthew?"

"Yes. I tried to get Mama to come, but she'd have none of it." She opened the Bible and read a passage from First Thessalonians, beginning, "'For since we believe that Jesus died and rose again, even so, through Jesus, God will bring with Him those who have fallen asleep. . . .'"

When Suzanne finished, she closed the Bible and looked at the sky. "You'd best fill it in. It's bound to start raining again."

Dane replaced his hat, went to the mound of earth, and set to work. Having filled the grave in and patted it down, he set the crude cross up at its head and said, "Good luck yonder, Matthew."

"Dane . . ." Suzanne said.

"Yes, ma'am?"

"Let us walk back to the house. Mother has softened toward you, it appears. She spied on you from the door and was much struck by your industriousness."

Dane replaced his hat, and they started out silently, Dane leading Pard. When they got to the little orchard, she said, "You tried to tell me about Minnie. I was not inclined to listen then. But I've heard stories about her. Perhaps I . . . Oh, tell me what happened, won't you?"

He told her. She nodded. "Perhaps I was too quick to judge. I don't know why it mattered so much to me. It's not as if we . . ."

"No, it's not as if . . ."

They fell silent, and when they reached the house, she said, "Come around back. There's a lean-to we use as a laundry. I've poured some warm water in a tub there. Clean up the best you can and wipe your boots.

You are then required—I am commanded to tell you this—to come in for coffee and biscuits."

W HEN SUZANNE WAS a schoolteacher, she would bring my biscuits and a little bacon to school for the children who had no breakfast," Mrs. Marrin said. She sipped her tea from a delicate blue-flowered china cup. They were sitting on wooden chairs in the small sitting room, near a Franklin stove. "Quite a few families then were just scraping by."

"She was a schoolmarm?" Dane asked. Suzanne, pouring herself some more tea, smiled at his surprise.

"Oh, yes, for three years, until her papa died, and then she had to stay here and help with the upkeep. When my husband was alive, we had sufficient funds—for he had inherited a fair sum—and we sent her to finishing school and the ladies' college in Kansas City. But after he passed, we ran through the money—had to have the barn rebuilt after a twister took it down, new fences built. Our crops were destroyed, and our horse was killed in the storm, and we needed to buy another. . . ."

Dane deduced Mrs. Marrin was being congenial now because her hired hand had died and the farm needed a workman's hand. Dane's hand. She knew that he was sweet on Suzanne and would work for nothing. This plan of hers, he realized, was going to work. He was sipping coffee and looking at the rainwater trickling from the ceiling into a basin on the floor. Mentally he was planning on making some shingles, if he could get the proper wood for it, and repairing the roof. *Do it today if possible. Sunday afternoon otherwise.*

Love makes a man a damned fool, he told himself.

Then he decided he should repair the barn's roof, too . . . after he fixed that fence. . . .

I T WAS A cold Friday morning—but Squint Brewster had felt colder—out on the gently rolling plain that eventually eased into the Willow Grove Hills.

"What makes you think this here's the right time, Ferry?" asked Squint. Hans, Ferry Johnson, and Squint rode to the miles-long fence closing the Circle X's herd off from the open plain.

"Because I saw a fella I know from Cimarron. Hoyt Gassaway. And I found out Hoyt's going to be all alone out here on watch this afternoon. And I know somethin' else, too—that ol' boy's got a taste for laudanum. Went to cowboying to get away from it. Mortal afraid of going near a druggist shop."

"He drinks that opium liquor?"

"He does. So I knew I could tempt him if I carried some out to him, which I did, mebbe two hours ago. And he started in a-swilling' it before I could tell him it was a friendly gift. . . . Well, half an hour later, he was lying on the ground, snoring, and there is nothing going to wake him. And his horse wandered off. . . . And here we are, boys. Now, let's cut out some cattle."

"You sure these cattle are unbranded?" Hans asked.

"This is the last of 'em unbranded. Kept here till they're ready to do it, which is tomorrow. We got here jes' in time! You see there—" He pointed to the east. "You can see the hophead fool lying there under that little cottonwood, snorin' away."

"He got any money on him?" Squint asked, not at

all restrained by the deputy's badge Jipps had pinned to his coat.

"Wouldn't bother. Never saved so much as a Confederate dollar. There's the gate. Let's get it open, and then we got to cut out ten fat ones. . . ."

"I don't care for this cowboy business," said Hans, shaking his head as he got down off his horse to open the gate. "A man could fall and get trampled or gored. For me, I only want to see beef on the platter."

Ferry, who knew a little about cowboying, chose the best beeves, and after an hour of chasing about, having to start over several times, they got twelve longhorns driven out through the gate. Hans dismounted, hastily closed the gate, and, grumbling, remounted and joined the others in harrying the small herd toward Willow Canyon.

"How we going to get those Quinlans interested in 'em?" Ferry asked. "Trent never said nothin' about it."

"I believe Trent Grady has a notion about that. . . ."

I S THIS NOT your day to howl, as you cowboys call it?" Suzanne asked as Dane led Pard into the barn, early Saturday afternoon.

"Ma'am," said Dane, taking Pard's saddle off, "I do not howl. Never took it up. A man could get a sore throat."

She patted the horse and said, "If you like, Dane, you can call me Suzanne once more. I've been reluctant to confer the honor because my mama has you in mind for a volunteer handyman and nothing more, and I don't wish to hear her warnings."

"About cowboys?" He put the saddle against the

wall and tied Pard up close to a bucket of water and a pile of alfalfa.

"Yes. Cowboys. We were almost prosperous, and she has dreams of returning to our former glory. Mama says all cowboys are either broke or soon to be broke. There seems no middle ground."

Dane laughed. "She's not far wrong."

"And especially if they go about doing free carpentry. It's usual to be paid."

"I have been paid in biscuits, jam, coffee with fresh cream, and even a dried-apple pie." *And occasionally spending time alongside Suzanne Marrin,* he thought. "Can't say better than that."

He picked up the box of tools, and they walked out to the gate by the roadside. "How's the roof holding up?"

"It's quite snug now. We thank you for that, Dane."

"I'm relieved to hear it. I'm not an artist in the roof-work line. I'm more of a builder of sheds and fences. I admired how Matthew built his coffin. He sealed up the joins with pitch, and every nail was flush."

"Do you know, he used to tell us he couldn't do much of the carpentry we needed, that he hadn't the skills. Not till I saw his coffin did I know he was deceiving us!"

Dane chuckled and bent to examine the wide front gate. "Sags, does it?"

"Terribly."

"It's the leather hinges. They don't last long. Iron would do better."

"Iron is too costly."

"I'll see what I can do with what we have." The clouds broke, and sunlight shone through, warming his face. He looked up at the cloud rack, about the peeping sun, and admired the glow about the opening. He glanced at Suzanne. "How is it that when . . . when you and I are—" He broke off, realizing he was saying aloud what he had supposed himself only thinking.

"Yes?" She looked at him, her eyes searching his face.

"It's just . . . quite a fluke of chance—how the sun comes out when you . . . when you're . . ."

"This sudden elegiac sentimentality seems unlike you, Mr. Dane," she said softly, smiling gently at him.

"It's me, prattling like a schoolboy." Feeling a fool, he busied himself digging noisily about in the toolbox. "I'm sure I saw an old wood drill here. . . ."

Suzanne watched him for a long moment and then went back to the house. Angry with himself, Dane set furiously to work. Two hours passed. . . .

Suzanne brought Dane a basket with dried applies, a ham sandwich, and a cup of fresh water. She looked at his handiwork, her eyebrows raised. "Don't tell me you've made hinges out of wood!"

"I did. There were some good solid oak boards. I cut 'em up, drilled through the ends there for the pivot, found a couple of old bolts. Should last longer than the leather."

"You missed your calling, Dane."

"Maybe so."

But what was his calling? He was afraid of what it might be. That day in the street, with Sterly Meagan, Dane had felt he was a hairbreadth from shooting Sterly dead. More and more lately, he felt like something was emerging in him, something better left in the dark.

* * *

Y OU COULD KILL him right now and be done with
it," said Ferry Johnson as he and Trent rode by
the Marrin Farm. They were only about fifty yards
from Dane, who had his back to them as he swung a
gatepost shut. He seemed to be testing it. They knew
him by his frame and his hat and the wool-lined jacket.

A tempting target indeed, thought Trent Grady. "But
you see, there's a woman going into the henhouse and
another hanging laundry. They would hear the shot and
see us. I'd have to kill those women, too."

"What of that?"

"That would require getting in close. Those women
surely have a shotgun. It could get messy." He added
dryly, "Of course, I could send *you* in to do it."

Ferry shook his head. "Not me. I know fer a fact
that Dane is a hard man to kill. And there's no women
living alone out here lacking in guns."

"Furthermore," said Grady, turning his horse away
from the farm, "killing three people generates three
times as much talk, three times as big a posse, three times
as much willingness to find the killer. If Jipps tried to shut
it down, the town would go to a federal marshal. And
killing two women? It'll get into the papers in the most
feverish manner. Questions will be asked by the governor. All of that."

"I reckon," Ferry said as they cantered their horses
toward town. "Leastways, the weather broke."

"Yes, it's a welcome change. I'd like to get this job
done and head south before winter sets in."

They made good time to town and put up their
horses at the livery. Gunderson looked daggers at

them. He had seen Ferry with the two new deputies, whom Gunderson was known to despise, but he took their money quick enough.

Outside the stable the two men instinctively paused, checking the street for trouble. It was a peaceful Saturday afternoon in Smoky River. Wagons and horses plied the street, a drummer's boy was banging a tom-tom and ladies were walking with parasols in the unseasonal October sun. "I'll just go into that saloon and get me some ham and bread and a beer," Ferry said, rubbing his bristly jaw. "You coming?"

"No, I shall sate my appetite elsewhere. I'll find you if I need you."

They parted, Grady heading off to Sing's eatery. He wondered if there was any way to send Ferry Johnson back to Steeple Rock. Shine had put him in charge of the three men, but he found Ferry particularly vile company. The odor of Ferry Johnson took a long time to leave a man's nose. But Grady supposed Ferry might be useful at some point—if only to draw gunfire away from himself.

Grady ate a passable meal at Sing's, then went to Clemson's Silver Goddess. He found a poker game and took a power of money off a series of fools until it was evening and time to search out the Quinlan boys.

But they found him. Ben and Dirk approached the table. They'd both been drinking, and they were rambunctious when they came to his table. "Well, it's that gambler feller," said Dirk. "Earl, was it?"

"That's right," said Grady. "Edmund Earl. Will you boys take a hand?"

"Not me," said Ben. "Looking you over, mister, I feel like I'm beat before I start."

He went to the mahogany bar to sit beside one of the pretty girls urging drinks on the customers, but Dirk sat down beside Grady, rubbing his hands and chuckling to himself. "Some days I just know when I'm gonna be lucky."

"Maybe I should beat a quick retreat," Grady said, signaling to a waiter. "I don't wish to buck your high luck."

"Now, don't run off till I win my money," Dirk said, tossing a handful of bills on the table.

The waiter arrived, and Grady said, "Drinks for the table, whatever these gentlemen prefer. I'll have the French brandy."

The drinks came as the cards were being dealt, and Dirk, as Grady had hoped, drank his off in a trice.

Grady won a hand—careful not to make the pot more than Dirk could manage—and he bought Dirk another drink. Then he let Dirk win for a time. Pleased and drunk, Dirk was soon downright chummy as he raked in the pots. "Mr. Earl, I am taking a shine to you. Buying me good whiskey and indulgin' my lucky streak. You are quite the feller."

"Perhaps I'm off my game," Grady said. "I'm rather fatigued—had another look out at those hills near the Horseshoe W today. Don't think I'll be building a house there, not with cattle running about so free. Why, they might stampede right through my garden."

"Whose cattle?" Dirk asked, counting his money.

"I've no notion for they were unbranded. Oh, at least ten of them. Out toward Willow Canyon it was. Just this morning!"

"Is that right!" Dirk peered at his cards. "Just this morning?"

Despite the cowboy's feigned indifference, Grady could tell Dirk was intrigued. "Yes, indeed . . . My, look at these cards. Well, I believe I'll play them anyway. . . ."

He began to win again—folding hands as needed, betting big on the good ones—and in another hour, Dirk had lost every penny. Ben Quinlan arrived to stand behind him and seemed to notice Dirk had no money on the table. "Dirk, you shouldn't be let nowhere near a card table."

"Never you mind!" Dirk stood up and, swaying, said, "Let's get on out of here. I've lost my all."

They left without another word, and Grady smiled to himself. Dirk Quinlan was doubly eager now to rustle those cattle.

Now, Grady thought, *time to get the other pieces in play. . . .*

CHAPTER NINE

Dane was spending Sunday morning doing personal work in the bunkhouse. He'd sewn up a pair of torn trousers, washed mud off his boots, and cleaned and oiled his Colt, and having discovered dust in the barrel of the Winchester he'd bought in town yesterday, he was just finishing brushing it out when Blue came looking for him.

Dane glanced up as the Indian came in. It was hard to read Blue's emotions, but Dane had an eye for subtleties, and the taut set of the man's lips spoke of worry.

"Dane—I got word that Ben and Dirk were caught rustling at dawn this morning. Circle X cattle, too."

"Again?"

"Yep."

Growling to himself in exasperation, Dane removed the long brush from the barrel of the Winchester and set to loading it. "Where'd you hear this?"

"One of the men who pretends he's a deputy now told Jim French, kinda laughin' about it, and Jim thought he ought to tell us."

"Ben and Dirk at the town jail?"

"Nope."

"Why not?"

"I wondered, too. But when I told Willoughby about it, he says maybe the boys are pulling the same shady deal—got hold of unbranded cattle that broke through a fence, which means a lawyer could argue it's not legally cattle rustling. And the Circle X figures that means they have to lynch them to get justice."

"Lynching is against the law, and if we had a straight sheriff, he'd be handling it. But we got Jipsell. Where are they?"

"Out in Willow Canyon—they were caught with the cows near there, and Hollander decided to take them into the canyon, where there's fewer witnesses."

"Then they've hung 'em by now."

"We got to find out for certain, Dane."

"I know." Dane put the rifle down and buckled on his gun belt, then holstered his Colt. "Who's out there from the Circle X?"

"Hollander and the Meagan brothers and that big yellow-haired son of a gun—the other one playin' deputy. He's the one told the Circle X their cows were being taken."

"What's Jess say to do?"

"Jess says get a couple of men, look into it. Buck's already saddled. Jess wants Rand here to keep an eye on the spread."

"All right. Let's ride."

* * *

DANE AND BLUE were in the saddle, with Buck siding them, heading at a gallop across the easy-rolling prairie for Willow Canyon. On the eastern horizon, the morning sun was banked by cloud cover, turning the clouds into a fiery orange. An occasional light rain swept over them and quickly went on its way.

Dane pictured the canyon, trying to figure the best way to approach it. The canyon must've started as a valley between two hills. Rockfall from the hills had made it into a box canyon. The north side of the canyon was rocky escarpment.

The hills to either side provided little cover. But the grass, gone yellow now, was still there, fairly high.

They rode on, and it seemed to Dane that Pard was enjoying this all-out gallop; he went for it harder than he had to. Dane had to tilt his face down to keep the wind of their passage from blowing his hat off. He hoped the mustang wouldn't step into a prairie dog hole at a full gallop. That'd be the end of them both.

A mile, two miles, three—then they reached the trail into the hills, and they slowed a little to look over a group of cattle peacefully cropping grass.

"Must be the ones," Blue observed. "Looks like the breed they favor."

Dane nodded. "No brands." They rode on, cantering now, Dane leading the way along the dirt track as it wound through the hills. Pard was blowing with the exertion of the long gallop. "You'll have rest and water soon, my friend," Dane told him. They cantered for another two miles, and the trail opened wide into a copse of willows growing near the thin creek that trickled out of the spring in Willow Canyon. The creek was only there when it rained enough, and it didn't have a name that Dane knew of, but he knew just where it led. He reined the horse to a stop and waited till the others drew up beside him. "Seems like we might be smarter to ride up the creek."

"Well, now," Buck said in his slow drawl. He paused and rubbed his chin. "That is surely not the way we usually take. We cross the stream, Dane."

"That's right, Buck. But I don't want to follow the trail in. They might be trigger-happy. And . . ." There was another reason—just a foggy suspicion. Maybe it had to do with Squint Brewster telling Jim French about what was happening up here, knowing Jim would tell the Horseshoe W. "I'm a little wary, is all. I can't tell you fellas where to go, but this is how I'm going. It's actually shorter, I think . . . only you can't ride all the way in."

He spurred Pard to the left, trotting upstream. Blue followed. And Buck said, "Well, hell . . . if you fellas are . . ." He followed Blue. It was shadowy in this gulch between rocky hillsides—colder, too.

The creek here dropped in a short waterfall, about six feet high, about ten yards ahead. Dane rode up onto the narrow clay bank, dismounted, and tied Pard to a woody shrub within reach of the water. He took his Winchester from its saddle holster and carried it to the steep hillside to beside the waterfall. It was tricky climbing with the rifle in one hand, and he slipped back a yard once.

"Look out now!" Buck called out behind him.

"Not so loud, Buck," Dane said in a low voice.

In a few minutes, they reached the top of the hill, hunkered down in the high, sere grass. A small outcropping broke up the grass enough so they could see into the canyon from here. Dane made out two cowboys standing by their horses. The rest were out of Dane's line of sight.

He crept forward and knelt behind the outcropping where he could see the whole box canyon. The men in the canyon were about fifty yards off. There were a few willow trees toward the back of the canyon, near a little pool around a spring. One of them was a tree big enough to hang someone from, and two ropes dangled from its thickest branch. The Quinlan brothers were sitting on their horses, hands behind them, under that tree. Dirk had one of those ropes right around his neck, and Ferry was sitting on his horse a little behind Ben, preparing the other Quinlan's noose.

Ben was jawing, not audibly from here, either cussing or trying to reason with the men holding guns on him. Dane recognized Sterly Meagan, and there was another cowboy, as fat as Sterly was thin, who might have been his brother, standing by their horses. Both of them had their guns drawn, pointed at the Quinlan boys. Dane wondered if Sterly's willingness to play along with this was about getting his own back after the humiliation on Main Street.

"That's Tater Meagan there with Sterly," Blue whispered. "That short fella on the other side, in the high-heel boots and the tall hat—that's Gabe Hollander. And there's that big yellow-haired deputy of Jipsell's. Name is Hans something."

Buck came up beside them and whispered, real slow, "They sure . . . took their . . . time. . . ."

"They did." Dane scanned the hills around the canyon and the rocky escarpment at its back. There—a faint glint of metal. "Someone put 'em up to that. And there's someone up atop those rocks, back of the canyon. He's got a rifle out. Can't see him, but . . ."

A vivid image rose into his mind then. He was walking through a shallow valley with the other soldiers. Blue uniforms. Everyone with their rifles in their hands. A glint of metal up on the ridge—and a muzzle flash. The soldier in front of him staggered and fell, dying, shot through the throat. "Down!" Dane shouted. Another shot came. . . . Someone screamed. . . .

He shivered at the sudden memory.

"A sniper," he whispered.

Dane set his own rifle, like a sniper would, on the V-shaped crack in the outcropping. Sighting in.

"A whut?" asked Buck.

"Expert long-distance rifleman" Dane said. "The Confederates used them. War of attrition. This one was expecting us to come down the trail. You boys draw your guns, and when you hear me fire, fire at that big rock at the top up there. Just plug away at it, to keep him down. He—" Dane broke off, seeing that Ferry was about to lower the noose over Ben's head.

Another flash of memory. Ferry . . . Ferry Johnson, his name was . . . putting a noose around the neck of a scared young man, no more than twenty. The name "D'Enfer" bobbed up into Dane's mind. Ferry was grinning, tightening the noose around the weeping boy's throat.

Something took hold of Dane then. He aimed, he fired, and the rope tightening around Dirk's neck parted. The gunshot startled his horse, and it ran forward. Ben was ducking under the other noose, his own horse rearing at the gunshot. Ferry drew his gun and was about to shoot Ben Quinlan in the back. Buck and Blue were shooting at the rocks that concealed the sniper.

Dane swung the rifle around and fired. Ferry Johnson fell backward off his horse, shot in the left shoulder—which was the spot Dane had aimed for. He didn't want to hang for murder if the law took this interference the wrong way.

Terrified by the gunfire, Ben's horse galloped away from the tree, Ben clamping the horse hard with his legs because his hands were tied behind him.

Dane was cocking and firing the rifle fast as he could, hitting the ground around Hollander and the Meagans and Hans so that they sprinted for the cover of the willow trees. The Quinlans' horses rode out of the canyon the way they'd come in, down the trail.

"We . . . done it!" Buck said as they ducked down behind the outcropping.

"We did," said Dane.

"But there'll be trouble over it," said Blue.

"There will," said Dane. The crack of a bullet and fragments of rock sprayed from the outcropping as the sniper on the escarpment fired at them. "Flatten down and crawl back. He won't be able to see us," said Dane.

Buck was already scrambling on his belly. "Surprising how fast a man can crawl if he has to," Blue observed.

He and Dane followed suit, and soon they had the hill between them and the sniper.

D ANE CAUGHT UP to the Quinlan boys where the trail crossed the creek. Their horses had stopped by the stream to drink, and the cowboys were struggling to loosen their bonds. Dirk still had a noose around his neck, the broken rope trailing after him. They had lost their hats, and their hair was in wild disarray.

"You'll only tighten the knots way," Dane said as Buck and Blue splashed up the creek behind him. Dane rode up between Ben's and Dirk's horses, then used his knife to free their arms.

Dirk pulled the noose off angrily, started to throw it aside, then said, "Nope, I'm going to keep this. Might have a use for it." He put the noose over the saddle horn and coiled the remaining rope. He looked at the others with an uncharacteristic seriousness and spoke in a scared whisper. "Boys—I've got religion. I was saying a prayer, and that rope parted! It was a miracle!"

"The . . . miracle—he's . . . right there," said Buck, pointing at Dane.

"Another shot for the history books," said Blue, nodding. "From on top of a hill with a Winchester."

"Luck," said Dane. "That rope wasn't holding still. Coulda missed it easy."

Ben and Dirk looked at him in awe. Finally, Ben said, "And you were the one who fired those shots that scared the ugly . . ." He let loose a string of cusswords describing the men who'd almost hung him.

"Now, aren't you quick?" said Dane. "But stupid enough to get roped into stealing cows. Who told you about 'em, Ben?"

Dirk looked abashed. "It was me he told. That gambler fella. Edmund some-dang-thing. I was drunk, and—I talked Ben into it."

"I saw the gambler riding with the very man who put a noose over your head. The gambler set this up."

"Maybe he was on the back ridge with the long rifle?" Blue suggested.

Dane nodded. "I'd bet my pay on it."

Dirk was drinking thirstily from his canteen. He wiped his mouth and handed it to his brother. "The varmints wouldn't even give us a drink of water."

"Why'd the gambler fix all this up?" Ben asked.

"He was luring me to an ambush," Dane said. "I have a feeling I've got some history with Shine O'Hara. The gambler, those so-called deputies—they work for him. A few years ago someone shot me three times and left me for dead out by Steeple Rock—likely it was them trying to finish the job."

"You kill any of 'em?"

"I shot Ferry."

"Is he dead?"

"Don't believe so. Wasn't aiming to kill him. Could go sour in court."

"Court?" Ben blinked and licked his lips. "You think Jipsell will arrest us?"

"He might. Not sure he could talk a jury into convicting you."

Dirk looked at his brother. "You want to risk it?"

"Hell, no! That Hans is one of his deputies! He'd look to hang us right in the jail!"

"Riders coming," said Blue, looking up the trail.

Dane couldn't hear them, but he'd learned not to doubt Blue's keen senses. "Ben—I don't think Willoughby is going to welcome you back. He didn't want to see you hung—but you throw too wide a loop. Best you take this knothead brother of yours somewheres beside Smoky River. And without those cows. You try to herd them anywhere, I'll catch you myself and let them hang you."

Dirk blanched. Ben nodded. "Yeah. Come on, Dirk. We'll head to Burrister and think where to go from there."

They nudged their horses into a trot and then spurred them to a gallop. They were only just gone around a curve in the trail when four men rode in from up the trail: Hollander on a high-stepping roan, Hans on a steed along the lines of a draft horse, the Meagans riding cow ponies. They all reined in their horses and glared at the three men blocking the trail.

Dane slipped off his horse and put a hand on his gun.

Hollander had a rifle in one hand, its butt propped on his knee. Hans was just reaching for his gun, after seeing the hands from Horseshoe W. The Meagans, waiting for orders, were just gaping, the slim one and the hefty one with the same stunned expression.

When Hans reached for his gun, Dane's Colt was instantly in his hand. Blue had a Henry rifle at the ready, and Buck had drawn a shotgun from its saddle holster.

Hans saw that Dane already had a bead on him.

"You holster that gun," Dane warned, his voice harsh and loud, "or, deputy or not, I'll shoot a groove through the middle of that big head of yours. Couldn't hardly miss it."

Hans holstered the gun. "You'll be arrested for pulling a gun on me, yah," he said.

"You were pulling on me first. And my guess is there's a whole lot of towns you can't visit without being arrested," Dane told him. "Be interesting to send some telegrams and find out."

Hans's face went rigid at that.

Dane glanced at the men siding him. Buck had his shotgun leveled at Hollander. Blue just waited, his hand on the Henry. He had a disconcerting confidence.

"What the devil are you about here?" Hollander demanded. He had a rough voice but high-pitched. His face was shaped by a lifetime of surliness. "You people shoot one of our posse?"

"Posse!" Blue snorted. "Lynch mob's more like."

"Where's Ferry?" Dane said. "I didn't shoot to kill him."

"Up the trail," Sterly Meagan said. "Stopped to fix himself up some."

"I'm arresting those Quinlan brothers," Hollander snarled. "Where are they?"

"Why . . ." said Buck, "they're . . . on their way to their mama's house . . . down to Texas. You . . . put a scare in 'em."

"South!" Hollander said. "Then get out of my way, or I'll see you installed in the calaboose!"

Dane shook his head. "You're the one might be going to jail, Mr. Hollander. Attempting to lynch two men. Against the law, last I looked."

"Some judges allow it if there's good evidence," Hollander said, the words almost a grumble. As if he wasn't sure of them.

"What evidence? I saw those cattle back down the trail. You can take them on home if you think they're yours. They're unbranded. They could've been wild longhorns—the runaways gone wild drift up from Texas."

"That's what Ben Quinlan said," said Sterly. "We figured they were lyin'."

"You can't hold us here like this!" Hollander declared. "Pointing guns at honest citizens!"

"Where's the man who tried to ambush me?" Dane asked.

"What the dickens you talking about now?" Hollander said, snorting.

"He was up on the cliff back of the canyon. Took a shot at me, too."

"I did see someone up there shooting," Tater said.

Hans turned angrily to Tater. "You—shut up! You don't know what you saw!"

Hollander turned to look sternly at Hans. "You know something about this?"

"He's seeing things, Mr. Hollander."

"You kept delaying us up there, or we'd have gotten the job done. Might be more coming we could hang, you said. Made no sense. We could've hung 'em and . . ." He shook his head. "You pullin' something on me here, Deputy?"

Hans gave one of his mountainous shrugs. "This man Dane is wanted in Steeple Rock. Dangerous man. A killer. Some bounty hunter up there might want to catch him unawares. That's law business, yah."

"There's no posters on me anywhere," Dane said.

Hollander looked at Dane, and his frown was now one of confusion. "I don't know which way to jump. But—I'll tell you this. If we catch those boys, next time we'll arrest them and take them to Jipsell. That I know. And I know you shot at us!"

"If I'd shot at you, you'd be dead," Dane said

"Now, that's probably so," said Sterly knowingly.

"Ferry pulled his gun like he was going to plug

those boys in the back. I just gave them cover to get away."

"That's how it was," Blue said. "I saw it."

"Me, too," Buck said.

"Come to think of it, Ferry did look like he was fixing to—" Tater began.

His words coming out between clenched teeth, Hans said, "Tater, I'm telling you one last time to *shut your mouth*!"

Dane smiled. Maybe Tater at least wasn't so bad. Seemed to prefer the truth.

"I'm inclined to let your gunplay pass," Hollander said in an easier tone, "given we were about to hang men you've worked beside for a spell. I know how that goes. And Ferry—he'd be no loss to the world."

"Good choice," said Dane. "You don't want a war with Jess Willoughby. He's had war enough."

Hollander gave a grudging nod. "But you need to get out of my way. Now."

Dane shrugged. "Holster that rifle, and you can ride by."

Hollander growled to himself but he slid the rifle in its saddle holster.

Dane kept his gun leveled as he led Pard out of the way. Blue and Buck reluctantly drew their horses off the trail.

Under the muzzles of Dane's Colt and Buck's shotgun, the four would-be lynchers rode across the shallow steam and then hurried off down the trail to go after the Quinlan boys.

The men from Horseshoe W watched them go. "You really think we should've let them go by?" Blue asked.

"Could've held them longer. Give the boys a better chance to ride clear."

"The trail southwest," Dane said, "is all churned up by our horses and those cattle. Won't be easy for Hollander to track them. He'll take the southern trail. But Dirk and Ben went northeast to Burrister. After a long ride to the south—and after all that's happened—I don't think Hollander will double back. He'll go home."

"What about Ferry? Maybe we should just shoot that walking pigpen. No one'll miss him."

"He'll be back along the trail to the canyon, nursing his wounds, and probably got himself set up somewhere he can keep an eye on the trail. One of us is likely to get shot if we go looking for him. We'd have to kill him. And I'm not sure the law is with us on it. Let's see if we can get back to the cookshack in time for lunch. Ike said we could have the leftover pork chops."

THE BULLET WAS lodged against the bone of Ferry Johnson's left shoulder. When he poured canteen water over the wound to wash off the ooze, he could see the base of the bullet clear as day against the pink-blue bone. He thought he saw a crack in the bone, too. Might could heal good, might could heal bad. And when he moved his shoulder, it hurt worse than a broken heart—that was an expression the orderly had used in the orphanage where he had spent seven years before running off. *"We'll whup your ass hard if you don't take a bath, boy, and it'll hurt worse than a broken heart."*

Taking a pint of Overholt's whiskey from his saddlebag, he sat on a low boulder in as much sun as he could find, picked up the quirt he used to whip his horse, and stuck it between his teeth. Ferry bit down hard and poured the whiskey over the wound. He groaned and cut into the leather quirt with his teeth in his pain. He poured whiskey over his knife blade and set to digging the bullet out, moaning deep in his throat and chewing at the quirt till he popped it out.

He poured a little more liquor over the wound. A sheriff in Deadwood had told him about using liquor to stop gangrene—the same sheriff who'd shot him in the arm for pulling a knife and who had then watched with glee as the barber poured on the whiskey and pried the bullet out, there being no doctor in the little settlement. But it had worked; the wound hadn't festered.

Now he poured some whiskey on an old bandanna and tied it over the wound as best he could, saying, "All that pain you give me, Dane, I'll give back to you ten times. Fer I know it was you. I'll shoot you in the back so you don't die quick. And then I'll see to your dying. I'll see to it slow. . . ."

CHAPTER TEN

"D ANE, OR WHATEVER your name is," Jess Willoughby said, "you're fired."

"That's your privilege, Mr. Willoughby." Dane was not surprised. Jess Willoughby had local politics to consider. "Mind telling me your reasons?"

Dane had just finished supper and was in the barn, rubbing Pard down, when Willoughby came to him, carrying a lantern in one hand and a handful of dollars in the other.

"My reasons? You shot a man riding with another rancher's posse."

"He was going to shoot Ben in the back of the head."

"Ben Quinlan had helped steal ten of Hollander's beeves."

"Doesn't justify murdering Ben. And those beeves had no brands on 'em. They were found away from Hollander land."

"They *say* they found them there. But someone cut 'em loose from the pen—the tracks are there. So Hollander tells me. One of his men rode over with a letter about it. And I don't want any more trouble with him. Says you also shot at him and his boys!"

"Near 'em, not at them. I just wanted the Quinlan boys to get away—"

"Yes, yes. I don't want to see anyone lynched either. It's good they left the area. I'd have hided them out of here myself. But there's something else—that deputy says you're a wanted killer."

"There's no warrant or poster out on me. That deputy works for Shine O'Hara. Word is, his men are responsible for McCutcheon and Hanrahan being—"

"Enough! You know there's no proof of any such thing. I also heard about you humiliating one of Hollander's men with a gun—shot his pants off!"

"That's a trick I wouldn't know how to do, Mr. Willoughby. I just shot the buckle off his belt. He was turned sideways, and—"

"Doesn't matter how you did it. Here's your pay." Willoughby handed Dane the money. "You did some good work, and I'm sorry to lose you, but you're going. You understand?"

"Yes, sir. I'll get my things." Dane put out his hand.

There was regret in Jess Willoughby's eyes as he shook Dane's hand. "Good luck, Dane."

R IDING INTO TOWN through a dark night, the moon and stars hiding behind clouds, Dane was haunted by uncertainty. Should he stay on in Smoky River? Or should he give up on this corrupt town?

He'd always wanted to have a look at Oregon. Settlers were still moving out there. Towns growing. Said to be green, a country rich with timber and fish and farmland. Lots of work out there.

Dane tried to imagine simply getting on his horse and setting out for the Oregon trail. But . . .

But of course, there was Suzanne. *"It's not as if we . . ."*

He smiled, remembering that when she said it, there was a certain wistfulness in her voice.

That gave him hope. No, he couldn't leave. Not yet.

But the fragmentary memory came again into his mind like a scene from a magic lantern show. It had happened atop a hill, under a lone, lightning-charred pine tree, a couple miles from Steeple Rock. It was at sundown, and the young man sitting on a horse with a rope around his neck was silhouetted against the bloodred sunset when Dane rode up.

When Dane rode close enough to see his face, he saw the boy was weeping. And a grinning Ferry Johnson was tightening the noose. And then . . .

He recoiled from the memory, and it faded. But he felt it was still there, like a door waiting to be opened. The truth about who he was, about his whole life, was pressing against that door. Pushing somewhere in his mind to be let out.

Dane shook his head. He had more urgent things to think about.

There was a good chance Hans Husman or Squint Brewster would find an excuse to arrest him after what had happened in Willow Canyon. It didn't matter that Hollander wasn't going to press charges.

Best to talk to Conrad. Likely they had stories to share.

A cold rain started up, slithering down his neck every time he leaned forward in the saddle, and Dane picked up the pace. Should he stop at Suzanne's?

He was running out of things to repair at the farm. He'd done the barn, the gate, the back fence by the grave, the roof of the house, another fence, a new post for the porch. . . . Maybe the well could use some work.

But Dane kept on past Marrin Farm, though now he could see the lantern light from the window of her little house.

He kept going till he got to the edge of town, then rode around to the dirt road behind the eastern row of buildings on Main Street. He tied up behind the hotel and went in the back way.

Dane paid for a better room than the last time, took his spare clothes and such up to the room, then led Pard between the buildings to the street. He looked up and down, didn't see anyone about, and took the mustang quickly over to the livery. Gunderson was just locking up.

"Got room for one more, Roy?"

"Why, here you are, just in time to keep a man from his supper!" But Roy seemed glad to see him, though the hostler tried to cover it up as he opened the stable doors and brought in the lantern.

Dane took some time brushing Pard, and paid Roy to give Pard his best grain. And a couple of apples, if he had them.

"You a-flowin' with gold now?"

"Not for long. Got into trouble at Willow Canyon, and Willoughby fired me."

"I heard that Swede telling Brewster something about it after he rode in. 'Didn't work', he says. 'That fellow Dane shot Ferry,' he says. 'Quinlans, they run off,' he says."

"You always have your ears pricked up round here, don't you, Roy?" Dane said, grinning.

"Best I do, the way things are."

Dane nodded. "They tried to hang Ben and Dirk for rustlers, and they tried to set me up for killing."

"You know Jipsell made that Brewster and the Swede into deputies?" Dane shook his head. "Folks accept that?"

"It's his privilege, according to the mayor. You better watch your back, Dane. I'm starting to think it's plain natural for some people to want to kill you. You always find a way to raise their hackles." He lit his pipe and blew smoke at a spider building a web in the rafters. "Those boys steal them cattle, Dane?"

"Depends on your point of view. But . . ."

"Not again!"

"Yep."

D ANE SAW HIM through the window. It was cheap glass, a bit warped, but he could see Arthur Conrad was working late, spectacles low on his nose as he sat at the desk, fluttering the quill pen to scribble on a document. Dane knocked and was called in.

"Dane! Good to see you, lad! Got some news for you—none of it good. Sit down. Have a drink."

"No, I thank you. But I'll take the seat." He sat on an old leather settee that squeaked a complaint at his weight. "That quill's leaking ink on your pants there, Arthur."

"Hellfire!" He tossed the quill pen on his blotter. "Well, it does not signify. Already stained these pants at the print shop. I'll never see how Joe kept himself clean. Messy work."

"I saw a banker use one of those fountain pens once. Seemed less troublesome than a quill."

"I'm a small-town lawyer. Get paid in apples and fish from the river as often as cash. Can't afford a fountain pen. You hear about our disastrous town meeting?"

"Some. Not much."

"We seem to have lost before we got started playing the game. Jipsell insists we're mighty unfair to Clemson and O'Hara. And he produced a killer for McCutcheon and Hanrahan—a drunken thief who could never have got the job done. Who got himself conveniently shot by Jipsell's new so-called deputies."

"That's some brass all right. Then that's three murders. I ran afoul of one of those deputies today. That's what I come to see you about."

Dane told him what had happened in Willow Canyon. Conrad whistled. "Saw that Ferry Johnson going up to Doc Greeley's a few hours ago. So it's you who sent him there."

"You think they can arrest me?"

"In a decent town—no. Not given the circumstances, Dane. But here—anything's possible."

"Might be time to ask Bat if he can send that circuit judge along."

"By God, you're right. I'll send a telegram. Then we'll have some supper and talk it over."

"There's more than one telegram to send, Arthur. Might need to send quite a few . . ."

* * *

D ANE HAD FINISHED his breakfast and come back
to his hotel room to shave—when a pounding
came on the door.

"Dane!" It was Gunderson. "Open the door, you
damned fool!"

Dane crossed the room and opened the door, a razor in one hand. "Roy, what am I a damned fool for
this time?"

"For coming back to this town at all with three bent
lawmen running the place! You got to get out of town.
They got a warrant from the justice of the peace for
you. They're gonna throw you in jail! You're like to
end up like Hanrahan!"

"Can you bring my horse?"

"He's already tied up out behind the hotel! And
they'll be here any damned second!"

"Thanks, Roy. I think I'd better used the window."
Dane closed the door, locked it, quickly threw his few
things in saddlebags, and went to the back window. He
unlocked it, raised it up, and looked through it. At least
they weren't out back yet. Pard was under the window,
tied to a drainpipe. Dane whispered, "Hey, Pard, I'm
coming down!" He was too heavy to jump onto the
horse from up here, but he dropped his saddlebags over
the horse's withers. Pard startled but stayed put, ears
cocked, listening for Dane.

Dane heard voices in the hall, Gunderson yelling, "I
tell you he's got the worst hangover a man ever had!
He's like to shoot you!"

"Get out of the way!" Brewster's voice.

Dane climbed through the window, lowered himself to the end of his arms, and dropped beside Pard. The horse startled again and pulled at his reins so they broke the drainpipe, but Dane vaulted into the saddle and spurred for a gallop, and they were galloping into the October morning fog as bullets from the hotel window cracked past.

The fog closed around him as he rode toward the end of town. Was it the smart thing to do? He figured it probably wasn't. Folks knew he'd been working out there. Gossip had him sweet on Suzanne, and for once, gossip was right. Marrin Farm would have been one of the first places Jipsell would look for him.

But he wasn't going to stay long. Just long enough to ask Suzanne a question.

The fog swirled as they galloped along, and in under fifteen minutes, Pard had carried him to the farm.

The horse blowing, Dane reined in at the gate. Suzanne was coming out of the barn with a milk pail in her hand, one shoulder sagging a little with the weight of it. She was wearing her work jeans, a light blue blouse, and a shawl. She had no bonnet on, and her coppery hair, though held by a horn clip, licked about her in the slight wind. "Kind of late in the day to do the milking, ain't it?" he called out in a teasing voice.

She looked toward him, surprised, and tilted her head, shaking it as if to make fun of him saying the obvious. "Yes, it is! Come on through the gate, Dane."

Dane dismounted, opened the gate, led Pard through, and closed it again, thinking he wished they had more protection from danger here than the rickety fence and the even more rickety gate. The sheriff would just let himself in, and he'd have his gun in his hand.

He got Pard a bucket of water and tied him to the little hitching post in front of the house. He might need to leave right quick.

Suzanne came out and joined him, bringing Pard a handful of dried applies. She held them in her palm as the horse lipped up the treat, and she said, "You've had him running hard. Heat's coming off him like a stove."

"We galloped here from town."

She let Pard finish the apples and then patted him. "You're a darn good horse to carry this big ol' heavy man so fast."

"Suzanne . . ." Dane took her hands in his and gently turned her toward him. She gave a small gasp but didn't try to draw her hands away. That was a good sign, wasn't it? It was one of those things he couldn't quite remember. "Suzanne . . ."

"I believe you said that already, Dane."

"You like me a little, don't you?"

She blushed, but she smiled and said, "I shall admit no such thing."

"Isn't saying that the same as admitting it?"

"Now you're acting like a lawyer!"

He drew her closer very gently. Her lips parted, and her eyes got wide. And then he kissed her. Her lips were astonishingly soft and warm. She stiffened for a moment—and then relaxed and kissed him back. The sun chose that moment to break through the clouds.

Then she pushed him firmly away. "Dane . . ." She was breathing hard, brushing her hair back from her forehead. "That was . . . sudden."

"If you're saying I shouldn't have done, I will apologize, ma'am."

"I . . . am not sure. I . . ."

"You kissed me back.

"Dane!"

"Didn't you?"

She tugged her shawl around herself and looked at the ground. "Yes. You sound like a lawyer again."

"I had to do it before I asked. I had to know."

She looked up at him and seemed to catch her breath. "Oh—I . . ."

"Would you come away with me? We could be married, say, in Kansas City."

"What? You mean—elope? This *is* going fast!"

"I haven't got a lot of time. Let me tell you what happened." It all came tumbling out. Willow Canyon. The interrupted lynching. Shooting the rope and Ferry. The Quinlans escaping. The rifleman on the high rocks. And he told her his reasons for believing he was the real intended target of the occasion. "Maybe they know how I feel about lynching."

"You're saying the deputies set you up so you'd come out there to help the Quinlans—and you'd . . . you'd be killed?"

"You know how Elias Keggum found me under that cliff. The men who shot me there wanted me dead. I'm not exactly sure why. But Elias warned me they'd come after me if they knew I was alive. It was at Steeple Rock—that much I know. And that's where these men are from. They work for Shine O'Hara."

Suzanne came a little closer and put her hand on his arm. "You're remembering more of your past!"

"I believe I am. It's coming in bits and pieces. What happened to me had to do with Shine O'Hara. He was involved with a lynching. . . ." He shook his head. "It's close, but—I can't reach it." He let out a long breath, then turned to look at the road from town. "I figure they'll come out here after they try the Horseshoe W. I don't reckon they know I was fired. I don't want to put you folks in danger by staying here too long, Suzanne. Seems like if I want to stay here, I might have to kill a couple of men wearing badges. That man who shot at me at the canyon—he is surely being paid good money. He'll try again. And he doesn't fight fair."

"Can you make peace with this O'Hara?"

"No. The deputy said I did something in Steeple Rock. He said I was a killer, Suzanne. Maybe I am. I don't remember."

She shook her head slowly. "No. You lost your memories. But you can't lose your character. If you killed anyone, it's because you had no choice."

"I don't know." His voice broke a little when he said it. He looked away, embarrassed.

"You say you want me to go away with you, Dane." She took his hand. "I feel like—I've been waiting for you all these years. I feel like I said *no* so often because those men weren't you. But, Dane, if you don't remember your life but for the last three years, you might be married. You might even have children. Haven't you considered that?"

"I have. It occurred to me. It doesn't feel like I do. But . . . you're right. I can't know. Not yet."

"And I could never marry you unless you knew for sure you weren't married. Anyway"—she looked back at the house—"I couldn't abandon Mama. She couldn't live here alone, Dane."

He nodded. There was a strange thickness that

seemed to obstruct his throat. "I understand, Suzanne." Dane realized then that he just plain wasn't leaving town. He wasn't going to leave Suzanne behind.

But he had to keep clear of Marrin Farm, at least for now. "Well, I'll stay hereabouts—somewheres away from here—till the right time comes."

"And when would the right time be?"

"Bat Masterson offered to send a judge down. Maybe I can go to his court. Arthur Conrad will defend me. And if there's a fair judge and jury, it'll go my way. Maybe it'll all quiet down."

He untied Pard from the gate and put his hand on the saddle horn—and then she punched him in the shoulder. "You are not leaving here in that fashion, Dane."

He turned to Suzanne. There were tears in her eyes. "You *will* give me another kiss. And then you can go."

"I admire a woman who knows what she wants."

Dane took her in his arms and gave her a long, slow kiss. At last she pulled back. They were both breathing hard. A sticky, living warmth seemed to fill the air between them.

"Oh, Lordy," she said, stepping back. "You'd best get out of here fast right now. Or I won't let you go at all."

He made himself turn away and climbed on the horse. She reached out and held the horse's bridle. "Wait—where are you going?"

"You tell them when they ask I went to Oklahoma to get some work. But I'll be going to Burrister first thing to talk to the Quinlan boys. Then I'll find a place to lie low and do some figuring."

"But you'll be back?"

"I'll be back."

She let go of the bridle and turned away without a word.

Dane nudged Pard into a trot, then into canter. He headed toward the hills overlooking the road to the Horseshoe W. Despite the danger he was in, he felt real elation. She'd let him kiss her. Twice. She'd said she had turned all those men down because she was waiting for him to come along.

He'd still thought of himself, despite the shining up, as just another broke cowboy, not much more than a saddle tramp. But now anything seemed possible. Suzanne was like a miracle.

Better think about where you're going now, he told himself.

Horseshoe W to have a word with Jess Willoughby. He couldn't take the road—Jipsell and his deputies, maybe even a posse, would be out there looking for him—but he could ride parallel to it.

He left the road, riding up into the low hills that followed alongside it at a distance of about an eighth mile. There was a sparse trail along the hilltops, and he headed west on it—just like those riders had followed it to watch him that first day he'd ridden out to the ranch. He rode on, staying in the trees as much as he could. A quarter mile on, he saw the riders from afar.

They were riding hard, guns loaded, murder in their hearts. Looking for the man known only as Dane.

CHAPTER ELEVEN

THERE WERE FIVE of them riding hard to the west. Even at this distance Dane was sure of three of them: Jipsell, Brewster, and the Swede. Who were the two others? One might be the gambler who called himself Edmund. The hat looked like his. The other was a stout man in town clothes too big for a long ride. Armbruster!

Not much of a posse. Lot of folks in town, Dane figured, no longer trusted Jipsell enough to sign on with his posse.

The riders were headed out to the Horseshoe W. Dane drew Pard deeper into the trees atop the hills and let the riders pass on. Then he rode on, too, more slowly, staying to the deer trail tracing the hilltops. It was cold and damp in the woods. The trees had lost half their leaves and more spun down around him with every gust of wind. The mustang's clopping passage scared up a grouse, its wings whirring.

Dane was within a half mile of the Horseshoe W when he saw the posse ride back toward town again, more leisurely this time, having discovered Dane was no longer at the ranch. Armbruster seemed wobbly on his horse. Dane watched them ride back to the east and out of sight.

They'd go to Marrin Farm now. Jipsell wouldn't allow the women there to be hurt—there were dealings even a crooked sheriff couldn't have a hand in—but it bothered Dane that the likes of Brewster and the Swede would be talking to Suzanne, even interrogating her. His hand tightened on the reins at the thought so that the mustang came to a stop. "Sorry, Pard. Let's get to the Horseshoe W. They're going to be surprised to see me back there."

Dane snapped the reins, and Pard trotted ahead. Soon Dane found a gentle slope and took them back down to the road. Another twenty minutes took them up to the gate of the Horseshoe W.

Jess Willoughby was there, standing beside a buckboard with a draft horse cropping on weeds. Willoughby was watching Blue attach a lock to the gate.

They both looked up as he arrived, Jess looking surprised and Blue showing none. Blue went back to using his screwdriver on the steel hasp.

Dane slid off the horse and went to stand by the gate, the reins in his hand. "Morning," he said.

"Didn't expect to see you again anytime soon, Dane," Willoughby said with a slight frown. "Especially after a posse was just here, less than an hour ago, looking for you."

"I'm not staying, Mr. Willoughby."

Willoughby grunted. "Since you're not working for me, and we know each other fairly well now, just call me Jess. Most folks do."

"Jess—I'm going to find the Quinlan boys if they're anywhere near. They might have to testify in Smoky River. On my behalf."

"They won't want to," said Blue, standing up, screwdriver in hand.

"No, they won't. I hope to persuade them. I'll testify on their behalf, too. Even if they aren't willing, I'd like to see how the damned fools are doing. And, Jess, I was hoping you'd trust me with their pay. Maybe you think they don't deserve it. But they worked hard, and they've got two weeks coming. If I can't find them, I'll send the money back to you. You have my word."

Jess Willoughby hesitated, looking at the lock. "Just do one more tightening there, Blue, all round." He took a deep breath and said, "Yeah, come on through, and I'll give it to you. You never gave me a reason to think you were a thief."

"You going to Burrister?" Blue asked.

"Yep. They might still be there."

Blue nodded and went to tightening the screws attaching the lock hasp to the gatepost. When he'd finished, he opened the gate and remounted and Dane rode through.

"Looks good," Willoughby allowed, peering at the hasp. He took the lock from his pocket and snapped it in place. "Let's find some other work to do."

Willoughby and Blue got into the buckboard, Blue holding the wooden toolbox in his lap, and Dane rode beside them as Jess drove to the ranch.

"You feel like you need that gate locked now?" Dane asked.

"Those fellas claiming to be a posse just opened my gate and let themselves in. I didn't like their style. Next time they'll have to work harder to get onto my property. Goes for the Quinlan brothers, too—I no longer trust them."

THE REFURBISHED SALOON had reopened just yesterday, with its new sign up top: *Clemson & Farragut ~ Fine Drinks for Lucky Gaming.*

Standing at the bar, nursing a beer, Arthur Conrad was bemused by the changes in what had been called Farragut's Saloon. The walls were now covered with red felt, a new mirror behind the bar reflected the backs of bottles of good whiskey, and the moldings were painted gold. The stocky, red-cheeked bartender had flaring mustaches and a red velvet vest over his puffy-sleeved white shirt. He looked more like a Gypsy musician than a Kansas bartender.

The second such saloon on Main Street, Farragut's had till now been quite shabby, making Rusty's place look spruced up by comparison. But now that Clemson had bought a controlling share, in a remarkably short time, Farragut's had been decked out and newly furnished with green felt gambling tables and a fine new carved mahogany bar that had come in on a barge just two days earlier. Farragut wasn't here, nor was Clemson, and, in fact, the place was actually owned by Shine O'Hara. Having handled the paperwork, Conrad knew that Shine had bought Clemson's debts and a very large controlling interest in the Silver Goddess. O'Hara had arranged for Clemson to buy Farragut's for him as a way around town ordinances.

The two gambling tables, that late afternoon, were already full of ranch hands and merchants evidently letting their assistants do the work at the shop. Cards were flipped at one table, and a roulette wheel spun at the other.

Conrad noticed Armbruster, looking dusty, tired, angry, and already drunk, alone at a corner table, drinking shots of whiskey with his beer. Armbruster shifted on his seat as if he had a sore rump. The posse had not gone well, or so Conrad had heard. Word had it they'd searched the town on both sides of the river, losing Dane at the Main Street hotel. They'd gone out to the Horseshoe W and the Marrin Farm and scoured the orchards and trails nearby. Suzanne Marrin claimed Dane had gone to Oklahoma, looking for work. Anyhow, it was clear Dane was well away from Smoky River, and Conrad was glad for it and sorry for it at the same time. He scarcely knew Dane, but the man's character seemed carved in him, as in stone. Conrad had seen him disarm Sterly Meagan in the most alarming way conceivable, too.

Conrad had hoped Dane might someday become town sheriff. But it seemed that was not to be.

A dance hall girl came and nestled close beside him at the bar. She was wearing more or less the same revealing demigarments as the Silver Goddess girls, except she had more gold in her outfit. She had her blond hair piled artfully atop her head and wore a cameo around her neck on a black ribbon. It didn't seem to go with the rest of her getup.

"Buy a lady a drink?" she asked in a tone that went with the velvet on the walls.

Conrad almost said, *They ask a lot for a cup of cold tea here.* He knew that was what the bartender gave the girls: tea poured out of a whiskey bottle. They needed the girls sober and wanted to save money on liquor. But there was a sadness in this handsome woman's eyes. She looked like she'd worked a few too many small Western camps and towns.

He decided to order a drink just to ease her way a little. "Yes, ma'am, if it's a drink I can afford. I'm but a poor country lawyer."

"Abe Lincoln was a poor country lawyer, too," she said, signaling the bartender. "And he got to be president. Maybe it's your turn now."

Conrad smiled. She seemed sharper than many of the saloon girls he'd met. She sounded like someone who could read and write. He hoped they weren't making her "take the gentlemen upstairs" here. It hadn't been tolerated on this side of the river, but he'd heard that the Silver Goddess flouted the rule. "What's the name they give you here?"

"I use my real name. It's Alice."

"Like in the book?" He was curious as to how well-read she was.

"Surely. I've surely gone right down that ol' rabbit hole, too."

Conrad had been trying to identify her accent. "South Carolina?"

"You have a good ear, sir."

"May as well call me Arthur. I use my real name, too."

She laughed. The bartender brought her drink. "And for you, sir?" he asked, beaming at Conrad.

"I believe I'll have another glass of suds."

"Arthur," Alice said after the bartender had poured his beer and moved on, "I have to take someone upstairs tonight if I can, and I've taken a shine to you."

"Don't you as a matter of professional course take a shine to every man who comes in?"

She pursed her lips at that and looked at her drink. He saw he'd hurt her feelings. "Those women have armored their souls," his father had said of girls who worked in such places. Alice apparently was more vulnerable than most.

"I'm sorry," he said. "That was rude of me. If I was prone to . . . to 'going upstairs' . . . I'd take you before any other. Even now, if I had the extra money, I'd just give it to you for standing here with me. Maybe sometime when I get a good fee."

She gave him a soft look of gratitude. "I thank you kindly for the thought, Arthur." She drank a little of her faux whiskey, for appearance's sake. "You know, I bought that book by Mr. Carroll the instant it came out. I owned my own place then, and I could afford such luxuries."

"You owned a saloon?"

"A small place for gents to hire a woman to dance. We served beer and wine, and we had a trumpet player, a fiddler, and a piano player. I was fixing to hire a percussionist when the county sheriff came in and told me I had to give him forty percent of my earnings, or he'd put me out of business. Even though the girls did nothing but dance with the fellows. He soon ran me out of business anyway at that rate and into debt. I started this kind of work. Mostly just . . . socializing. Dancing with gents. Until recently. That man O'Hara . . ."

"He insisted, did he?"

"Yes. In Steeple Rock and now here. I haven't managed to put much aside, so I don't quite know where I'd go. . . ." Alice gave a laugh of self-mockery. "Listen to me, prattling on about my troubles." She looked at him sidelong. "I don't usually do that with real gentlemen."

"I'm honored," he said. He found himself wanting to help her. And from somewhere in the back of his mind, the thought of making her an honest woman arose. He was a lonely man, after all. Too old for the available ladies in town and too young to forget about holding a woman in his arms.

Two beers and you're having foolish thoughts, Arthur Conrad, he told himself. *Set the notion aside. She's likable right enough, but no doubt she'd tell the same sad story to many a man.*

Conrad didn't believe that though. He wasn't sure why. And the foolish thought would not quite go away.

"What the hellfire are ye up to!" came a harsh shout from one of the tables.

Conrad turned to see a young cowboy in a long brown leather coat standing at the poker table, talking to a saloon girl with thick black hair entwined with red ribbon. She was half turned toward Conrad—and she looked scared. "I know that play!" the young, bony-faced cowboy said. "I saw it in Sweetwater. She stands behind a feller like she's his friend and looks at his cards! Then she fools with her hair or her earring—and it's a signal. She's working with that crooked tinhorn right there!"

Conrad had noticed the gambler around town. Said

his name was Edmund Earl. He was immaculately dressed, a round-faced fellow with muttonchops who looked as dangerous as ice cream. But now he stood up and put his hand in his coat pocket. "You're calling me a cheat, sir?"

The cowboy swung to the gambler and jabbed a fore-finger at him. "I've seen it before—same movements! Met a girl used to do it. One for aces, another for kings—why there's something for most any hand!"

"I am, in fact, here at the invitation of Mr. Clemson, and he will vouch—"

"Vouch, hell! I'm going to wait till you're—"

That was all he got out. Edmund Earl pulled a hide-away gun from his coat pocket and shot the cowboy through the heart. The bar girl screamed.

The cowboy staggered back, swayed—and fell dead.

The saloon girl turned to the gambler. "You didn't have to do that! I told you, no—"

"Shut up!" Earl snarled.

Conrad could not help himself. He went to the ta-ble. "That looked like murder to me, sir. I didn't see him reach for a weapon. You'd best give yourself up to the sheriff."

The gambler gave a small ironic smile at that. "Oh—the sheriff? Yes, I shall, so that all is legal and above-board. But, sir—the cowboy was reaching for a pistol." The gambler put his hideaway back in his coat pocket.

Conrad shook his head and bent to look into the cowboy's coat.

"You! Stay away from that man!" It was Jipsell standing in the door to the street.

Unnerved, Conrad stepped back.

Jipsell came over and knelt by the body. He reached into the dead man's coat. "He does have a gun there!" But the sheriff didn't pull a weapon out into sight. Jipsell scowled at the gambler. "He was going for his gun when you pulled?"

"He was!"

Jipsell nodded, but he didn't look pleased. "You shot him, you help me carry him!"

The gambler's jaw worked at that as he ground his teeth. But he put his bowler on his head, raked in his winnings—careful to leave the house its share—shoved them in his pocket, and went to take the cowboy by the legs. They carried him outside, leaving only a small trail of blood.

Roy Gunderson sidled up to Conrad. "Well, here we are again, Arthur."

"Why, Roy, I didn't know you were here. What do you think of all this?"

"I think that boy had no gun in his coat," Gunderson said in a low voice. "And I think Jipsell will find one for him."

"Yes. Another murder goes unpunished. I'm going to get out a special edition—"

"There's some danger in that, Arthur."

"Oh, they wouldn't— Well, they *would* dare, wouldn't they? But I must do it anyway."

DANE HAD MADE a camp on a flattish ridge overlooking Burrister, within a copse of junipers and red cedars. He'd found a low spot, ringed by junipers and spruce that would hide away most of the light from his campfire, and he sat cross-legged there now, chewing salt beef, drinking from his canteen, and gazing into the fire.

He'd observed the town for some time in the afternoon from a series of vantage points in the brush and outcroppings. He had picked out Ben Quinlan, who looked quite drunk already, but no one else he knew, although there were men he recognized as certain types. Men who found ways to get along without working or by doing as little as possible. Some who looked like road agents, too. There were few women. Burrister was twenty miles from Smoky River, and he saw no sign of the posse—but Jipsell might well send the deputies up there, perhaps tomorrow, to look for him.

Nevertheless, he would go into the little town and take his chances.

"You should have your guns closer to you," said a voice from the darkness.

Dane reached for his gun belt, which was lying on his saddlebags. Then it occurred to him he knew that voice. "Blue?"

Blue came out of the darkness and sat beside him. "I caught a couple of game hens," he said, tossing the birds on the ground. "I'll pluck and clean one if you'll do the other."

"Something better than jerky would be welcome." Dane picked up one of the game hens. "You were quiet coming in here. You move . . ."

"Like an Injun?"

Dane smiled. "You could've called out to the camp."

"And miss seeing you jump for that gun you left too far away?"

"Fair enough. How'd you find me?"

Blue looked at Pard, dozing not far from the fire. "Big man on a mustang—easy tracks to follow."

"What brings you out here?"

"I told Jess he should rehire you. I said what you did was right. We disagreed. And I didn't feel right about staying. Anyway, you'll need somebody to side you. This place is a nest of back shooters."

"Can't be that bad."

"It's what I heard. Couldn't hurt to have a man watching your back."

"Good. You head out first, and I'll watch your back."

Blue actually smiled at that.

D ANE WOKE THE next morning to Blue saddling his paint pony and whistling to himself as he did it— probably to wake Dane up.

"Is that a tune you're whistling?" Dane asked. "Does not sound like one." He stretched, feeling twinges from sleeping on the cold ground.

"Must be a tune somewhere. Maybe China. I went to look at Burrister. Asked a runaway Comanche who lives there about the posse. An old man who doesn't miss much. He says no sign of them. He knows Squint Brewster—says he's an owlhoot, passes through Burrister fairly regular. Was tolerably surprised to hear he's a deputy now."

"You see the Quinlan boys?"

"Nope. Too early for them to be up if they're not being paid for it. But I saw their horses in a big old shack that passes for a livery stable."

"If Squint and the Swede are still working for O'Hara, they'll be looking for me in Burrister—after they've tried everywhere else. And that long rifle sniper will be along, too."

He got up and grained Pard from the bag Gunderson had sent along. "Blue, maybe we ought to do a wide circle around the town, see if that sniper's hunkered up on the hills."

"Already did it before I came back to camp."

Blue-Snake Thompson is a good man to ride the river with, Dane thought.

They broke camp and followed a game trail through the brush to the main road. Keeping a wary eye on pretty much everything he encountered, Dane rode slowly into Burrister, Blue at his side. The rutted road led straight into the one-street town. The street was crammed with saloons and a few shops, one of which promised *Medicaments and Barbering.* There was a combination grocer and feed store next door to a tackle and gun shop that also provided some blacksmithing. There was one bawdy house, and Dane spotted a ramshackle hotel with a sign claiming *Fine Eats.*

Cabins were wedged between shops and saloons. More dotted the hillside above the town. It was fairly quiet as they rode in, though a couple of drunks, probably up all night, were arguing by a water trough, and two women were physically fighting, their makeup smeared. Several cowboys were snoring in the straw of a long lean-to, where a dozen horses were tied up.

"This street got a name?" Dane asked.

"Nope," Blue said.

"How'd the place come to be called Burrister?"

"Used to be a mining camp run by a man named Burrister. Lead and zinc. Ran dry, so Burrister himself left, and now it's just a place for some people to hide out and other people to charge them money for doing it."

"Got a church?"

"Are you joking?"

"How about a lawman?"

"There is a fellow named Dan Dugmire. Used to be a mining engineer back when. Declares himself sheriff and judge and mayor—does it every New Year's Day. Most people seem to accept his authority. He's got some kind of gang around him."

"Sounds like you were here before today."

"Came with my brother a couple years back, trying to look out for him. He's buried out on the west side of town in something kinda like a cemetery though there's no tombstones except for my brother's."

"Get himself shot?"

"He did. Drunken argument. Never had a chance."

"Anybody pay a price for it?"

"Not in a court. But I saw to it. Tossed him down an old mining shaft." The matter-of-fact way Blue said this was disquieting. But Dane couldn't blame him much.

"Let's see if they have coffee in Fine Eats."

They tied their horses up at the water trough—the drunks having wandered away—and as the thirsty mounts drank their fill, Dane and Blue sauntered to the hotel with the *Fine Eats* sign. On the way, Dane scanned doorways, rooftops, windows, even the hills overlooking the town.

It's a hard way to live, he reflected, *having to watch your back all the time.*

The flyblown eatery was just a series of benches along dirty wooden tables. All except for one angled across a corner of two walls; a nicely carved and fitted oak table sat there, and a lean, long-necked man in a tired black suit took his ease in an overstuffed easy chair, his back to the corner. He was facing the front door. *Not a man who wants to be snuck up on,* Dane thought. He had an underbite that thrust his chin forward and a splendidly curling mustache. His receding long black hair was swept back and speckled with gray. He was toying with chess pieces on a board, coffee steaming at his elbow. A dragoon revolver lay within reach by the coffee.

"Well, gentlemen!" he said, glancing up. He had a nasal voice and deep-set dark eyes glaring from under bushy eyebrows. "Take a seat. There're some rags somewhere if you wish to wipe the table. You're kinder early for this town, but we can rustle you up some coffee and eggs and beans, if you've got two dollars between you. Eggs are fresh. Raise the chickens m'self."

"That'll do fine," said Dane. Blue nodded.

They scuffed through scraps of food and broken crockery that lay amongst sawdust on the floor and sat at a table only moderately befouled. They, too, sat facing the door.

"Karl! Eggs, beans, and onions for two gentlemen! And coffee!"

Someone grumbled from beyond a curtained door to one side of the proprietor.

"I'm Dan Dugmire, boys, mayor, sheriff, sometimes judge. And your host. Call me Dan."

Dane thought about giving a false name but decided he wanted to see if Dugmire reacted to his real name. "Just call me Dane."

"Blue," said Blue.

"We clean the place once a week on Sundays," said Dugmire, looking around as if he'd just noticed the state it was in. "But it might've slipped m'mind last Sunday."

Dane brushed some crumbs off his table. "I noticed a creek a little ways behind the buildings on this side. Does it have a name?"

"No, we can never agree on one. A man was, in fact, shot in an argument over naming the creek. He insisted it be named after him. But who wants to live next to Hank Shischneller Creek? Same problem with the street name. Can't agree. I think it should be Dugmire Street. But there are a couple of old-timers who insist it's Burrister Street."

"Anyone killed over that?" Blue asked.

"No. Only wounded."

A little time passed. Dugmire fooled with his chess pieces. Then he noticed his coffee had gone cold.

"Karl! Damn it!" he roared.

Grumbling without intelligible words, Karl brought out two wooden plates of eggs, beans, and onions each with a wooden fork stuck in the food. The squat, red-eyed cook wore a long apron gone brown with grime, and he had an enormous mane of bushy blond hair—though so coated with soot, it had become black in places—and a forgotten beard laced with equally forgotten drippings.

He slapped the plates down before the two customers and stumped back to the kitchen. Dane pulled a long beard hair from his food and set to eating. The coffee was slapped down shortly afterward, some splashing on the table.

They ate, and drank the coffee, and hoped they wouldn't get food poisoning.

"What brings you gents to Burrister?" Dugmire asked, trying to checkmate himself on the chessboard.

"Looking for a couple of friends, Dan. Got some business with them. The kind they'll appreciate. Ben and Dirk Quinlan."

"Met 'em. Not much trouble yet. One fistfight. I refereed. Dirk won it. I lost two dollars on the betting. Last I knew they were sleeping in the horse shed. Ran through their money last night."

Dane and Blue finished their meal, waved goodbye to Dugmire, and went out to find the Quinlans.

After they'd gone, Karl came out and looked out the flyspecked window after them. "I seem to recognize both them fellers."

Dugmire nodded. "As did I. The man calling himself Dane came through here about four years ago, give or take a few months. Came from Dodge, was headed for Colorado."

"You remember all that, boss?"

"I couldn't forget that man. That was before you came to town, Karl. That man stopped here to water his horse and buy some grain. The Silmers were here. Three of the gang. They recognized him when they saw him go into Molly's for a beer. Said he'd shot Bud Silmer. Said they were going to get him for it. I was in the Painted Lady, having myself a libation, and he was there, too, drinking a beer just as peaceful. He said goodbye to the saloonkeeper and turned to go, and there were the Silmers, rushing at him with their guns out. He drew and killed all three of them. Two of them got off a shot. One of the balls cut into his side. Didn't do much harm. The other one busted the bar mirror. He shot one of them in the head and the other two

through the heart. I never saw such a thing. He hardly
blinked an eye. He turned to me, calm as could be, and
he apologized for the ruckus. He opened his poke and
took out a hundred dollars in gold to pay for the dam-
age, and he thoughtfully added another six to pay for
the burying of the dead men. I pointed out those men
had prices on their heads. He said he didn't kill men
for money. He wished me good day, went to the barber
to get his side patched, and rode out without another
word. I tell you, he seems a decent sort—but that man
fair gives me the chills."

"You didn't act like you knowed him when he come
in today."

"Ah! When as regards dangerous men, Karl, Dan
Dugmire is the soul of discretion. . . ."

CHAPTER TWELVE

D ANE AND BLUE took their horses from the hitch—
and then Blue said, "My Henry's gone!"

Dane saw that the gun was indeed gone from its
saddle holster. "Someone stole it—and maybe there he
goes!" He pointed at a man running around the corner
of a building across the street. He was carrying something, trying to hide it, but Dane glimpsed the rifle
barrel. "Blue—"

But Blue was already sprinting faster than Dane
had ever seen him move, crossing the street double-
quick.

"Blue, wait—you haven't got a gun! He does!" Blue
rarely carried a pistol.

Dane ran after him, heard a gunshot—then a thump

and a grunt of pain. When he reached the mouth of the narrow, trash-strewn alley, he saw Blue standing over an unconscious and very scruffy man. Blue had his rifle back in his hands.

"Where'd he shoot you?" Dane asked.

"Missed me. A man can't shoot straight when somebody's running straight at him and looking him right in the eyes."

"Should we bother the so-called law here about this?"

"No. He's out cold, and he's got a broken nose. That will make him more thoughtful."

"This town's probably got more thieves than anything else."

"We'd best get back to our horses before someone steals them."

"Pard would never let anyone steal him, but I'm not so sure about your horse."

They returned to their horses and led them down the street to the long lean-to horse shed. An old man with but a few teeth in his head appeared out of nowhere. He wore oversized pants held up by a single suspender, a red undershirt, and no shoes at all. "Dollar a day to use the livery," he said, sticking out his hand.

"How do we know you're the owner?" Dane asked, looking him up and down.

"Wayll, I sleep right there on that cot, I got my fire barrel right over there, I got my pots right here, and ain't nobody smell more like horses than me."

"You have me there," said Dane, taking out two silver dollars. He jingled them in his palm. "Now, that's for all of today and tonight. Right?"

"All the way till noon tomorrow."

Dane handed him the silver dollars, and they tied their horses up in front of some moderately clean hay. "Costs far too much for whatever this lean-to is, but I'm not in the mood to bargain with a toothless, barefoot old man."

They found Ben and Dirk about four horses down, sleeping by their cow ponies, both of them snoring. Ben was lying on his back, head on his saddle, hat down over his eyes.

Blue walked up to him and kicked Ben's boot. "Hey, drifters. Wake up."

Ben tilted his hat back and knuckled his eyes, then peered up at them. "Dane? Blue?"

"Figured it out first crack out of the box," Dane said. "Jess said you could have your pay. We brought it."

Ben yawned. "That's good. That's real good." He took off his hat and held it out like a panhandler. "Put it right in there."

Dane took four silver dollars from his pocket and dropped them in the hat. "That's for the two of you."

"Four dollars? We got two weeks' pay coming!"

"And you'll get it. That's for breakfast and coffee, maybe lunch, maybe hair of the dog, depending how you spend it. I'm not going to trust you with anything else right now, seeing as how you gambled away what you had in this hellhole."

Ben sat up and winced. "Oh, Lord, my head. They have the worst whiskey here I ever tasted, and I drank a lot of it. Don't know as I can think of food or liquor. Or gambling. Or even women. Meanin' you can give me the rest of the money."

"Nope. Not yet. Something I want to talk to you about."

Ben scratched his head. "The law looking for us, Dane?"

"Could be. Not sure they're bothering with you two now. They're looking for me though."

" 'Cause you shot that fella at Willow Canyon? Hell, you had a reason."

"Didn't do him much harm anyhow. But that's their excuse, right enough." Dane pointed at the hills over-looking the town. "See that middle hill there with the notch in it?"

"I expect I do."

"See that oak on the top? Only real tall tree up there. There's a game trail leads up to it. We're camping in the spruce just down from there. We'll have supper for you. I have no reason to stay around this town. Good place to get shot in the back."

"Someone stole my Henry," Blue said. "I got it back."

Ben stuck out his lower lip and nodded. "You hurt him much?"

"Has to have his nose set now. You come up there at sunset. That good, Dane?"

Dane nodded. "Sunset. Both of you."

Ben shrugged. "Sure. We'll be there. I'm gonna see if I can catch me some more winks."

He lay back on the saddle, covered his eyes, crossed his arms over his chest, and two seconds later went to snoring.

"Blue, maybe we should do some hunting, pass the time and stay out of sight," Dane said. "Get up some kind of real meal. Gather some roots, too, maybe.

Might have some purslane still growing out the woods. Keggum showed me that one. . . ."

"Good," Blue said, sounding pleased. "We'll hunt, and there's that stream that goes by here. You don't want anything from it downstream of this place, but upstream it's okay. I got some fishing line and a couple hooks. . . ."

They got their horses and rode up into the hills and began their hunt. It took some time to find a fresh track and to follow it to their prey. Blue leading the way with remarkable quietude, they soon came upon the elk. Too big for their needs, Dane figured. But a man hunting for food is unlikely to be choosy, for game is unpredictable, and Blue fired his rifle with only a second to aim. The elk started off, stumbled—and then fell dead.

"Good shot," Dane said as they walked up to the kill. "Kinda big howsoever."

"We can salt the rest of the meat or sell it. That one's lived a long time. Had a lot of fights. You can see it in his antlers. He had a limp, too. He was ready to go and join the great circle."

"Great circle? Those missionaries must not have been convincing."

"I liked that Jesus. He's got some good things to say. I like that brother of his, James, too. Cares for the poor. And I liked them who taught me."

"How'd you end up with missionaries?" Dane asked as Blue grabbed an antler and started dragging the elk to a tree. Dane took the other antler and helped.

"I grew up with my people till I was eleven. Hunk-papa Lakota. We got shoved onto a reservation, and my folks died of the cholera. The missionaries took me in. Baptists. Dunked me in the water. Gave me some good books to read though. Fenimore Cooper. Tennyson. Nice people. But I see the big circle."

They hung the elk from the fork of a half-grown oak tree, upside down to bleed out, then returned to their hunting. Blue set grass-rope traps in the brush where there was grouse sign.

They returned to the horses and ate a lunch of corn cakes from Blue's saddlebags and hazelnuts from a tree growing beside the unnamed creek.

"We could name this creek if no one has," Blue said.

"How about Drunken Thieves Creek?"

Blue smiled.

They went out again, checking the grass-rope traps Blue had set for grouse. They'd caught a fat one, which Blue killed. With the grouse dangling from Blue's belt they returned to the elk. Blue methodically skinned it, then sawed up the meat with a serrated knife he'd brought for the purpose. The two of them scraped out the hide and rolled the haunches and venison steaks in it, tying it up into a bundle that Blue slung in front of his saddle horn.

They returned to the creek, where they dug out cat-tail tubers and wild onions Blue found near the bank to cook with the meat. Then they set about fishing. Three leisurely, mostly silent hours passed before the rainbow trout began biting. They caught five of them, using shreds of offal from the elk for bait.

It was getting toward dusk when they rode into town, Blue stopping in at the general store for a cooking pot and some salt. Off-key piano and fiddle already sounded from the saloons. A couple of gunshots banged from the far end of Burrister's only main street. One man, waving a knife, chased another from the Bouncing Bosom Saloon. An elderly lady wearing a lot of rouge tried to beckon Dane up to a hovel stuck between the general store and the hotel. "Won't charge you much!" she shouted.

Dane just tipped his hat to her. He was relieved when Blue came out with his goods and they could head to camp.

"Burrister makes Smoky River seem a beacon of rectitude," Dane said.

THEY COOKED UP the meal as sundown streaked the sky: a stew of venison and the starchy cattail roots, with purslane and wild onions, and spitted grouse, rubbed with salt. Dane had eaten little in the last twenty-four hours, and the smell of the stew, especially, was tantalizing.

Dane had cleaned the fish and set them up on sticks to be smoked by the fire, Blue tended the spitted grouse, and they both glanced at the sky from time to time. Sunset was ending. Next time Dane looked up, it was getting dark.

"You think they're coming?" Blue asked.

"Maybe I gave them enough money to gamble with."

It got darker out. Still they waited. Then came a rustling in the bushes—at which Dane put a hand on the butt of his Colt in case it wasn't the Quinlans.

It wasn't. A boy of about twelve stepped out into the firelight. He was gaunt, had unkempt brown hair with bits of dry leaves stuck in it, and wore dirty trousers.

"Um—hello the camp," he said, staring at the stewpot.

"Hello," Dane said, taking his hand from the gun. "Come on in and set."

"Thank you, sir." But the boy stayed where he was. "I got a sister, and there's my mama, too. We was passing down below and saw your fire. I come up to see if I can ask for some food. Least for Mama and Teresa. We don't like to beg, but something happened and—we don't know what else to do. We haven't eaten but for some wild cabbage for two days—and nothing for two days before that neither." After a moment, he added, "And I ate some grubs last night."

"What's your name, son?" Dane asked.

"Calvin."

Dane nodded. "Bring 'em up, Calvin. Plenty to eat."

The boy vanished into the brush. Blue said, "Suppose they have a daddy they're not mentioning. Suppose he's using those kids as a decoy so's he can bushwhack us."

"That's a melancholy turn of thought. There's such a thing as being too careful."

Blue shrugged. "I lived this long without getting shot." He picked up his rifle and laid it across his lap.

About fifteen minutes passed, and once more the brush thrashed, and Calvin drew a small, hollow-cheeked girl into the firelight. She wore overalls; her long brown hair was braided. Behind them came their mother, shivering in the cold and breathing hard from the climb up the hill. She had lank brown hair and large, frightened brown eyes. Truly looked like she hadn't eaten for a while. She wore a dirty yellow frock over a man's trousers, and a shawl. The three stopped just inside the ring of light and stared at Dane. Then at the stewpot. Then at Blue. Then back at the stewpot.

"That everyone?" Blue asked.

"Yes, sir," said the mother, her voice quavering.

"Ma'am," said Dane, "you can call me Dane. My friend here is Blue. We've already met Calvin."

"I'm Isabel Cummings. This is Teresa."

"Pretty names! It's a privilege, ma'am. Please sit down, and we'll serve up some food."

They filed in and sat on a log, side by side, on the other side of the fire. The woman's worried eyes told Dane she was wondering if she could trust these two men.

Blue picked up the wooden plates and began to spoon stew onto them. The children watched his every move with wide eyes. "Now," Blue said, "this here's almost cooled off. A couple of no-account cowboys was going to join us, but they have not shown their faces, so you can have theirs, too. But seeing as you haven't eaten in a while, I'm going to give you each a smaller amount, first helping. You eat it and sit with that for a while. And if it stays down, you'll have some more. Corn cakes and grouse, too."

Dane got them his canteen and handed it to Mrs. Cummings; she handed it to the children, who drank thirstily.

Blue passed out three plates and three wooden spoons, and they all set to without hesitation. Partway through, Isabel remembered her manners. "Won't you fellas be eating?"

"Oh, yes, ma'am," said Dane. "Blue, have your dinner, and then I'll have mine." They had only four plates.

"The hell you say," said Blue. "I can go without longer than you can." He spooned stew onto the last plate, added one of the game bird's legs, and passed it over.

"Suit yourself, tough hombre," Dane said, picking up his spoon.

"Slow down, children," Isabel said. "The man was right."

"I feel good," said Calvin. "I don't think I'll have any trouble eating more."

Dane finished, then handed Blue his plate. "That'll do me for now."

He looked at Isabel and thought that, despite her shabby appearance, she was a woman of real dignity. "Ma'am. Calvin mentioned something happened . . . ?"

She wiped her mouth with the back of her hand, and drank a little water before passing the canteen to Teresa. "Yes, sir." She took a deep breath. "Something did. First thing was, my husband died on us. He worked into a cold night bringing the crops in and got caught in a rainstorm. A norther blew in, and the rain froze to his clothes. Caught pneumonia. And in ten days—he passed. He was a good man." She paused and pinched her lips together, and her eyes glistened in the firelight. "This was in Texas, halfway up the Panhandle. Crescentville. After that, we thought we might go and join my sister, Belle, in St. Louis. We packed everything in our wagon, sold our stock except for the draft horse, and set out."

Blue looked at her in surprise. "Alone?"

Calvin frowned. "I was with 'em. I had my pa's buffalo gun."

"Didn't do any good," Teresa said, looking at her empty plate.

"It misfired on me or I'd'a got one of them!"

"If it hadn't misfired, Cal, they'd probably have killed you," Isabel said.

"Who, ma'am?" Dane asked.

"Two men came along and robbed us of everything. One of them, the big man, his name's Tandy. Didn't hear the other's name used. Short fella with a derby hat and a stub nose. They took the wagon, everything."

"Pa's watch, too," Calvin said.

She nodded. "Your papa's pocket watch, too. Four days ago. They hitched their horses to the wagon and drove it up this way. Made us come along. And on the way, Tandy, he . . ." She glanced at the children, not wanting to say it, in front of them. Maybe not wanting to say it at all. But she wanted Dane to know what kind of men these were.

"I understand, ma'am," Dane said, feeling that familiar cold anger rising in him.

"They didn't feed us. They said they didn't want us to have the strength to run off. Couple days' travel, we saw no one else on the road. I heard Tandy talking to that other man about what they might do with us, and it sounded mortal. They were taking us into Burrister. Said they'd kill us if we spoke to law or complained the least bit, and we were to stick with them and do as they said. So the children and I hatched a plan, and when they started out again in our wagon, we jumped off the back and ran into the brush. One of them fired after us, but he missed. They didn't trouble to come after us, and we set out into the woods . . . slept under leaves and such. Two nights now, trying to find our way to somewheres safe. Holding each other to keep warm. Drinking from puddles." Her lips quivered.

"Don't have to say any more," Dane said. "Blue—
you think those fellas would still be in Burrister?"

"Ma'am," said Blue, "how much money did they take
from you?"

Her eyes flashed in anger. "Three hundred and forty
dollars and a fifty-cent piece!"

Blue nodded and turned to Dane. "They're still in
Burrister, all right."

FERRY JOHNSON WAS feeling a burning pain from his
wound and weak from loss of blood. But he stood
upright in front of Shine O'Hara and told him the
story straight.

"And so," he finished, "he shot me off my horse."
He jerked a thumb at his bandaged shoulder. "Still a
power of hurt."

Shine nodded thoughtfully. "Dane's a former Union
officer. Seems Grady was outmaneuvered in Willow
Canyon." Leaning back in his seat and tenting his fingers, he went on. "Grady should have figured Dane
wouldn't come into that canyon like a salmon in a fish
trap. Where are those Quinlans now? I wonder."

"That fella Buck from the Horseshoe W says they
rode south into Texas. But Brewster thinks they might've
gone to Burrister."

"If you find them and bring them back for trial, why,
Dane may come looking for them. Come out of hiding.
Which is just how I want it." Shine opened a drawer,
took out a bottle of whiskey and a cigar. He poured
himself a drink in a crystal goblet. Ferry watched but
didn't dare ask for any. Shine flicked a match alight

with a thumbnail and lit the cigar. He took a drink, then puffed at the cigar, looking at the ceiling as if there was something special to see up there. At last he said, "I might have to look into this myself, being as how Dane's got the bulge on Grady—and you and those two deputies can't be trusted to button up your shirts without them turning out crooked."

"Shine, I did everything I was supposed to do! It's not my fault Grady had it wrong—"

"Ferry—shut up."

"Sure, but—" He didn't like the warning in Shine's eyes, so he said, "Yes, boss."

"I'll tell you what's going to happen now. You will get yourself a room at my third-best hotel, and you will sleep. You will not go to a saloon. And in the morning, the two of us are riding out with Henderson and Flayle. We're going to Smoky River, where I will see to my new establishments and peruse the new help. Have to pay off certain councilmen, too. And then I'll personally see to it that Dane pays for murdering Johnny O'Hara."

A LONG ABOUT TEN o'clock, Dane was sure the Quinlan boys weren't going to show up. One of them must've won a handful of cash off some other fool, and now they were drinking up the proceeds.

Dane stood, stretched, and pondered Isabel and her two children, all of them sleeping by the fire in the blankets Blue had given them. Dane had laid his rain slicker over the two kids and his duster over Isabel, just in case rain clouds rolled in. It was a cold night, but

Blue had built the campfire up considerably, and the sky was clear. Stars peered curiously down at them. "Leastways doesn't look like it'll rain on them," Dane said softly. "Let's go find those lunkheads."

Blue nodded. "I'll saddle us up. Those kids—a thunderbolt wouldn't wake them."

Isabel opened her eyes and blinked around skittishly—then remembered where she was. "Dane . . ."

"Yes, ma'am?"

"Mr. Dane, Mr. Blue—thank you."

"That's all right. Have enough to eat?"

"More than enough. I think my stomach shrank to the size of a poor man's purse."

"There's more if you wake up hungry. I'll leave you my canteen. And there's the smoked fish and some corn cakes—make a good breakfast."

"Are you coming back?"

"We are. We're going into Burrister on an errand. Those cowboys supposed to meet us here are likely getting in trouble, and we need to herd 'em up here. They're good boys at heart, and they'll be glad to meet you. You rest, and we'll be back. And, ma'am?"

"Yes, sir?"

"You're safe with us."

She smiled and closed her eyes.

IT WAS ABOUT ten thirty when Dane and Blue rode into Burrister. It banged and squawked with music and shouts, and a bottle crashed into something and broke somewhere down the street. A low fog had crept in from the creek back of the town, and a woman stumbled through it, laughing, hand in hand with Dugmire's cook, Karl. He half dragged her, still laughing, into the hotel.

Lantern light from the saloons seemed to make ghosts of the curls of fog.

"Look!" Blue pulled up his horse and hooked a thumb at two men standing at a wagon about sixty feet away. Dane reined in and considered the strangers.

The two men—one big, the other little more than half his size—were arguing at the back of the wagon. The wagon's draft horse was hitched to a post beside the water trough. A couple of riding horses were tied to the rear of the wagon. Both men had their holsters tied down on their hips, and both had the scruffiness of men who had spent a lot of time running from the law, sleeping rough when they had to.

"You will give me my share now, by God!" said the shorter, stockier one in the brown leather vest and derby hat. "You've pinched some of it off! That was three hundred forty dollars, and where is it now?"

"Most of it's where I hid it, and keep your damn voice down!" Tall, big around the middle, freshly shaved, he wore a wide-brimmed hat with a low crown. Both men had seen the barber today, Dane figured. "You think I'd be fool enough to leave it in the wagon? Come on, I'll buy you another drink, and we'll ponder on it."

"Nothing to ponder," said the man with the derby hat. But he stalked sullenly back toward a saloon. The bigger man, shaking his head, followed after.

"Three hundred and forty dollars," Blue murmured.

"Yep. Forgot the fifty-cent piece." Dane contemplated the saloon.

Over the doorway hung an old, fading canvas banner in place of a wooden sign: *Molly's Parlor: Leisure and Good Times.*

Dane rode to a hitching post. "Blue, let's see if Ben and Dirk are in Molly's Parlor."

Molly's Parlor. The name of the saloon seemed familiar to Dane. Why? Had he been to this town before he lost his memory?

He and Blue tied up their horses and crossed the street to the saloon. Inside, they found nothing reminiscent of a parlor. It was a typical saloon with a long wooden bar, and the two men bellied up to it matched the description of the men who'd robbed the Cummings family. Beyond them was a row of bottles; many of them—probably moonshine—were without labels. Over the bottles a painting of a rather plump naked woman reclining invitingly on cushions hung askew. At her feet there were two bullet holes in the painting. Perhaps someone had been shooting at her toes.

The walls were blackened with soot from the smoky stove to one side of the bar. The air was gray with tobacco smoke. Men crowded around oaken tables, some of them splintery.

He knew the place. "I was here once before," Dane murmured to Blue. "I almost—"

"There's Ben and Dirk!" Blue nodded at a table in a corner. They were playing stud poker with Dugmire and a weathered, brown-bearded man in a bison-fur coat, all of them squinting past their smokes to see their cards.

"Just who I want to see," Dane said. Four strides took him to the table.

"Well, well," said Dugmire, glancing up at him. "Mr. Dane, I believe."

"Why, Dane!" Ben said, gaping at him. "Is it past sunset?"

"It's hours past it," Dane said. "You must've won some money."

"Sure did! I took one of those dollars and got into a game, and it grew! I got— Well, I had fifty dollars. Down to eight now. Still, more'n I started with. And I staked Dirk, too. How's about the rest of our money?"

"You're not getting your pay till we're headed out of town."

"Where we going?"

"We'll talk about that at the camp."

Dane noticed a curious onlooker standing against the wall near Dugmire, smoking a small cigar: a very small, bald man in a rumpled suit and thick spectacles. Something about him made Dane wary. He had a tumbler of whiskey in one hand, and he seemed to be singing to himself under his breath. Sounded like "The Little Old Log Cabin in the Lane."

Dane turned to Dugmire. "You bring your sheriff's badge with you, Dan?"

"I did not. Don't like to wear it less'n I have to. Some will regard it as a bull's-eye to aim at—do you see? You have a complaint about our noble citizenry?"

"Two men from out of town."

"At any given time, at least half the men in Burrister are just spending time here before they run out of coins. Can you be more specific?"

"You see those two at the bar? The one with the dented derby hat and the big man next to him?"

"Yes, they came in a couple days ago. They've been

some trouble, but it wasn't necessary to call the vigilance committee. We came to an agreement."

"One of the men is named Tandy. Don't have a name for the other."

"The man in the derby is Clonnick. The big fella does, in fact, go by Tandy."

"They robbed a woman and her two children of that wagon hitched across the street. Stole the wagon, their horse, their rifle, a watch, and three chests of other goods, mostly clothes, tools, and pots and pans—and three hundred and forty dollars cash. We just now heard them talking about the money with exact specificity."

"The lady told us what they looked like," said Blue, "and what their horses looked like. It matches up. They violated the lady, and she and the kids ran off when they overheard those varmints making some right ugly plans for them."

"You know this family, do you?"

"Isabel Cummings and her two children," Dane said. "Little girl is just nine. We met them earlier today, half starved and half frozen. They're resting at our camp."

"I see. Well . . ." Dugmire rubbed his chin and squinted at Clonnick and Tandy. "If all this can be proven beyond mere allegation . . ."

"Their papers are likely still in that chest in the back of the wagon," Dane said. "Would have Mrs. Cummings's name on them. There'll be clothes she can describe without you opening the chest first. There's their testimony, description of the men, her knowing the big man's name. . . ."

Dugmire looked inquiringly at him. "You a lawman?"

I don't know, Dane thought. But aloud he said, "Everyone knows that much about the law."

The little bald man with the spectacles had inched closer, seeming to listen to the conversation closely.

"I heard a story about the way the law works in this town last time I was here," said Blue.

"What story is that, pray tell?" Dugmire asked, scowling at him.

"That the law changes for you depending on how much you pay it," Blue said. "Even those two, they could pay a 'fine' for everything they did and go free."

"We do have expenses to pay around here. If what you say proves out, we'll confiscate the wagon and the money and take our fee from it and return the rest to the lady."

"And those two?" Dane asked, nodding toward the bar.

"Why, we'll hold them a few weeks and take their guns and horses and sell those as part of their fine. Then we'll let them go—too much trouble to keep them locked up. We don't hang for robbery. Might put them on a work detail though."

"They're guilty of rape, robbery, and kidnapping. They should be in the territorial prison for some years to come!"

"We have our own way of—"

"Of robbery?" Blue asked.

"Now, hold on!" Dugmire said, standing up. He swept back his coat, showing his dragoon pistol. "I'm the sheriff here!"

"You're no more a sheriff than I'm the governor of

Kansas," said Dane. "If you pull that dragoon, I'll kill you."

"You won't have to," Blue said, pointing his Henry rifle at Dugmire. "I'll do it. Give that dragoon to Ben there, Dan, real careful—and sit down."

Dugmire handed the bemused cowboy the gun and sat heavily down.

"What do you intend to do now?" Dugmire asked, looking at Dane.

"Seeing as I can't trust you to do the lawful thing, I'm going to take those two, hog-tied, to Dodge City. Turn them over to Bat Masterson. And the Cummings family will go along, if they agree to it, as witnesses."

The little man with the spectacles edged away and walked, as if casually, over to the bar. Dane watched him walk right up to Tandy. He tugged on Tandy's sleeve and whispered to him, nodded toward Dane, then stuck out his hand, expecting to be paid for something.

Tandy shoved him away, nudged Clonnick, then turned to glare at Dane. Clonnick turned from the bar, one hand on his gun.

"Who's the little bald gent?" Dane asked, letting his hand drop to his gun butt.

"Hm?" Dugmire looked. "Oh, that's Burl Chalmsey. Used to run an inn here. Lost it—he's got the laudanum monkey. Lives from spying on folks now. I see he's alerted your two robbers."

Till now Dane had been of a mind to disarm the two men before they knew what was coming. Dane had no desire to kill anyone. But now it looked like an armed confrontation was afoot.

Dugmire said, "Listen—you with the Henry rifle. Mind if I move away?"

"Do it and keep your mouth shut."

Dugmire got up and backed away from the table, farther out of the line of fire.

Clonnick whispered something to Tandy, who gave a grudging nod and started toward the door as if they were intent on riding out. Both men had hands on their guns. The bar had gotten quiet. Everyone was watching. A few men near the door slipped outside.

"Tandy, Clonnick," Dane said sharply. "Hold it!"

The two men kept walking.

"Stop or I'll gun you down," Dane added.

Clonnick stopped abruptly so that Tandy bumped into him. Tandy cursed him and spun toward Dane. "What the hell you want?"

"We have met the Cummings family. You're going to drop your guns and come along. I'm taking you to the law in Dodge."

"I don't know what the devil you're jawin' about!" growled Tandy. "That wagon is mine! The whole kit 'n' caboodle."

"I didn't say anything about a wagon. But as for that—let's go to the wagon, look through it, see if we can find any papers belonging to Isabel Cummings. She'll be along with us, once I've got you tied up, to testify. It'll be finished and done, Tandy."

"You the law? I don't see a badge!"

"Not the law. Just going to take you to it."

Tandy looked at Dugmire. "I paid you forty dollars to see we were square, Sheriff!"

Dugmire cleared his throat. "Afraid matters have

taken an unforeseen turn, gentlemen." He looked at Dane, then back at Tandy. "I recommend you drop your gun belts."

"All right," Tandy said, sighing. He unbuckled his gun belt and dropped it—grabbing the pistol as the holster fell to the floor. He whipped the gun up at Dane.

Dane's hand seemed to make up his mind for him. He drew and fired before Tandy got his weapon leveled.

Tandy staggered back, his pistol discharging loudly into the floor. Then he went to his knees, staring at Dane in surprise. And fell flat on his face.

"Yahhh!" yelled Clonnick, running for the door.

Blue's Henry rifle fired, and the impact caught Clonnick hard just as he had one foot in the air, spinning him to fall on his back.

"Dang it," Blue said. "That's what I get for shooting from the hip. Just trying to wound him."

"He looks tolerably dead, however," Dane said, holstering his gun.

"Never saw that trick with the gun belt before," Blue said.

"I don't think it was new to me," Dane said. "Can't quite recall."

The air was even darker now with gun smoke; the burned powder stung Dane's eyes. It was a familiar sensation. He felt little else. This was the first time he could remember killing a man, but if anything, he felt a sense of relief. It was a long trip to Dodge City.

"Well," said Dugmire, shaking his head in disgust, "that's *four* men you've killed in here, Dane."

Startled, Dane stared at him. "I was here before?"

"You don't remember killing three men in this room? You're a cold one, all right."

"Why'd I . . ."

"They were gunning for you. The Silmer gang. You'd killed their boss."

Dane nodded as if he remembered. And the memory was, in fact, padding around in the underbrush of his mind, like a stealthy cougar waiting to spring.

Silmer. Another name that sounded teasingly familiar.

He had a passing vision—men running at him in this very room, their pistols out. . . .

The memory was almost there but refusing to come clean out of hiding.

Dane turned to the Quinlans, who were gawping at him with identical expressions. "You boys coming to the camp, or you just going to sit there, looking like a couple of confused frogs?"

"Sure, Dane," Ben said. He licked his lips. "Not feeling an urge to cross you."

"I'm coming," Dirk said, nodding his head rapidly.

Dane sighed. "I'm not forcing you. But it's for the best you come along."

He turned to Dugmire. "You can keep the forty dollars, though it's probably stolen money. Use it to bury these men. Everything else they have, excepting their clothes, goes to Isabel Cummings. Including their horses."

"And saddles?"

"And saddles. You in agreement?"

"Do I have a choice?"

"To be blunt, Dan, no, you don't." He turned to the

watching crowd of awestruck men. "I'm going to search these two dead outlaws for the money and the pocket watch they stole. I'll leave their guns here."

He did as Blue watched the crowd, rifle in hand, in case the dead men had friends here. Dane found a silver pocket watch and sixty dollars in folding money.

"He said he hid some," Blue said when Dane told him.

Dane turned to Dugmire. "Where they been staying?"

"My hotel. Room six. I'll come along so you don't have to bust the door."

They went directly to the hotel, Dugmire calling out to Karl, who was just then coming out, tucking his shirt in his pants. "Karl, two dead men in Molly's. Check 'em for anything we missed of value, take their guns and belts, and get Dick to bury them. Oh, and Chalmsey. If he hadn't mixed in, we wouldn't have this mess to clean up. Make him do it, too, and don't pay him."

HELLO THE CAMP," Dane called, as he, Blue, Ben and Dirk approached the firelight. Dane was carrying a saddlebag over one shoulder.

"Oh, it's Mr. Dane!" Teresa cried.

He pushed through the brush, and she grinned happily at him. "Did you bring more food?"

"We've got some more venison hidden away," Dane said, taking off his hat and smiling down at her. "We've got something else, too." He looked up at Isabel and Calvin, standing behind Teresa, their faces gaunt in the campfire light. "First off, we've got a couple of no-account cowboys." The Quinlans and Blue emerged from the brush. "That one's Ben. This one's Dirk. Boys, take off your hat for the ladies."

The brothers took off their hats and nodded to Isabel. "Ma'am."

Teresa laughed because they said it at exactly the same moment.

"Got something else for you. Calvin, is this your pappy's watch?" He took it from his pocket and held it up by its chain.

"It is!" the boy cried. "But Mama give it to me when Daddy passed."

"Come and get it, then." The boy rushed up and took it from his hand.

"And give this to your mama." He handed over the saddlebag.

Calvin brought it to his mother. "What's in it, Mama?"

She opened it—and saw the money inside. Folding money, gold and silver.

"There's two hundred and forty dollars and fifty cents left, Isabel. They spent some, and they bribed the sheriff with forty dollars, too. But we found most of the rest in their room. Tandy cut a slit in a mattress and hid most of it there."

"Oh, my Lord," Isabel said, tears in her eyes. "I never thought we'd see any of it again."

"Calvin," said Blue, "this yours, too?" He had brought along the one-shot buffalo gun they'd found in the wagon.

"Yes!" The boy ran over and took it from Blue. "Thanks, Blue!"

"*Tanyan yahi,*" Blue said.

"What's that mean?"

"Means 'you're welcome.'"

"What about George?" Teresa asked. "Did they kill him?"

"That the draft horse?" Dane asked.

"Yes, sir!"

"He's just fine. We grained and watered George, and he pulled the wagon up close to the hill. Didn't complain once. He's resting down in a little piney woods not far from here by the wagon. And he's got a couple of new friends. You folks can have the horses belonging to the robbers, too. Along with the saddles and tackle. Might make up for most've what those . . ." He started to use a cussword and thought better of it. "What those men spent."

"You saved George, too!" Teresa ran to Dane and threw her arms around him.

He smiled—a broad and entirely involuntary smile. He'd never thought much of the idea of having children. But he was starting to change his mind.

Isabel came to him and took one of his hands and one of Blue's. "Thank you. Thank you both."

Both men, somewhat abashed, just nodded.

"Those men going to hanged?" Calvin asked as Teresa ran to look at her papa's watch.

"Won't be necessary as it happens," Dane said. "They're dead and buried."

Calvin's eyes got wide. "You killed 'em?"

"We had to. They didn't want to come peaceful."

"It's sinful to say so," Isabel said, dropping their hands, "but I'm glad."

"We're going to Smoky River," said Dane. "It's not

perfect, but no town is. If you folks want to come with us, I think I know a place you can stay for a while and catch your breath."

It would be a good place if the man was willing. They'd be out of the line of fire there.

Because it might not be safe for anyone to be around Dane. Not in Smoky River . . .

CHAPTER THIRTEEN

"BEN, YOU EVER see anyone pull a gun faster than that?" Dirk asked in a low voice as they rode across the rolling plains on their cow ponies. A wind slapped a thin rain at them in the gray morning light. They were a fair distance ahead of Dane and Blue, who were riding alongside the wagon.

"You mean in Molly's? I think he drew even faster shooting that rattlesnake."

"Well—you ever see anyone shoot a man that coldly before? He didn't even blink, Ben!"

"That—yep, I noticed it. Cool as a cucumber. Best way to be if you got to do it."

"He did it like he's done it a lot before."

"Kinda figured that, too."

"You really think we ought to go Smoky River? I'm starting to think maybe we oughtn't to."

"We told Dane we would. He says it's for our benefit

as much as his. We need to have it clear in the court records that we didn't rustle those cows."

"If the judge finds that way, Ben."

"There's sure some risk. But most folks don't hold with lynching. And those cattle weren't branded."

Dirk was silent. There were only the sounds of the horses occasionally snorting and their hooves slowly thudding on the trail. "We're up ahead, Ben, quite a bit. We got our money. Was we to head off in a gallop . . ."

Ben shook his head. "I said we'd come along."

"We didn't give our words! And he said it was our own choice."

"I know. But where would we go?"

"Texas is where."

"You can go, Dirk. Can't bring myself to do it. You know why?"

"Well?"

"Because that man saved your life—twice. He saved both of us at Willow Canyon. And what he done for those folks back there— Why, that's not a man you turn your back on."

Dirk thought about it. Finally, he nodded. "I reckon you're right."

M AYOR COSTIGAN AND Howard Armbruster were looking at Conrad with fixed expressions of doubt. Both sat in wooden chairs in Conrad's law office. Costigan—in his frock coat, his top hat in his lap, and wearing his best gently grave expression—looked more like an undertaker than a mayor in Conrad's view.

Arthur Conrad was pacing, sometimes with hands

in his pockets, sometimes gesticulating, trying to convince them that the town was in moral crisis. Armbruster was newly a member of the town council and in Conrad's view was following the mayor around like an obese puppy dog.

"Gentlemen," Conrad declared, "I saw a man shot dead for calling out a card-game cheat in O'Hara's new saloon! And it was a cheat, I assure you. Why, Howard here was there himself!"

"I didn't see what happened. Sheriff said the man was reaching for a gun under his coat. Good enough for me."

"That gun never did make a public appearance," Conrad said, stopping his pacing to point a finger at Armbruster.

"Don't point at me in that manner, sir!" Armbruster blustered. "Do you accuse me of some wrongdoing? Why, what I did see in that saloon was you being mighty cozy with a woman of loose morals and quick fingers!"

"Alice? The woman is more sinned against than sinning." He turned to the mayor. "It's not just that one cheat—one which I've no doubt was approved by O'Hara, long as the saloon gets its cut. There's a roulette wheel controlled by a foot pedal—"

"That's so the croupier can set it to spinning without getting out of his chair, I believe, Arthur," said Costigan mildly.

"The pedal is not to be used to *stop* the wheel—but I saw him stop it to the detriment of those who'd been on a hot streak. Saw it over and over!"

Costigan gave a sympathetic shake of his head. "In the smoky confines of a saloon, and after a drink or two, your eyes are likely playing tricks."

"Indeed? What of the framing of a mere petty thief who never owned a gun with the murders of Hanrahan and McCutcheon? What of the persistent rumors that certain council members are being paid off to ignore the—"

"What's this!" Armbruster cried, getting to his feet, hands balled into fists. "Are you now saying we're taking bribes?"

"I am not sure of their identities—"

The mayor stood up, too, more serenely, and put on his hat. "You cannot heed mere rumors, Arthur."

Seeing the men were about to leave, Conrad said angrily, "A special broadsheet is being distributed right now. I've hired young Lem and Ellie Waters to do it. They're handing them out to all and sundry!" He went to his desk, found a copy of the two-page edition, and handed it over to Costigan.

The mayor glanced at it. "Rather messily printed, Arthur. Tsk!"

"I have not the gift for printing that Joe had, but by gosh, it's legible!"

Costigan scanned it with bobbing eyebrows. "Dear me! These are quite possibly actionable accusations! There is such a thing as libel, Arthur! Calling O'Hara the boss of a criminal gang! Are you aware the man is here in town, staying at the Smoky River Hotel? He may have words with you!"

"Let him have his words, and I'll have mine, Mayor!"

Costigan folded the broadsheet and handed it back. "I don't think this will end well for you, Arthur."

He turned and led Armbruster, who was snorting and shaking his head, out the door.

* * *

FED AND CLEANED and with their best clothes back, Isabel and her children presented a nice picture as they sat by the fire in Jess Willoughby's sitting room. Teresa had coiled her mama's hair up on her head in braids, and they both wore clean clothes and white bonnets from the wagon.

There were nine people gathered around the fire in the big stone-built fireplace. Rand stood beside the Quinlans, his arms crossed, listening in wonder. The Cummings children and Blue sat on an Indian rug spread on the hardwood floor, happily gazing at the big fire and the enormous elk rack over it. Dane and Mrs. Cummings were on a leather settee pulled close to the fireplace, Willoughby sat, hands clasped, in an easy chair.

"And that's the story, Mr. Willoughby," Isabel finished. "We're beholden to Dane and Blue forever."

She'd left out the part about being violated by Tandy, and Dane didn't blame her a whit.

Jess shook his head. "Ma'am, that there are men like that at all—very sad." He looked at Dane. "You did good. Both of you." He turned to Blue. "But, Blue—you ran out on me. I guess I'm glad you were there to help, but . . ."

"Hell, Blue," Rand put in, "I tried out two men to take your place, and they didn't half measure up. I sent 'em packin'."

"We have some business in town, Dane and me," Blue said. "When that's done, if you still want me around, I'll come and help out."

"Blue," Dane began, "you don't have to come to town with me."

"Yes, I do," Blue said flatly.

"You know anything about horses, Calvin?" Willoughby asked.

"Yes, sir!" Calvin said. "And we got *three* horses now!"

"So I hear. Well, maybe you can help Rand out while you're here." He smiled at Isabel. "You folks are welcome to stay as long as you need to. I've got an extra bedroom."

"I'm grateful past words, Jess," Isabel said softly.

Willoughby's smile melted away as he turned to the Quinlan brothers. "And you two—! You knew better than to take up those cows."

"I believe they were set up for it, Jess," Dane said.

"Makes no difference. But"—Willoughby shrugged resignedly—"I am short of hands. Ben, Dirk, if you desire it, I'll try you on one more time, in a *probationary* fashion."

Their faces lit up. "Yes, sir!" Ben said. "Leastways for me!"

"And me, Mr. Willougby," said Dirk. "Gets too durn hot for me in Texas anyhow."

Jess stood up and shook hands with Ben, then Dirk. "Now—get out to the bunkhouse and give it a good cleaning."

"But we—" Dirk began, blanching.

Ben clapped a hand on Dirk's wrist. "We'll get 'er done, Mr. Willoughby. Come on, Dirk."

Dirk shrugged and followed his brother to the door.

Dane looked at Teresa and Calvin warming themselves at the fire and their mother gazing fondly at them. But he saw a shadow in Isabel's face—a pain she was trying to veil away. Dane guessed at its source. That which should only have been for her to freely give had been taken by brutal force. By the man Tandy.

She was a strong woman. Dane could sense it. A woman had to be strong to be a wife, mother, and farmer on the frontier. On the way to Horseshoe W, she'd spoken of that last harvest with her husband. She had worked beside him all day, trying to get it in before a winter storm set in, and she had been in the barn shucking field corn when he decided to go out again on that cold night. . . .

And she was a proud woman. She'd insisted that she and the children, though not fully recovered, collect water for the canteens, wash the wooden dishes and forks, and help pack up the camp.

She was a frontier woman. Like Suzanne.

Was Suzanne well? What had happened to Isabel and the children made him wonder if Suzanne was safe living away from town with only her mother there. Not even old Matthew was around to keep an eye out.

Dane shook his head. He should be with her. She'd as much as said she would marry him if the situation was set right.

It was dark out, too late to show up at her farm. But he made up his mind that tomorrow he'd ride to see her, before he went into the lion's den. . . .

A RTHUR CONRAD WAS humming to himself, that early morning, as he packed his buggy with his rain slicker, lunch, and fishing pole. The weather had become more kindly—it would surely be the last clement day this fall. He knew where there was a fishing hole downriver. He could find some peace there and think things through as he tried to catch some catfish and maybe bass.

The buggy had new rubber wheels on its tire rims, but still it was a jarring ride on the rugged trail that followed the bank downstream on the Smoky Hill River. Conrad's mind was so full of the affairs of Smoky River, he scarcely noticed it. Nor did he hear the hoofbeats of the three horsemen riding after him, muted by the sounds of the rushing river—running high and fast after a period of rains—and the squawking of his buggy springs.

There was a road following the river on the other side, too, occasionally visible through the screen of willows and cottonwoods. It was the more traveled route to and from Smoky River. Through a gap in the trees, he glimpsed someone he recognized there. The Lakota ranch hand, Blue-Snake, riding alone toward town. Conrad waved to him, and Blue-Snake Thompson raised his hand in return.

Half an hour later, Conrad reached a wide, deep place in the river, an indentation in the bank that he chose to regard as his personal fishing hole. It was especially murky and deep, perfect for a few hours' fishing.

"Should have come earlier, Jocelyn," he told his horse as the mare cropped grass along the bank. "Had trouble sleeping. I don't suppose that happens to you."

Conrad was just stringing the fishing wire on his rod when three men rode up behind him. He turned to them—and the greeting froze in his mouth unspoken. It was the two jumped-up deputies, Squint Brewster and the Swede, and Ferry Johnson, whose left arm was in a sling.

Brewster waved a copy of Conrad's broadsheet. "These here slanders cannot be tolerated."

"Mr. O'Hara's exact words, more or less," said Ferry.

"Well, if they're exact—" Conrad was stalling, hoping for a chance to run. But the river was behind him, and he was hemmed in by armed horsemen.

Hans pointed his pistol at Conrad. "You come up here, yah. On the road."

Conrad looked at the pistol. Then he walked up to stand close to the three horses.

"That way," Ferry said, pointing down the road away from town. "Start walking."

"You know, I have many friends in town. Bat Masterson is going to come back and . . . ah . . ."

"Oh, Masterson's too smart to do that," said Brewster, balling up the broadsheet and throwing it in the river. "Do what you're told, or we'll gut-shoot you." He drew his own pistol and aimed at Conrad's belly.

"Where are we going? If you're trying to frighten me, you've already succeeded."

"And 'cause you're scared, you'll say you won't publish any more insults against Shine O'Hara," Brewster said, nodding. "You'll be lying." He rubbed the back of his hand over his nose to wipe away a drip and said, "What do we plan for you? There's something we call a Shine ride. You're going on one."

"Except you was going to make him walk," Ferry said.

"True enough. It'll be a Shine walk."

"Is this how you did it with McCutcheon and Hanrahan?" Conrad said, looking over his shoulder. There was no one visible on the far bank.

Brewster cocked his pistol. "All right, let's see if I can shoot right through your belly button."

"You can't see it," said Ferry.

"I'm gonna guess. That's the fun." He aimed carefully.

Conrad raised his hands. "I'll do as you ask." He turned and started down the road. They rode slowly up behind him.

"This is too blamed slow," Brewster said. "Get a-running!"

Conrad began to jog along, thinking about making a quick dart into some brush. He might jump in the river and try to swim for it.

He looked at the brush to his right—

A bullet kicked up dirt between Conrad and the brush, the gun's report echoing across the flat landscape to their left.

Conrad gasped and looked pointedly straight ahead.

"You won't get two steps if you try it," Hans said.

Minutes passed, and Conrad began to breathe hard.

"Still kinder slow," said Ferry.

He fired his gun at the ground behind Conrad, who thereupon found the strength to run faster.

Soon he was sweating. His lungs began to ache. Arthur Conrad was a man who spent most of the day at his desk, and he was in no shape for running.

Are they just trying to frighten me into silence? Conrad wondered. *Or do they plan to kill me?*

A quarter mile on, they came to a hill with a bluff overlooking the river. The road rose up the hill, and Conrad gasped his way up it, stumbling along by the time he reached the grassy top. A couple of oak trees stood near the bluff, one of them with roots reaching out of the bluff toward the river. Part of the hill must have collapsed.

"Slow down and walk over to your right till I tell you to stop," Brewster said. "If you run, I'll shoot you in the spine. Then you'll have to crawl where we tell you to go."

Conrad slowed to a walk. He wiped sweat from his forehead and thought, *They're going to kill me. May as well run.*

But there were three men with guns pointed at him. He might dodge one gun but not three. The threat of a bullet in the spine . . .

"Stop there!" Hans barked.

Conrad stopped, ten paces from the edge of the bluff. It was perhaps fifty feet down to the river. If he sprinted, perhaps he could leap into the water.

"I can see you gettin' ready to run," Brewster said. "Don't try it."

The horses trotted up close to him, behind. Hans was saying, "I chust think we should knock him a good one on the head, toss him in."

"I was figuring something like that," Brewster said. "Just a drowning. What they call a misadventure."

"Maybe so," said Ferry. "Sure would like to string him up though. Nice big oak over there. Could be suicide, too."

Conrad just stood there, swaying, wiping sweat from his eyes. Everything seemed shockingly vivid. The trees, the clouds blowing along the horizon, the smell of the river rising to him. Ravens called somewhere near.

My last experience of life, he thought.

D ANE AND BLUE rode hard alongside the river, the wind in their faces. Dane's hat blew off, but he didn't stop for it. Blue had seen Brewster and the others riding up behind Conrad, and he'd ridden fast to rejoin Dane, finding him on the road just before Marrin Farm.

Dane wondered if they were too late. Would they shoot Conrad and bury him out here somewhere? The river was handy. Maybe they'd drown him.

He bent over and whispered in Pard's ear, "Give me all you got, Pard! Come on!"

The mustang seemed to understand, and it extended its neck and galloped even faster. Dane had to hold on tight.

There—at the top of the hill up ahead. He saw three riders sitting on their horses. Now one of them was getting down. . . .

Dane and Blue rode up the hill, and the riders turned to face them just as they arrived. Dane reined in, and Pard skidded to a stop. He slid from the saddle, one hand on his gun. Blue took his Henry from its saddle holster.

"Don't fire unless you have to, Blue!" Dane called, taking in the tableau. As Dane had hoped, his pounding arrival had startled the gang's horses so that they reared. The men had to get control of their horses before they could ply their guns smartly.

Dane stepped forward, one hand on his gun but the other lifted in a gesture calling for restraint. "Hold your fire!"

Arthur Conrad had turned to face the new arrivals, his eyes alight with hope. "Oh, thank God. . . ."

"Holster your guns and ride peacefully out!" Dane said. He was still reluctant to shoot at the Swede and Brewster. They had deputy badges on their coats. Shooting lawmen, even bent ones, was frowned upon by the Kansas judiciary. Ferry had his Colt pointed at Conrad.

Brewster and Hans got their horses under control. Hans pointed his gun at Dane—

"Drop it!" Blue shouted, aiming his rifle at Hans from the saddle of his blowing horse.

Hans looked at Blue, saw that he had the drop on him. The Swede dropped his pistol.

Brewster was trying to get a bead on Dane, but the mustang was in the way. Dane was hesitant to draw and start a general gunfight. Conrad would almost certainly catch a bullet.

"Drop it, Brewster, or I'll blow a hole right through the side of your head!" Blue shouted.

Brewster dropped his gun and raised his hands, but Ferry Johnson stepped behind Arthur Conrad and put his pistol to the back of the lawyer's head.

"This man stays with us!" Ferry shouted. "We'll let him live—but he comes with me!"

Dane shook his head. "You shoot him, I'll kill you," Dane said. "I have a notion you know I can do it, Ferry."

Ferry snorted. "You haven't even got your gun out."

"Then cut me down," Dane said, growling the words. "Or drop your gun. You don't drop it, I'll kill you, whatever you do."

Ferry licked his lips—and then jerked the pistol's muzzle to aim at Dane.

Dane drew and fired before Ferry could pull the trigger. Ferry spun, shot through the forehead, and fell flat on his back. His body twitched a time or two and then went limp.

"Holy cats," Conrad muttered, turning to stare at the dead man.

"You murdered him!" Brewster said. "Just like you murdered Johnny O'Hara! I saw both killings!"

Johnny O'Hara. That name . . .

Dane shook his head. "Ferry pointed his gun at me."

"You're a liar! He had his gun out to protect our prisoner! We were going to question him and take him back to town! He's accused of slander and fraud!"

"They were going to kill me," Conrad said, walking unsteadily over to stand beside Dane. "They were discussing how to do it. Ferry decided to knock me on the head and drown me!"

"Lies!" Hans said. "Yah, that is a lie! The sheriff, the mayor—they will believe us! We are lawmen, not you two! You are wanted men now, pointing guns at lawmen! Killing a member of our posse!"

"Ferry Johnson was wanted in Texas and Oklahoma on suspicion of murder, Dane!" Conrad said. "We got telegrams back on him and Brewster and Hans here. Hans is wanted in the Dakotas for rape and robbery. Brewster's wanted for questioning in Denver—on a murder case."

"Don't matter you got your friends to tell lies in telegrams!" Brewster said. "A telegram's no proof of anything!"

"And Bat Masterson," Conrad went on, grinning, "has dispatched that judge out to us. Justice William Peebles! Has a reputation of being a righteous man."

Dane smiled. "Good news."

"You and Blue are my good news. What're you going to do with these vile miscreants who style themselves lawmen?"

"They still have the badges. They can ride out. They can take their guns in their saddlebags—not in hands or holsters. And they can take this man's body with them if they choose."

"Yah, we take his body to show the murder!" Hans said, climbing down from his horse. He picked up Ferry's body and carried it to his horse, slung it over the big horse's rump. He used a coil of rope to tie it in place and picked up his gun.

Dane said, "Mine's still drawn, Deputy."

Hans shrugged and dropped the gun in a saddlebag. He picked his partner's up, tossed it. Brewster caught it and—noting Dane's gun swung his Colt Army pistol his way—he dropped it carefully into a saddlebag.

"You'll hang for this, Dane," he said. "And for murdering Johnny O'Hara."

Then Squint Brewster and the Swede galloped off for town.

CHAPTER FOURTEEN

"WHO'S THIS JOHNNY O'Hara?" Conrad asked, climbing into his buggy.

"Wish I could remember," Dane said, standing by his horse at the fishing hole. He was dusting off his hat, which was somewhat worse for wear, found on the way here.

"What do you mean, you wish you could remember?" Conrad asked, looking curiously up at him.

"I'll tell you about it as we go," Dane said. "Not much of my past is yet known to me. But it's starting to come back a little at a time."

Blue sat on his paint pony and mused, "We should all three ride away from town a piece. That long-rifle man is like to be round there. We could be shot off our horses and never see the shooter. There's another bridge about four miles on. . . ."

Dane nodded. "We can circle back on the other side of the river. I expect Jess will take one more in for a day or two till we get things figured."

They were crossing the low, almost flooded log bridge, far less substantial than the one in town, as Dane finished answering the lawyer's questions. The bridge was just four logs shorn of bark and lashed together, the chinks closed up by packed mud and gravel. The riders and the buggy caught spray as the fast, high water threw itself against the bridge, and Dane was glad when they made it across the slippery logs. "That bridge is going to be washed away one of these days," he said.

"Everything gets washed away sometime," Blue said. "Best marry her."

"What?"

"Suzanne. You ask her?"

"Why, it's none of your . . . Well, that is . . . Yes, I did. She almost said yes."

"Ask her again."

"Blue, why are you suddenly so opinionated on my personals?"

"Because someday, the bridge will break up and wash away."

Puzzling over that exchange, Dane rode up beside the buggy. "Forgot to ask if they hurt you any, Arthur."

"Just my pride. And my feet. Maybe we should all lay low till the judge arrives."

"Maybe."

The day was getting cloudy, Dane noted, as they rode down the west-side road. There was a snap in the wind from the north, a hint of the coming winter.

Five miles and they were back on the road that led toward Suzanne's farm.

"Arthur, I'm going to see Suzanne. And act on some advice. Blue will ride with you to the Horseshoe W. Tell Jess what happened. He can be a reserved snob of a man; he's a grouchy, overdressed son of a gun. But Jess Willoughby's a good man. He needs to know about all this."

Dane waved and turned east toward the Marrin Farm. When he got there, Dane found Suzanne outside, taking advantage of the rainless day by hanging clothes on the line. She wore her work clothes and a woolen jacket, and she had her hair tied back in a braid.

He tied Pard to the fence and walked over to her. "Miss, can you wash my socks for me?"

She turned and smiled. "Here you are. Back to stay?"

"I'm drawn back here like iron to a magnet. But things have gone from bad to worse, Suzanne. I just killed Ferry Johnson."

"You killed a man today?" She shook her head. "The magnet for you is trouble, Dane."

"He gave me no choice. I had to shoot him dead. He and those deputies had abducted Arthur Conrad. They were going to kill him, and Ferry was about to shoot me."

Suzanne put her hand over her mouth. "Oh, Lord. And the deputies?"

"I let them go."

"They'll say shooting Johnson is murder!"

Dane nodded ruefully. "They already said so. But Blue and Conrad are witnesses that it was self-defense. And those deputies may have to head for the hills. Arthur got telegrams in saying Brewster's wanted for questioning for murder in Denver and Hans is wanted out in the Dakotas for robbery and worse. Still, to get a fair break, I'll need a fair judge. That could be Bat's friend Justice Peebles." He took a deep breath. "Suzanne, I—" He broke off and took her hands. "There's another judge I want to make my case to. I want to talk to your mama."

"And ask her for my hand? I'm a grown woman, Dane. I'll make up my own mind about that. Anyway—" She sighed. "I think she's come to like you—but I doubt if she'll give it her blessing."

"Let me come in and talk to her anyway. I'd feel better. I don't want to hide things from your mother."

"Come on, then."

He led Pard around to the back of the house, where there was water and grass, and then followed Suzanne inside, hat in his hands. Mrs. Marrin was sitting in a chair by the fire, squinting at her sewing in the fireplace light. "Mr. Dane! You know, I was just thinking of you. That crank on the well is all to splinters."

"I'll see to that, ma'am. I have come now to tell you that, if all goes well, I plan to ask Suzanne to marry me. I am hoping for your blessing."

Mrs. Marrin laid down her sewing. Her mouth was quirked into a puzzled frown. "I saw you two canoodling not so long ago. You've done it all behind my back."

"It was our first kiss, Mama," Suzanne said. "And some overdue at that."

Mrs. Marrin clasped her hands in her lap and shook her head firmly. "I cannot give my blessing to a marriage with a wanted man."

"It's a misunderstanding, Mama. Everyone knows the sheriff is crooked."

"I won't know it till the court declares it so. When I was in town yesterday, Mr. Armbruster said this man came to the rescue of a gang of rustlers!"

Dane was trying to think of how to lay out the real story when Suzanne said, "Mama, I am not ready to marry Dane—the impairment of his memory makes it impossible to know if he's already married."

"I don't think so," Dane hastened to say.

"But you don't know for sure?" Mrs. Marrin said, looking at him sternly.

"Well . . ."

"Mama, his memory is beginning to return to him. And if it doesn't come back completely, why, we could trace him somehow, find his hometown. Learn the truth that way. It may take time, but it does not matter. I will marry no other man my whole life long."

Dane was taken aback at that and deeply moved. "Suzanne, I—"

Then he heard the drumming of hooves out on the road. And a gunshot.

One hand on his gun, Dane strode to the window and looked out to see eight men on horseback gathered outside the gate. He made out Sheriff Jipsell, Brewster, the Swede, Armbruster, and the gambler who called himself Edmund Earl; with them was a man in a colorful suit and a cream-colored homburg, a face tantalizingly familiar, and there were two men with him Dane had never seen before. They had the look of hired guns; one had a Winchester in his hand, the other a cocked Colt. Dane noted that Earl carried a long rifle in a saddle holster, and on it was a telescoping sight.

Jipsell had his pistol pointed at the sky. He'd fired the shot to get their attention, and now he fired once more.

"What is it?" cried Mrs. Marrin.

"Mama, get into the back room!" Suzanne said. "Go!"

"I demand to know what is going on here!"

"It's one of those phony posses Jipsell favors," Dane said, his heart sinking.

He was surprised to find a shotgun poking beside him, aimed toward the window. He turned to see it was in Suzanne's hands. Her face was angry, determined. Beautiful.

"Come out without a gun and your hands up, Dane!" called Jipsell. "You're wanted for murder! We know you're here! You were seen! Surrender so the ladies aren't threatened by gunfire!"

Dane nodded to himself. He had no choice with the ladies here. Eight gunmen could riddle the house with bullets. Suzanne seemed ready to use the shotgun, and that would draw fire to her. He must surrender. "Suzanne . . . my darling . . ." He put a hand on her arm. "Step away from the window." He took off his gun belt.

"Dane—no! They'll lynch you!"

"Why, I have friends in town. They will see I get a trial," Dane said. He hung the gun belt on a peg and opened the door a little.

"Dane!" Suzanne cried out. "Don't!"

"Suzanne, get away from that window!" Mrs. Marrin hissed, coming to drag her back.

Dane flattened beside the door, opened it a crack, and yelled, "I'm coming out! Hold your fire! I am disarmed!"

"Then, come out, hands up!" Jipsell responded.

"Mama," Suzanne was saying, "let go of me!" She pushed her mother away and stepped to the window, shotgun still in hand.

Dane opened the door and stepped through. The gambler was now nowhere to be seen. He raised his hands. . . .

"Dane, look out!" Suzanne said. He threw himself flat, and a bullet cracked into the doorframe just where he'd been—he saw the smoke from the Springfield rifle in the gambler's hands. In a split second, Dane realized that the assassin had moved off to the left corner of the yard for a better shot at the man he had been hired to kill—a place where the posse would not interfere. He had to make sure his fee wasn't given to a hangman. And then a boom from the house and a tinkle of glass, and the assassin screamed and spun around, cut down by Suzanne's shotgun.

The two new gunmen with the posse fired—one at Dane, the Winchester bullet slashing over him and ricocheting in the house. A woman screamed as the other fired his pistol at the window. More glass shattered.

"*Suzanne!*" Dane shouted, scrambling back, rolling away from the door. Suzanne was trembling, crouching under the window, looking openmouthed at her mother, who was lying on the floor in a pool of blood.

"Hold your fire till I say!" Jipsell shouted. "Get down—behind the horses!"

Dane stared at Mrs. Marrin in shock. *She was hit by the ricochet. By a bullet meant for me.* He got up to a crouch and grabbed his pistol, turned to see Suzanne step to the door; she stood just to the side of it and shouted, "You've killed my mother! You—you immoral imbeciles! You've *killed her*!"

Dane took her arm and tugged her back from the door. "Get down, Suzanne, for God's sake!"

"Oh, Lord!" Armbruster's voice. "No one said we'd be killing women!"

"Shut up, you fool!" snarled Jipsell.

His head whirling, heart pounding, Dane tried to see the way forward. Then he noticed that Suzanne's arm was bleeding.

"You're shot!"

"No . . . it's broken glass from when they shot in the window. . . . It's not bad." She began to sob, pressing her forehead to his shoulder.

"I'm sorry, Suzanne. This is my fault."

"No!" she said sharply, looking at him in wild fury. "No it is *not*. It's their fault! And it's the sickness in the town that no one speaks about, Dane! It's the fault of those without courage to stand up to them!"

Dane nodded. "You're right. But . . ."

Then he heard the men outside talking. "I told you we need this kerosene, yah!" Hans was saying. "Chure, we use it now!"

"Swede! Wait!" Jipsell's voice. "You fools have gone too far!"

"She'll make trouble for us!" came another voice. A familiar voice. But still without a name.

"Hans—come back with that!" Jipsell yelled.

Dane went to a crouch at the window and saw Hans running toward the house, his gun in one hand and a gallon of kerosene in the other. In the open jug was a burning rag. He lifted it to throw at the house—

Dane fired, shooting the jug. The burning rag caught the fuel as the jug burst, and it exploded into flame. Hans screamed, a figure of fire running, trailing flame, firing his gun at nothing. . . . He ran back toward the horses—and in an act of mercy, Jipsell shot him in the head. He fell, burning, near the gate. The horses reared and whinnied and tried to run. Cursing, the men struggled to control them.

"Suzanne, if I fight them here, they'll take cover and fire into the house. That's six heavily armed men out there. They'll splinter the house with bullets, honey. Now, I want you to go out back of the house. Pard likes you. He'll let you ride him. You ride through the orchard, open the fence gate back there, head west. Maybe you can fetch Blue and some others at Willoughby's."

"Dane—don't go out there."

He kissed her hand, then went to the door. "Sheriff! You give me your word you'll take me alive into town, and I'll come out!"

There was a muttered, inaudible colloquy. Then Jipsell called, "You have my word!"

"Dane, no—"

He turned to look at her. She looked so pale, so wild-eyed. "Get on the horse and ride. They might decide you have to go to town with us. We don't want that. Keep the house between you and those men till you're well away. I love you, Suzanne."

Then Dane stepped to the door and threw his gun

out. "There's my gun!" He took a step through the door, raising his hands, expecting to be shot down.

With relief, he heard Suzanne running through the house to the back door.

He could see six men, just getting their horses back under control. Armbruster was gaping in horror at the body of Hans Husman. Black smoke was swirling up from the still burning body. Dane glanced to the left, saw the still form of the dead assassin.

Good for you, Suzanne, he thought. What a woman she would be to ride the river with.

"Come out farther," said the man in the cream-colored homburg.

Dane walked out, keeping his hands high, looking at Jipsell, who was climbing onto his horse. The others came into view, training their guns on Dane. "Some say your word isn't worth much, Jipsell. I'm taking a chance on them being wrong!"

The man in the homburg climbed on his horse, raised a silver-plated pistol to take careful aim at Dane. . . .

Jipsell pushed the man's hand down. "No. I'll not have it done like that. He'll be hung, and that's good enough."

"He'll talk about the dead woman," said the stranger in the fine clothes. There were diamond rings gleaming on his fingers and one in a stickpin on his lapel.

"That was a ricochet—Grady did it when he fired, and he's dead."

"We should finish this now!"

"I don't usually give my word, O'Hara. But I promised my pa that when I did, it'd be good. He's going to town with us."

"Very well," said O'Hara. "Maybe it's for the best."

O'Hara, Dane thought. *Shine O'Hara.*

The man's face came into full focus for him now. And the memories lined up and began marching back to him. . . .

CHAPTER FIFTEEN

DANE WAS RIDING toward Smoky River with a shot-gun at his back.

He was on the Swede's horse. Flayle, riding to his right, had hold of the horse's reins. Beyond him rode Armbruster, shaking his head and muttering under his breath. On the left were Jipsell and Shine. Henderson was riding behind Dane, the shotgun propped on his hip. Worried about Suzanne, Dane didn't much care. Shine had spoken of taking care "of that" later.

Dane listened to the men around him talking as they all trotted on their mounts toward Smoky River. Armbruster commenced something close to sobbing. "That woman, lying in there—that's Miz Marrin! I just bought two pies from her for the bakery just yesterday. . . ."

"It was an accident," Brewster said, shrugging. "We'll see she gets a fine burial soon enough."

"We can't be goin' around—"

"*Shut up*, Armbruster," said Jipsell, an icy warning in his tone.

"Where's the other woman gone, do you suppose?" Shine asked. "Squint, you look through that house close like I told you?"

"I did, boss! Looked under the beds and all. She wasn't in the house. The back door was open. Could be she rode out through that orchard. She's liable to cause trouble."

"We'll reckon with that when the time comes," said Shine O'Hara.

Dane had heard Shine use those same words another time. . . .

IT WAS A warm spring night in Steeple Rock, in a plush back room of O'Hara's dance hall. Dane was there. Working for O'Hara as a hired gun.

Dane was standing near the door, arms crossed, listening and watching. Seated in front of Shine's desk were Ferry Johnson, Squint Brewster, Tol Henderson, and Al Flayle. Johnny O'Hara, Shine's young cousin, was half perched on a window ledge; he wore a Stetson tilted back on his neatly cut brown hair, sported a weedy mustache and a fringed buckskin shirt. Dane had kept his distance from Johnny and the hires from the get-go. He just didn't cotton to them.

"We're not going to wait for D'Enfer to make his move," Shine said. "We're gonna stir him up and take him down. He was just in Hutchinson's place bragging how he's going to take his claim to the mine to the ter-

ritorial government. Now, that mine belongs to me and
we can't let him take it away."

"If it's yours, how's he going to take it?" Dane
asked. "Your claim will stand up, won't it?"

The others looked at him in disbelief. Did he know
nothing about Shine?

Shine O'Hara narrowed his eyes and looked at
Dane as if he'd never seen him before. "Of course I
own the claim! But—he disputes it. Said he had it first.
He's lyin'!"

"Easier to go to the governor yourself and show
your papers for the mine than to go to war over it."

"Remind me, what did I hire you for?" Shine asked,
his tone dripping with sarcasm.

The other men grinned at that.

Dane smiled. "Bodyguard mostly, you said. And to
defend your rightful claim. Anyone not appointed by
the law comes and shoots at you, I'll defend you. And
I'll defend a rightful claim."

"I told you not to hire a lawman, Shine," Henderson
said. He was a rangy man with crooked teeth, a handlebar mustache, and his mottled head shaved clean.
He had long arms and wore his gun belt low over his
denims. Dane had seen him spur a drunk into a fight
just so he could shoot him. On a bet. He collected the
money over the dead man's body.

"I'm not a lawman," Dane said. "I had the job for a
time. They asked me to resign."

"For killing too many folks, what I heard," said
Johnny O'Hara, smirking.

"Hell, I'd have given him a bonus for that," said
Shine, looking at the gleam in his rings.

The men laughed. Dane didn't.

"He's got a big reputation, but I ain't seen him show how's he got it," said Flayle. A stocky man with a scraggly beard, Flayle was usually grinning, oftentimes lopsidedly. He wore a long bison-fur coat he didn't seem to take off no matter how warm the room was.

"That's true, Al," said Shine. "Dane, you can show us how good you are tomorrow night. We're going to raid the D'Enfer camp. We'll toss some brands in there and wait till they start shooting. Then you shoot a couple of D'Enfer's men. He dotes on his miners—he'll come looking for us. We'll be waiting. And he *won't* be going to the governor."

Dane thought it over. He knew they'd call him yellow if he didn't go. But this wasn't what he'd signed on for. Plus, he was now fairly sure O'Hara had no rightful claim. "I don't shoot men down as part of a plan—not since I was in the Army. If anyone comes hunting you, Shine, I'll protect you."

"He's afraid he'll catch some lead!" Ferry sneered. He shifted his big quid of chewing tobacco, spit into a spittoon, and added, "He don't go with us, he's a waste of your money!"

Dane ignored him. "You riding along on that raid, Shine?"

Without a speck of embarrassment, Shine said, "Nope."

"Then I need to stay with you so I can watch your back."

"Lookin' for reasons to stay home," said Al Flayle.

"Shine . . ." Dane let out a long breath. "Supposing you hit those diggings and stir them up, what happens if D'Enfer hires his own professional allies? D'Enfer's men might come after you in force."

Shine pursed his lips, then shrugged. "We'll reckon with that when the time comes. You going to keep your mouth shut about this?"

"Nothing to tell." *Not yet anyway.*

Shine waved him away. "We'll talk later. You go on and wait for me in the bar, Dane."

Dane smiled. Shine didn't want to do any more planning with him listening. "Sure thing, boss."

He went down to the bar and ordered a beer. Shine never did come down for that talk.

The raid happened that very night—but it didn't work. Shine's men rode by the miners' camp, whooping and tossing burning brands. There was only one shot—the diggings sentry shot Flayle in the arm, knocking him loose from the saddle so he was dragged a piece by the stirrup. The sentry retreated behind the earthworks they'd put up around the mine, and no one else started shooting. They just waited back there for Shine's men to come closer. And Shine's men didn't want to do that.

Next day, Dane bought a couple drinks for the town assayer. Jude Haver was his name. The assayer's opinion was that D'Enfer legitimately had the rights to the mine. "I ain't a lawyer, but I know he got the papers."

Dane nodded. He decided that in the morning he'd give O'Hara his money back. And he'd ride out.

That night, Henderson, Ferry Johnson, and Brewster caught Russ D'Enfer coming out of a saloon, Cozy's Whiskey and Beer. Dane wasn't there when it happened; he heard about it from the saloonkeeper:

Russ had a fine new horse he'd bought somewhere out of town. Henderson knocked him down. Brewster took his gun and accused him of stealing the horse. Ferry said Russ D'Enfer was going to hang for it. Shine figured that would bring the senior D'Enfer gunning for him—and he could simply have him shot down.

Dane got to the hanging tree just in time to see them hang the boy.

A cold anger rose up in him, and his hand trembled over his gun. But there were eight men up there at the hanging tree, and he had no rifle in hand to shoot the rope. It was too late to save Russ D'Enfer.

Dane went to the Griddle Saloon, where the sheriff liked to do his drinking. The old man just shook his head sadly. "Can't help you."

"Shine O'Hara murdered that boy!"

"I thought you worked for O'Hara?"

"Not anymore!" Dane tossed a small leather bag of gold on the bar. "He can have that back. Let's you and me ride for Denver. We can get a US marshal up here."

"For what? Horse stealing's a hanging offense around here, Dane."

"He didn't steal that horse! They set him up." He raised his voice. "Shine O'Hara is a cheat and a murderer!"

"What did you say?" Johnny O'Hara was playing poker in the corner. But he threw his cards down and stood up.

Dane ignored him. "You going to do your job or not, Sheriff?"

The bartender—Gully, his name was—ducked down behind the bar, shouting, "Look out!"

Dane turned as he drew his gun and saw Johnny

O'Hara pointing a gun at him, and in pure reflex, he shot him. Johnny spasmodically triggered the cocked gun, and the bullet cracked into the bar. Then he fell facedown over the card table. The back of his head showed a terrible exit wound.

"Holy hell—he's killed Johnny O'Hara!" said the sheriff. He scowled at Dane and poked him in the chest with a gnarled finger. "You get out of town—now!"

"He drew on me."

"They'll come gunning for you. They'll shoot the place up. And you won't be the only one to die. Get going—get out of Steeple Rock, or you'll have to shoot me, too!"

Dane growled to himself, holstered his gun, and walked to the door—stopped there for a moment to look at Johnny O'Hara's body drooped over the table. The other players had backed off and were looking at Dane in horror.

Feeling sick, Dane went out, got on his horse, and set out for the road. Snow was falling thickly, whipped at him by a cold wind as he galloped away from Steeple Rock. It didn't feel good, riding out like this. But if he fought Shine's men, there'd be no end of killing.

The snow whirled, and the darkness thickened.

Dane was riding around the curve by Squaw's Cliff when something knocked him off his horse—the rifle's report reached him as he fell. The stallion ran off and Dane, shot in the left shoulder, was too dazed to chase him down. He got to his feet, feeling wobbly, and drew his Colt. Another shot from across the narrow canyon kicked up dirt at his feet. He fired at the muzzle flash, just glimpsed through the snowfall, emptying his gun. Hoofbeats drummed behind him. He turned to see

Brewster and Ferry Johnson and Henderson riding up, firing their guns at him—and he staggered back as a couple of rounds hit him. The second one knocked him off the cliff.

Then he was falling, snow swirling around him. There were tree branches and crunching sounds and the sharp smell of pine sap—and there was a *thump*.

The next think he remembered was Elias Keggum dragging him from the broken pine branches at the base of the cliff.

And he remembered—the absence of memory.

H IS MEMORY WAS restored—shoved at him, a torrent of images and feelings coming at him now, as the posse took him into Smoky River to be summarily judged and hung for murder.

Dane remembered his life. His parents were Marcus and Sylvia Dane. Marcus had been a carpenter—teaching his son the trade—before starting his own sawmill. He'd passed in seventy-one. Dane's mother was still alive—at least last time he'd seen her back in Gatesville, Missouri, where he'd grown up. He had a brother named Oliver.

He remembered it all clearly now. He was not married. No wife, no children. He knew it for a fact—a fact he'd recalled too late. If he'd known sooner, he might've been able to marry Suzanne, take her away from here.

He'd lost her and failed her, too. He should never have gone to see her at the farm today. That rash act had led to her mother's death.

They were almost to town now.

"I think we should hang him from that oak tree over by the bridge," Brewster said. "That's a nice spot for it. Right in the middle of things. Folks can gather. Ferry would've liked that."

"Y'know, Dane, you made one colossal, stupid mistake, killing Johnny," Shine said.

"He'd have shot me dead otherwise. His gun was cocked."

Shine dismissed Dane's assertion with a wave of his hand. "He had good reason to kill you. You were slandering me in front of the public! That cannot be borne."

The horsemen rode on in silence till they reached the sheriff's office. They tied up the horses, and Henderson reached up with one of his long arms, grabbed Dane's elbow, and pulled him out of the saddle. Dane twisted in the air so he'd fall flat, as he'd learned to do when bronc busting in Texas, to keep from breaking bones. He gasped for breath, the air knocked out of him.

Henderson stepped back out of reach and pointed the shotgun at Dane's belly. "Get up!"

Coughing, Dane rolled over and got to his feet. He was aware that townspeople were gathering nearby, talking in low voices. He thought he heard Roy Gunderson and Rusty among them. Armbruster was walking away from the posse, muttering to himself.

"Jipsell," said Shine, taking a cigar from his vest pocket, "go get that justice of the peace. We'll have a little bit of a courtroom in the jail."

Jipsell nodded and went loping after the justice of the peace.

"Shouldn't be long now," said Shine, smiling smugly, blowing cigar smoke at Dane. "Then we'll have justice for Johnny."

"It was you who taught him to be a damned fool," said Dane. "And that's what got him killed."

Shine's smugness fell away, and his eyes caught fire. "You are going to regret saying that. We just might have to spend some extra time hanging you. I've seen it done. It's an unpleasant sight!" He chuckled. "And maybe we'll bring that girl of yours so she can watch. After that— Well, some terrible accident will befall her, I'm afraid—"

Unstoppable rage took hold of Dane, and he launched himself at Shine. Brewster kicked out and tripped him so he fell short, his hands still trying to clutch for Shine's throat.

Flayle started in first, kicking Dane hard in the ribs. Brewster laughed and kicked him in the head. White specks whirled through Dane's vision. He almost lost blacked out, but he fought for consciousness. He heard Roy Gunderson and Rusty close by, shouting something he couldn't make out at Shine—and Brewster telling them to keep back "or get shot for interfering in the law's business."

"Get him up and hold him for me, boys!" Shine called.

Henderson and Flayle dragged him to Dane feet and held him tight. Brewster stepped behind him, grabbed Dane's wrists, and twisted them back. Cigar clenched in his mouth, Shine slugged Dane hard in the belly—Dane tensed his muscles to take the blow, but Shine kept on slugging, like a boxer hitting a sandbag, and at last Dane's muscles betrayed him, and he had the breath knocked out of him once more.

Shine threw the cigar at Dane's face, then set himself, catching his tongue between his front teeth; he cocked his arm for a roundhouse and slammed Dane in in the jaw. Dane's head rocked back—and darkness took him. Seconds later, he came to himself, lying flat on his back. He opened his eyes only a slit.

"Henderson, get some rope, tie his wrists" came Shine's voice.

Dane kept his eyes mostly closed as Henderson turned to a horse for rope. Through his slitted eyes, Dane saw that Brewster had Dane's own pistol in his right hand. Brewster knelt, reached under Dane with his free hand to flip him on his belly—and Dane sat up fast, his right fist rocketing at Brewster's chin, his left hand grabbing the Colt. His right connected, knocking Brewster back. His left jerked the pistol from the falling man, flipped it, and fired it. Not his usual way to shoot—but he couldn't miss at this range. The round caught Al Flayle in the chest; his next shot, in the same second, hit Brewster in the throat as the deputy was pulling his saddle gun.

Danc didn't see them fall; he was busy blowing a hole in Henderson's forehead as the gunman swung a shotgun toward him. Henderson fell. Dane got quickly to his feet as Shine O'Hara, stunned by the turn of events, clumsily tugged out his shiny pearl-handled pistol. Dane shot him in the face, and O'Hara spun and crumpled.

Suddenly feeling dizzy, Dane looked at Brewster, who was still alive but choking on his own blood. He would be dead in a minute or two. "Hold it!" shouted Jipsell, trotting toward him, his gun out. Dane turned toward him.

"I'll bet I can shoot before you do, Jipps," Dane said. His tongue seemed thick. It was hard to talk.

Jipsell froze. His gun hand was shaking. He dropped the gun. "Don't shoot me. I'm not in the fight."

Jipsell licked his lips and did as he was told.

"Where's that justice of the peace?" Dane asked. His eyesight seemed to rock back and forth. It was getting dark at the edges of his vision. That kick in the head maybe . . .

Jipsell said, "He heard from Armbruster about Mrs. Marrin's . . . about her passing. He didn't want to come."

Rusty and Gunderson ran over to them. Gunderson snatched up Jipsell's pistol, and Rusty caught Dane under the arms as he tipped over backward, falling into darkness.

I T WAS EARLY morning, not quite light out, when Dane woke. He was lying on a bed, facing a window. He could see the moon, not quite sunk away for the night.

Someone sat on the bed beside him. "Dane?"

Head throbbing, Dane turned over to see Suzanne smiling down at him. "How's that thick skull?"

"Feels thicker than ever." He reached up to touch the lump at the back of his head—there was a bandage over it. "Suzanne—my memory's back. All of it."

"Oh!" She stood up, looking startled.

"Came back to me when we were riding into town, soon's I got a good look at O'Hara."

"Are you—wanted anywhere?"

"No. I was a lawman for a good while. And not a bent one. I left that job, worked as a hired gun—a kind of bodyguard mostly. I got in a few fights, and some men died. But it was legal, self-defense. I hired on with Shine O'Hara for a short time till I saw he was crooked. And I saw his men do murder. I got in a fight with his cousin, Johnny O'Hara, and killed him. Shine sent his men after me—and I was shot."

"And you fell off a cliff! Where your friend found you!"

"That's right. My name's . . ." He hesitated. "Nathan Dane. My father was Marcus Dane. My mother, Sylvia, last I knew, is still alive. And I swear to you—on my word—I've never been married. I have no children. I—"

His head throbbed painfully, and he touched the bandage again.

"Leave the bandage alone, Dane . . . Nathan. Doc Greeley said not to touch it. Says you got a concussion, but you're likely to be all right. Same can't be said for Shine O'Hara. Or those others."

"More I'll have to answer for. They were threatening to kill you."

"I know, Dane. A lot of the town heard them say it and saw them beat you. Justice Peebles arrived in town about an hour ago."

"Where am I?"

"Arthur Conrad's office. He's keeps a cot there. Doc Greeley wanted you nearby."

"Your mother . . . Lord, I'm sorry, Suzanne."

Suzanne closed her eyes and nodded. Then she looked at him and said, "We're burying her tomorrow in the town cemetery." She sighed. "The Quinlan brothers and Blue came over and helped me with her body. I asked them to tear up the floorboards where she . . ." She swallowed hard and went on. "They're going to replace the boards with new ones. I just don't want to tread on even the slightest trace of her blood."

Dane nodded. "I understand." He looked around. "Where *is* Arthur? Where's Blue?"

"Right here." Blue was just coming through the door. He had his hands stuck awkwardly in his coat pockets. "Finally got here. Should have got to town sooner—we could've stopped that beatin'. We rode in half an hour late."

"It took Suzanne some time to get to you. And it's a long ride here. You came, that's all. Where's Arthur?"

"Arthur's talking to Justice Peebles."

Dane nodded—and regretted it. Nodding still hurt. "I'm surprised not to be in the jail."

Blue grunted. "Me and Rusty and Roy and the Quinlan boys—and about forty citizens—we persuaded Jipsell to back off on that. Folks are calling for him to be removed from office."

"Won't have to do it for Costigan," Suzanne said. "A citizen's committee threatened him with the law, and he's left town. Clemson's gone with him. Those men shooting Mama"—her voice broke—"that changed everything."

Dane took her hand. *That changed everything.* It probably changed her feelings for him, too. How could she marry him when he'd brought death with him to her home? When her mother had been killed by a bullet meant for him?

He smiled bitterly and closed his eyes.

Let her go, he told himself. *You haven't the right.*

Dane made up his mind he would not bring up marriage again.

* * *

THE SMOKY RIVER Cemetery was a quarter mile east of town in a fenced-off lot surrounded by sugar maples. The trees were barren of leaves that day as Dane stood by the open grave beside Suzanne, hat in hand; the gray-black clouds were slowly inching across the sky, like a line of ghosts viewing the burial; the jutting, often crooked wooden crosses were dripping from the earlier rain. The town had taken up a collection, and Mrs. Marrin would soon have a fine tombstone with her name and roses, her favorite flower, carved upon it.

Mrs. Marrin's coffin was already in the open grave, and the preacher at the foot of the grave, praising Mrs. Marrin's life. Dane and Suzanne stood with a small crowd of mourners. "She had her ways, surely," the preacher said, "but she was a God-fearing woman who came every Sunday to church, who donated what she could, who oversaw the bake sale to raise money for the bell, and who comforted the infirm. If someone was sick or dying, Mrs. Marrin always called on them. . . ."

Dane hadn't known that Mrs Marrin had visited the sick and the infirm. He'd thought of Suzanne's mother as something of a shrew and a bit too calculating. He shook his head sadly. Too often folks, himself included, leapt to judgment when they only saw one side of a many-sided person. Certainly, he'd seen her profound love for her daughter. . . .

The sky rumbled with the coming thunderstorm, as if to underscore the preacher's reading from the Bible. "'And God shall wipe away all tears from their eyes;

and there shall be no more death, neither sorrow, nor crying, neither shall there be any more pain: for the former things are passed away. . . .'"

Dane thought about Elias Keggum. He felt as if Old Keggum were there at this grave, nodding, as the thunder rumbled and the wind sighed. *For the former things are passed away . . .*

F IVE DAYS LATER, at the hearing, Dane was feeling better, almost back to himself. But he wasn't at all sure which way the judge was going to jump. Sitting in the front row at the town hall, he had plenty of time to study the man's demeanor.

Justice Peebles was surely a serious man. He'd been three and a half hours on that wooden chair, lips compressed, taking notes with a gold fountain pen at a small table brought in for the hearing. He was never seen to smile, always keeping the same hard, skeptical expression on his lined face during the testimony and asking few questions. He was about sixty-five, Dane reckoned; he had a drooping white mustache and thick white hair contrasting with his black suit and black string tie.

It was a cold afternoon. Hail was rattling the windows, and the fire had gone out in the Franklin stove, so the town hall was growing cold.

Most everybody who could fit into the building was there. Suzanne was sitting beside Dane in her best blue dress, and she was wearing her blue lace gloves. Jipsell was sitting uncomfortably a little behind and to the left of the judge. Jipps kept shifting, crossing one leg and then the other. He avoided the eyes of people in the audience, aware that they were doing some judging themselves. There wasn't much hope he'd be reelected sheriff. He'd barely avoided being arrested himself.

"And so, sir, your honor," said Bill Sharton, standing in front of the judge, wringing his small hands, "I felt my life was in danger if I didn't say Andy had been embezzling and . . . and if I didn't play along. Andy told me, the day before they killed him, he'd seen Clemson bribe Mayor Costigan and Harry Stannard."

There was much outraged comment among the onlookers at that.

"Quiet in the court," Peebles said emotionlessly. "Go on, Mr. Sharton."

"That Clemson, that Brewster, they told me if I spoke about it, I was going to go on a Shine ride. And they told me what that was. What they tried to do to Mr. Conrad! I'm sorry to everyone, all of you folks here—I'm sorry. I should have told the truth. Andy McCutcheon was right about the whole kit and caboodle. But, sir—I was not under oath."

Peebles nodded. "I understand. They threatened you. It was a tough spot to be in. You are free to go."

Letting out a long, relieved breath, Sharton hurried to the door.

Armbruster was called up next.

"You have, I understand, a statement to make," the judge prompted.

"I . . ." Armbruster cleared his throat. "I do. I sometimes drink too much and—"

"Is that relevant, Mr. Armbruster?"

The onlookers laughed.

"Well, sir—I was drunk when I said I'd go on that posse to Marrin Farm. I didn't know these men really, except Jipps. That Brewster and Husman, they had a bad reputation, so I should've known better. And . . . that man Grady, he was a hired killer! I heard Husman speak of it on the way to the farm. I'd never have gone sober. I wanted to go back to town soon's we got there, but . . . Well, what I want to say is, Mrs. Marrin was a decent woman, a churchgoing woman, and—" Tears in his eyes, he turned to Suzanne. "I'm sorry, ma'am. What happened—it was wrong."

She nodded to him and gave a wintry smile.

"Anything else, Mr. Armbruster?" Peebles asked.

"Yes, sir. Those men were planning on murder! Not justice but murder! I heard them speak of it. I have written everything down. Arthur Conrad there—Mr. Dane's lawyer—he has my full statement. It was going to be a murder under pretense of law."

"That corroborates, in fact, the substance of what we've heard today," Peebles said. "And I think I've heard enough. You may have a seat."

Armbruster went and sat down heavily, mopping his forehead with a large white handkerchief.

Peebles sat back and took hold of his lapels. "Every witness except the sheriff has spoken favorably of Mr. Cornelius N. Dane's character."

Dirk Quinlan hooted at that. "Cornelius!"

Dane grimaced.

Suzanne jabbed Dane with an elbow and whispered, "You told me Nathan!"

"Nathan's my middle name. I cannot bear Cornelius."

"Given the testimony of Mr. Blue-Snake Thompson and Mr. Arthur Conrad," Peebles went on, "I will not order that Mr. Dane be tried for the shooting of Ferry Johnson. As for the gunfight that ended with the deaths of Shawn O'Hara, Hamish Brewster, Albert Flayle, and Tolliver Henderson, *more than sixty* citizens of Smoky River signed an affidavit witnessing that the shootings were in self-defense. That in itself was very persuasive. I am reliably informed, too, that Mr. Dane received two medals for his service to the Union in the Civil War and a letter of commendation from General Grant. The testimony of Mrs. Isabel Cummings was—quite moving. And persuasive, too, as to the gentleman's character. I also am informed that he was an effective town marshal in Arizona Territory and that there is no warrant or indictment for him anywhere. Officers Bat Masterson and Wyatt Earp have sent glowing notices for him—apparently he was some help to Officer Earp when he was hunting a man in Tucson for Wells Fargo."

Dane nodded. That memory was coming back to him, too.

Peebles cleared his throat. "The sheriff here characterized Dane rather differently. . . ." At last, a small smile. "But I find that his opinion does not signify."

Chuckles arose from the onlookers. Jipsell switched his legs around again.

"Therefore," said the judge, folding up his notes, "I find that Mr. Dane cannot be tried in these matters. He is without fault and is free to go."

Suzanne gasped at that. Dane felt a weight lift off him he hadn't known he was carrying. He felt about a hundred pounds lighter.

There were whooping and applause from the crowd.

"Judge," Jipsell put in, "uh—there's the matter of these Quinlan boys here." He pointed to Dirk and Ben.

"Yes, yes, I've looked at that already. Without brands

on the cattle nor an eyewitness seeing them take the cattle from the owner's land, there is no proof of rustling, and they may go on their way."

More whooping from the Quinlan brothers.

"But"—he spoke sharply—"let them be more careful about what they round up next time."

The whooping ceased.

Peebles went on. "I do have something more to say to you, Sheriff Jipsell. I have every reason to believe you were bribed and may have suborned murder. The evidence is lacking, but if we work hard enough, we may well be able to find some. I could call in some favors to see that you are held in the county jail until that is accomplished. But I'll give you an alternative. If you place your badge on this table, pack up your goods, and ride out of town by sunset—"

The crowd erupted in cheers.

"I will let you go! You can join the former Mayor Costigan. It appears that he has 'fled town with all speed,' as the local paper had it."

Jipsell swallowed hard. "I . . . accept your offer, sir." He stood up, unfastened his badge, tossed it on the table, and hurried to the door.

"The hearing is adjourned," Justice Peebles said, getting to his feet and tucking his pen in a shirt pocket.

D ANE HELPED REPAIR the sitting room floor of Suzanne's house, insisting he was recovered from the concussion though every hammer blow seemed to resound through his head, and from time to time as he worked, cutting boards to fit, she came in and watched him. He did not look up from the sawhorse, and he said nothing. Mrs. Marrin's death was on his conscience, though reason tried to tell him it was not his fault. He felt he had no right to court Suzanne.

Immediately after finishing work, unwilling to hear her kind words of gratitude, Dane called out, "Good evening, ma'am," and hurried out to Pard.

"Looks like it's just me and you, Pard. Couldn't ask for better company."

He rode through the windy dusk out to the Horseshoe W to work on the new Cummings house. Mrs. Cummings had been hired as a housekeeper and cook, and Jess had hired Dane and a couple of town men to build a small house on the property for Isabel and the children. Calvin and Teresa, Dane saw as he dismounted in front of the Willoughby house, looked delighted as they rode together on the back of one of the horses that had been salvaged from the outlaws. Blue supervised as Calvin put the horse through its paces about the corral.

Dane set to work on the partly finished house, and he had just finished shingling the roof when Suzanne rode up. She sat on her saddle, looking quizzically up at him.

"You, sir, on the roof!" she called out. "Do you not see that it's grown too dark to work without a lantern?"

"Yes, ma'am, you're right," Dane said, taken off guard by her arrival. He climbed down off the roof as the dinner bell sounded. "There's our dinner bell, ma'am. Ike would be most pleased if you'd join us, I'm sure. He's cooking for the hands, and he has not Mrs. Cummings's culinary gifts, but he's a fair hand."

She dismounted and patted the horse's neck. "I would be honored."

Dane had invited her only out of custom and hoped she'd say no. For seeing her made his heart twist within him. It was difficult, downright tough, not to take her in his arms.

"Dane—" Suzanne hesitated, then seemed to make up her mind. He knew that look of determination. "You left the house so suddenly. It isn't like you! I felt . . ." She paused, swept an errant curl of copper hair from her face, and said, "I felt as if you were avoiding me."

"Ma'am—Suzanne—I do not deserve your company. I was the cause of your mother's death."

"Now, that is rubbish!" She surprised him with her vehemence. Suzanne took a step closer to him. "Dane—I understand how you must feel. I have always known you were a man of conscience. But do not let your conscience take on an unjust burden. You didn't know those men would be there. You didn't force them to open fire. A ricochet—you did not speed it on its way. Promise me you will not deepen the tragedy of her loss by . . ." She pursed her lips and went on, seeming a little annoyed. "I should not have to . . ." She shook her head and turned away. She covered her eyes, and her shoulders quivered.

Horrified that he'd hurt her, Dane stepped up to her, gently turned Suzanne around, and slid his arms around her. "I did not think that it was the time . . . if it ever could be . . ."

"I know. Oh, I know," she said, drawing him even closer. "Dane—do not make me ask you."

"I . . ." Did she mean what he hoped? "Suzanne—" But no, he should assume no such thing.

She pushed back from him, stuck out her lower lip,

and punched him in the shoulder hard enough that it stung. "You damned fool! Are you going to marry me or not—Cornelius?"

He rubbed his shoulder ruefully and grinned. "Promise to call me Nathan instead of Cornelius?"

She sighed. "I guess I can do that."

"Then I guess I'd better marry you before you give me another bruise."

And then he kissed her.

IT WAS A double wedding, a month later; Suzanne Marrin became Suzanne Dane in the Smoky River Church, alongside Arthur Conrad and Alice. The church was packed so that some had to listen to the ceremony from outside. Guests of honor were Roy Gunderson, Rusty, Mr. Sing, Blue-Snake Thompson, Rand Binch, Ike, Buck, the Quinlan brothers, Jess Willoughby, Isabel Cummings and her children—and W. B. "Bat" Masterson.

Suzanne looked nervous during the ceremony—nervous and beautiful with a bouquet of winter-blooming English primroses in her hands. But Dane thought Alice looked as happy as he'd ever seen a woman look. The preacher, far from spurning the "soiled dove," had been delighted when Alice came to him saying she wished to be washed in the blood of the lamb and to change her ways. She had come with Suzanne, who was a kind of mentor to her—and already a close friend. Alice was a constant figure about the church after that, and even Armbruster came to accept her. She and Suzanne had taken to having quiet teas with Sadie Danniger.

A special election to replace Costigan ended with Arthur Conrad becoming mayor. His first act was to ask—to beg—C. N. Dane to become town sheriff. Dane was reluctant. It was his fervent hope to never have to shoot another man. But he reflected that many a sheriff had gone their whole career without having to use his gun. "Only as an interim," he said at last. "Until you find a permanent sheriff. It is not work I take to. Not anymore."

"What work do you prefer, Dane?" Arthur asked over a beer in Rusty's.

"Farming. Perhaps a small ranch. Maybe some carpentry on the side."

"We're happy to have you for as long as you choose," said Mayor Conrad.

In January, Dane went to Doc Greeley in a great hurry. "Suzanne's come down with something!" he said as he rousted the doctor out of bed, and the look on Dane's face precluded grumbling.

Having examined Suzanne, Greeley shook his head gravely and said, "I'm afraid—she's come down with babies."

"What!"

"Perhaps only one baby. But you never know. Mrs. Smithson, who's no bigger than a whisper, had triplets."

IT WAS A bitterly cold but mostly peaceful winter. Dane had little to do as sheriff, apart from riding herd on drunks and petty thieves. In April he trailed and captured a small gang of actual cow thieves. Seeing who had come for them—a man who now had a fearful reputation in Kansas—the three rustlers instantly dropped their weapons without being asked.

In May, a drifter attempted to rob the bank. Dane, who'd gotten word in time from the observant Roy Gunderson, waited for the robber outside the bank. The man stepped out the door, carrying a bag of money—and Dane knocked him cold with his gun barrel. Doc Greeley bandaged the disappointed robber in the city jail.

In June, Dane and Suzanne were invited to a wedding. Jess Willoughby wed Isabel Cummings; he was impressed by her competence, her fearlessness, her diligence, and her cooking. The little house out back was taken over by Ike as Isabel and the children moved into the main ranch house.

Come late August, Dane found that he was the father of a little girl. And he was surprised to hear, as she nursed little Elana, that Suzanne shared his ambition to pack up and go to Oregon.

In September, accordingly, thcy sold the farm and most of their stock. Dane quit as sheriff—Buck surprised everyone by taking the job and being a clever and efficient if slow-talking lawman—and the Dane family set out in a covered wagon on their way to the Oregon Trail. For that was whcre Suzanne's ambition lay, the same as Dane's—a big new ranch in Oregon.

Dane drove the team, with Suzanne at his side, cradling the baby in her arms. Sherman the draft horse and Suzanne's horse drew the covered wagon, with Pard trotting along at the back. Dane had considered bringing Gravy with them, but Gunderson was happy to keep the mule in the pasture, and she looked so contented there, he hadn't the heart to take her on an arduous journey.

Dane wasn't wearing his gun belt. It was under the seat, and there was a rifle within reach. But he earnestly hoped never to have to kill another man.

The wagon was about a mile north of town when a rider cantered up to pace alongside them.

"Why, Blue!" Suzanne said, smiling brightly. "We just saw you at the goodbye party, and here you are again!"

"Perhaps I shouldn't intrude on you folks. . . ."

Dane snorted. "I was just wishing I'd asked you to come along!" He noticed that Blue had a considerable pack behind his saddle.

"I am always happy to see my friends!" Suzanne declared. "Are you heading our way for a time?"

"For the whole journey if you'll have me along. Have me a yen to see the Oregon Territory. Especially, with you saying you had a place waiting to ranch on the Oregon coast—I've never seen the ocean!"

Dane grinned. "It's a wonder! Saw the Pacific when I was in San Francisco."

"I've never seen the Pacific, and I long to," Suzanne said as the baby began squirming in her arms. The baby set to squalling. "We could ask for no better company than you, Blue—but little Elana will assault your ears with this squalling, I fear. She's a trifle colicky."

"Sounds like a strong child. She'll be fine."

Suzanne sighed and kissed the baby. "I did hesitate, wondering if we should wait till she was bigger for so long a journey . . . but Doc Greeley said she was 'strong as an alfalfa-fed horse,' so . . ."

The wagon creaked along, Blue's horse clopping

alongside, following a dirt road north through the plains. It was a warm, muggy day but overcast. "What route we taking?" Blue asked, his tone indicating he didn't give a fig what route it was.

"Many routes," Dane said. "Two thousand miles of them. Up to Kansas City first. We'll be following the Missouri for a while, then the Snake River, then cut across the Blue Mountains and thence to the Columbia Gorge. We'll follow the Columbia west a piece, then cut down to Oregon City. Rest awhile there, I expect. Then across the Coast Range to the Dane Ranch. Not much more'n a small valley two miles from the Pacific. I'm afraid you'll be drafted to help me build a cabin and a good deal more."

"Would be insulted if you didn't allow me to help," Blue said, gazing up at the cloudy sky. As he looked, the cloud cover broke, and the sun shone through.

Dane smiled. "You see that, Suzanne? When you're with me, the sun comes out."

Ready to find
your next great read?

Let us help.

Visit prh.com/nextread